THE FLORISTRY COMMISSION

THE FLORISTRY COMMISSION

by

Claire Peate

HONNO MODERN FICTION

Published by Honno
'Ailsa Craig', Heol y Cawl, Dinas Powys
South Glamorgan, Wales, CF6 4AH

A catalogue record for this book is available from The British Library.

ISBN 1 870206 746

Published with the financial support of the Welsh Books Council

Cover design: Vivid
Cover image: Jupiter
Printed in Wales by Gomer

For my Mum and Dad.

1

'Well, Rosamund, what do you think?'

Gloria twirled around her bedroom in an enormous fluffy wedding dress. I stared at her, eyes wide like saucers, not knowing what on earth she expected me to say. I was used to seeing Gloria dressed up in chic grey or black suits with her oh-so-smart shoes and her business-like handbags – this was too much of a departure from the norm for me to know how to deal with it.

'Well what?' she said sharply, turning her face towards me. 'Don't you like it?'

No I didn't. She looked like the doll my grandma used to disguise the spare toilet roll. What could I say?

'I do.'

Narrowing her eyes, she strode over to me, 'You *don't* like it do you? What's wrong with it? What? Is it too big do you think, too much skirt? I think it's wonderful, look…' and she spun round again, the netting billowing out around her.

Now I have never been what you might call a 'girl's girl', and I'd never really regretted not learning the skills required to be so.

Up until this point.

If I had paid attention and had bothered to learn the right girl-skills then I could have lied glibly, telling her that of course I liked it, I loved it. In fact, isn't that the most *gorgeous* dress I'd ever seen, and where, oh my God where did she find it? I could have cooed and flattered her and *secretly* disliked it. But no, I was not that woman. All I could think was that she wasn't particularly suited to being a bride and would have looked at home on my cistern hiding the toilet roll and that really *really* wasn't a very nice thing to be thinking. Besides which, being completely honest in tricky situations like this just wasn't the done thing; it was like seeing a friend's ugly baby: you pretend they're adorable little cherubs, whilst hastily stepping back from the pram and breathing deeply. But here was my good friend bound tightly into a hideous white dress, with bows, which made her look like a short, slightly chubby business woman in an enormous bundle of fabric. Which is exactly what she was.

'Oh!' she said, exasperated at waiting for me to come up with the goods. But she wasn't cross, not really. Gloria and I, you see, had known each other since our very earliest days on the playground, and there's always a comfortableness that comes with really old friends that you never get with friendships afterwards. Right from the start we were opposites, even in looks. She was always neatly turned out, hair in a blonde bob, short and on the plump side while I was tall and skinny with long dark hair that refused to be tamed by even the most ambitious of hair products. On a good day I was once told that I resembled a pre-Raphaelite muse, all wavy hair and big brown eyes, long skirts and a tiny waist. On bad days, however, I could be said to resemble a lanky wild-woman with bizarre tastes in clothes. Gloria used to despair at what I wore, primarily because it wasn't neat fitted outfits in the smart greys and blacks that she liked. My wardrobe contained a lot of long flowing skirts, bright jumpers and stripy scarves. So, no doubt, at this point Gloria was weighing up the idea that perhaps it wasn't such bad a thing that I didn't like what she was wearing.

'I'm sorry Glo, it's just… I don't know,' I searched for the right words. 'I suppose I'm just overwhelmed that's all. I mean, I'm really pleased for you, but it's so strange to see you in a wedding dress…' I petered out messily.

Gloria put down her enormous veil and came over to where I was sitting, flopping down beside me.

'Poor, poor Rosamund,' she said, taking my hand in her own tiny mitt, 'I'm so sorry. Here I am going on about me and my wedding, and you've had so much to deal with, haven't you? Poor Rosamund. You got here yesterday and I haven't even asked about you about all those terrible things you've just gone through, yet!'

It was true, she hadn't asked.

'Don't be so silly,' I said, patting her hand back, which seemed to be the right thing to be doing, 'and you look great. Really. It's just… unusual. You must agree; a wedding dress is a pretty odd piece of clothing when you think about it.'

She looked downcast for a moment, 'I suppose so, but it feels so glamorous…' and with that she got up and shimmied over to the mirror again, putting the veil back on and looking one way and the other experimenting with different looks; demure bride, sexy bride, shy bride, cross bride.

'God, I've got to lose some weight in the next two months, just look how tight this bodice is. I can hardly breathe.'

'Do you think you'll be able to?'

'Breathe?'

'Lose weight.'

'Probably not. Philip wouldn't notice anyway, so there doesn't seem much point.'

'Unless it stops you breathing properly, that would be a good point. Can you take in a full breath?'

She tried, and failed. Laughing, in small half-gasps, she said she could go about half way, which would be enough to get by, and with that she undid the side zip and got changed. I left her and went to unpack the rest of my belongings.

I was grateful to Gloria; she had been so kind when everything had gone badly wrong for me. Hidden away in her gorgeous old townhouse, in the middle of the lovely old town of Kings Newton, I felt safe and a whole lot calmer than I had been in a long time.

I don't know what had made me call her number when I got to the Gs in my address book. Over the past fifteen years we'd gone our separate ways, which seemed inevitable since we were such dissimilar people. She had become the successful businesswoman I knew she would be, pillar of the community and all that, while I had drifted around in London, doing jobs that were just good enough to push me on to greater things, but not good enough to be particularly interesting.

In fact, our relationship had been getting to the stage where I had even hesitated over penning a Christmas card to her last year, not having phoned or written since the Christmas card of the year before. So it had come as a real surprise to me when, phoning her up a week ago to tell her that I'd finally left Greg, she had suggested I stay with her over the summer while I got myself together and worked out what I was going to be doing with my life from now on.

The situation, however, was not without its benefits for her, the scale of which I was only just beginning to appreciate. Gloria owned her own florist's business in the town and had another opening in north Shropshire two and a half weeks before she was due to get married. Gloria being Gloria – completely unable to relax or pace herself when under pressure – had been trying to run the Kings Newton shop as well as coordinate the opening of the new shop. And on top of that she had taken it upon herself to organise everything for her wedding. It was all getting to be too much even for her. I was beginning to realise that when I had phoned out of the blue, she had seen an opportunity and grasped it with both hands. I would be working alongside her usual assistant in the Kings Newton shop while she dashed between the shop, the new shop and the wedding venue. It didn't sound too difficult, and it would occupy my mind, which is what I probably needed as I didn't want to spend my time pining over that waste of space that was my ex, or fretting about what I would do now that I'd given up my old life. In fact, I was rather looking forward helping out in the florist's shop in this beautiful little market town, with its old cobbled streets and gorgeous knick-knack shops. Flower arranging is quite a trendy thing to be in right now and what better place to do it than in the beautiful Welsh Marches during the summer?

And so here I was, folding up my small collection of clothes into the old chest of drawers in the corner of Gloria's spare room. Everything I now owned contained in one suitcase and a holdall. Why hadn't I managed to cram more clothes into the bag before I ran out of the house? If only I had my cherry coloured wraparound dress and my Jigsaw t-shirts.

Gloria poked her still-veiled head around the door,

'Did I tell you about the hen night?'

'No.'

'Well it's not a hen night as such. There's the annual fair coming to Kings Newton and I thought it would be really quite fun to go with a group of mates. It's the night before the wedding …'

'Really? Aren't you worried about hangovers or anything?'

Gloria looked taken aback for a minute, 'No! Good God Rosamund, we're not going to drink ourselves into a stupor! We're not at university now; we don't need to get off our heads to have a good time.'

Gosh it sounded fun. 'I just wondered that's all,' I said, wanting to change the subject from the sombre hen night topic. 'So… thirty nine days to go!'

'I know. God I can't believe it's all happening so quickly. It seems so long ago since Phil proposed. Anyway there will be you, me, and a group of friends from Kings Newton and Wrexham going to the hen night. Maybe I'll invite Alan too. He's the one I was telling you about earlier, the local boy who's my assistant in the Kings Newton shop. Maybe not though, he's so irritating.'

'Sounds good,' I said. Boy, I could lie for England!

'Roz, I'm glad you're here.'

'Me too,' I gave her a hug, still holding my folded pants in one hand.

'Have you called your mum since you moved out of Greg's

house? Does she know where you are? You know how she frets if she can't get hold of you.'

I hadn't called my mum. I really couldn't face calling her, she'd be so disappointed in me, that I'd left Greg, who I was convinced she loved more than she loved me. In fact she would probably be more devastated by the break up than I was.

What would I say to her?

'Yes, I've called her,' I lied. Again! It could get to be a habit soon, if I kept this up.

2

Gloria's Flowers was a small but busy shop in the middle of the market town just opposite the old cross in the town square. I had been in Kings Newton a week and had already got to know the layout of the town pretty well. There were plenty of boutiques and trinket shops in this area of the town, each with jolly wooden signs hoisted up front and bright shiny windows stacked full of colourful goods. Gloria's Flowers was slightly more subdued than the rest, with two bay trees standing outside, tied with velvety purple ribbons. The Victorian shop front was painted a glossy muted plum and on it was written 'Gloria's Flowers *Kings Newton 458275*'. Inside Gloria had gone for a country-cottage feel – the walls were covered in a gorgeous Farrow and Ball wallpaper with a pattern of intricate swirls in cream and off-white. Here and there she had hung giant gilt mirrors (not for sale) and some local art work (price on request) so that every inch of the place was busy with something to look at. The place smelt amazing; fresh cut stems and rose petals mixed with other more earthy scents and as I breathed it in I thanked my lucky stars that I'd been given such a break. This was *so much* better than working in a stuffy city office crammed with stuffy city people. It was exactly what I needed.

I was sitting on the old pine table Gloria used for wrapping the flowers, mug of tea in one hand, scissors in the other, watching my friend bind bouquets of roses. I was being inducted into the art of floristry, but it was still early days yet so all I was required to do was nod and 'mmm' every so often while she chatted away.

And so, while she went on and on about disgraceful town planning, something to do with the redevelopment of the small market town of Kings Newton, I stared out of the window and wondered what the hell I was going to be doing with myself in the next couple of months in this sleepy little place, and beyond that, what was I going to *do about* myself?

After the initial joy of being free from boring job and bastard boyfriend I found guilt was creeping in. My mother, who is and has always been my harshest critic was forever telling me not to be impetuous and hot headed. To think things through and – God, forbid – plan. My mum liked Gloria, who was the essence of thoroughness and forward thinking. Gloria liked Mum, too, and the pair used to sit and talk for *hours* about just what they should do about me.

Perhaps I shouldn't have run away. Perhaps I should have kept my job and moved out of Greg's and in with a friend in London. That would, I reflected, have made more sense, certainly from a financial point of view. And I suppose it would have been less stressful if I had kept some thread of continuity in my life. But then to hell with all that. Why not change it all and walk away – see an opportunity and grab it with both hands?

Or was it all down to semantics? Was I *walking away* or was I *grabbing an opportunity* or was I—

'Scissors!' Gloria chimed, holding the ribbon up to me. I snipped it at an angle, as I'd been told to do, and carried on swinging my legs under the table.

'I hate roses,' she muttered crossly as she hacked their stems, butchering them viciously.

'Do you want me to help you with trimming them?' I volunteered, with as little enthusiasm as I thought I could get away with.

'No. But watch what I do because you'll have to do this soon.'

'Where's your other shop assistant?' I said, 'Shouldn't he be working today… What's his name again?'

'Who? Alan? No, not content with having taken a week off work on holiday he's called in to say that he's going to a funeral today,' she said, rolling her eyes upwards in mock disbelief. 'That boy is so sensitive, as you'll find out for yourself when he comes back to work tomorrow.   Some elderly aunt died, and Alan was completely devastated. He just couldn't stop crying.' She shook her head as she put the ribbon in the cupboard, 'He'd only met her once, and that was eight years ago.'

A picture of Alan was forming in my mind – a lank, limp Goth type person; someone who revelled in the association of a dead relative and was no stranger to white face powder. Still, at least he wouldn't be telling me to 'cheer up' all the time, which is as far as Gloria's sympathy had extended over the past week. She hadn't once asked me about the details of what had happened in front of the fridge. Between Greg … and my sister.

The door opened, jangling the tiny brass bell that hung above it.

'Tom!' Gloria went over to the rather beautiful blonde-haired man who had sauntered in, and went to kiss him on the cheek. He dutifully bent down to let her, keeping his eyes on me.

'You're looking as beautiful as you always do,' he whispered, rather loudly I thought, to Gloria, who dropped her businesswoman-front and giggled like a teenage girl on Babycham.

'As are you Rosamund,' he said, making me jump, a smile playing on his lips. 'You *must* be Rosamund, right? Gloria told me all about you. It's always nice to welcome a pretty lady into Kings Newton.'

I meant to laugh off his smarmy comment, but, being unpractised, it came out as more of a porky snort. But no matter, neither of them had noticed me, they were talking intently to one another in hushed voices. I blushed quietly in the corner. Why could I not be more suave?

'Well …' Tom said after a few minutes, looking around and smiling at me like a cheeky schoolboy. 'You'll be wanting to know the news then?'

'What news?' asked Gloria hacking at the rose stems with renewed vigour.

Tom pulled up an old chair and sat down slowly, taking his time, which wound Gloria up immensely.

'Come on, what news?' she said impatiently. Tom looked pointedly at me for a second and Gloria waved off-handedly, 'Oh don't worry about Rosamund,' she said, 'you can say anything in front of her. She's not going to give any secrets away to anyone.'

Wasn't I? What kind of secrets? I was intrigued.

Tom leant towards us and in a portentous half-whisper said, 'The diggers arrived this morning.'

If pushed, I'd have to admit it wasn't the most exciting piece of news I'd ever heard, but Gloria clearly thought it was.

'No!' she dropped the flower stems, 'They can't have! I don't want diggers parked up outside my wedding. How dare he? Why has he got them there now – it's way too early!'

'A friend said he heard them driving up the High Street at about five this morning, and I've been to check; they're parked over by the woodland beside Weston Hall.'

'Bloody Richard Weston… I was told it would all happen after the wedding and now the whole thing will be a mud-fest. Oh my God, I'm going to be married in a quagmire!'

'What's up?' I asked, completely nonplussed by all this talk of diggers and wedding receptions.

'Oh it's a long story,' said Gloria, still looking incredulous at the news that Tom had delivered, 'but a lot of the land around Kings Newton is privately owned by the Weston family who live over at Weston Hall at the top of the town. You will have seen the boundary wall that marks the north of Richard Weston's estate by the side of the church. Anyway, his ancestors have owned the land around here since way back and as the last relic of the family Richard Weston is selling off plots of land around the town for redevelopment.'

'Really?' I asked. 'Seems quite old fashioned having a landowner. Does he have a title?'

'Yes. Wanker.'

'He's a Lord,' cut in Tom, 'but he never uses his title. That's the only modern thing about him. The whole situation is one archaic mess. The family home, Weston Hall, has been left to rot into a huge crumbling pile of bricks—'

'That I'm having my wedding reception in.'

'That Gloria's hiring for her wedding reception. But, apart from the rooms open to the public, the whole thing is in a pretty poor state and so, to raise money for the house and to fund his extravagant lifestyle, Richard Weston is starting to sell off land here and there regardless of what we, the people who live in the town, think. Arrogant ponce… Our gorgeous town is being ruined just to keep him in champagne, coke and sports cars.'

'They're building fifty eight homes on a site where the old town used to be – it's a massive development for Kings Newton –' added Gloria by way of explanation, 'and this early start probably means that they'll be digging while my wedding is taking place. I hope that they don't create an eyesore. Oh my God, think of the mud …'

'Well I was talking to one of my friends this morning,' Tom went on, 'I can't tell you her name—'

'Her?'

Tom gave a wry smile, 'As if you need to worry!'

I looked from one to the other. Were they flirting with each other? They were standing very close to one another and why did she not need to worry that he was talking to another girl? Now this was intriguing – a lot more intriguing than JCBs.

'So what were you talking to *this girl* about?' Gloria asked, half joking, but also I detected that some caution on Tom's part would be needed. Gloria's temper was ignited by the tiniest of sparks.

'Well she knows a lot of what's going on in Weston Hall …'

'Oh so she works up at the Hall then? It's Jo. Or Eliza …?'

'I'm not saying anything.' Tom enjoyed teasing her. Gloria, however, hated it.

'Oh get on with it then,' she said tersely.

'Well, *this girl* was saying that the redevelopment project hasn't been moved forward. The start date is exactly the same.'

'Oh. So that means the diggers aren't needed for another few weeks yet. Why would Richard Weston pay to have them on site so long before they're needed?'

'Exactly!' said Tom, 'This indicates that Weston must have got wind of the road block we were going to stage. He must reckon he's out-smarted us by getting all the diggers to the site early. So we couldn't stop them arriving as we'd planned to do.'

'So that means,' said Gloria, slowly, 'that Richard Weston was tipped off about the protestors' road blocks by someone who is close enough to him to make him trust the tip-off, and also is close to us and knows what's happening with the protest. Shit! We've been so careful to keep it secret.'

'Pre-cise-ly…' Tom seemed to be very excited about this and kept running his hand through his long blonde hair. 'We have a spy in our midst. Someone is passing on our protest plans to Richard Weston.'

'That's quite exciting,' I chipped in, 'having a spy! Do you have any idea who it might be?'

'No,' said Tom shrugging his shoulders.

'None,' Gloria echoed, puzzled.

'So what exactly were you going to be doing to stop the diggers getting in to the town?' I asked.

'We were going to be a human road-block, stopping the diggers from entering the main streets. There are a lot of us in town who have got the courage to stand up to Weston's plans. We've been peacefully signing petitions and holding up banners for the last six months to try and stop him selling off the land. All we've got to show for it is one rigged 'meeting' between him, his wily solicitors and us poor, honest townsfolk, which solved nothing, and a leaflet through our letterboxes to tell us what we can expect to happen to our town. It's pathetic. The fact that it's got to the stage of physical protests is entirely Weston's own fault. The man gave us no option; he didn't want to listen to us when we had something to say.'

They talked for a while about 'taking decisive action' and 'solicitors', venting their anger in conversation. It sounded pretty gripping; townspeople take on the aristocracy. The landowner sounded like a real tyrant. I bet he has a handlebar moustache and shoots foxes.

As soon as Tom had gone, Gloria pulled up the chair he had been sitting on and sat facing me.

'Well, what do you think?' she asked, watching my face.

'Of what?' The protest? The town development?

'Of Tom!' she said, with a look that implied 'who else?'

I looked at her for a few seconds. Handsome. Smooth. A charmer, with plenty of practice at charming and probably plenty of people to charm to boot. Those were my first impressions. But after the wedding dress charade I was more cautious about letting on what I thought.

'He's nice.'

'Nice?'

'Yes, nice. Why?'

'I just wondered, that's all,' she said off-handedly.

'Oh,' I went back to writing out the orders. She was still looking at me, wanting to talk about Tom.

'He's lovely isn't he?' she cooed, head in her hands smiling moonily.

I put my pen down, open mouthed with shock.

'You. Are. Not?'

'Not what?' she grinned sheepishly.

'Oh my God you are! You're *having an affair* with that man.'

'I know!' she clapped her hands together in excitement, 'Isn't he gorgeous?'

Everyone was at it! Everyone was cheating on someone.

'How long have you been seeing him?' I asked, incredulously.

'A few months…'

'How many months?'

'Eight.'

'*Eight months!* How on earth had she got away with keeping it a secret from Phil for eight months? Kings Newton was only a small market town; surely gossip was rife.

'Oh come on Roz,' she said, suddenly irritated by my questioning, 'you don't think that's really bad do you?   You had two relationships on the go when you were going out with Robert Smedley, so don't come the martyr with me.'

That was a stupid argument, I was fifteen at the time, but I didn't argue with her.

'No, no I don't think it's *bad*,' I said, trying to find a way out of the corner she had backed me into, without upsetting her. 'It's just that … you and Phil always seemed so happy together. And you've been together for so long.' And they were getting married, I wanted to add.

'Well, Phil and I are very happy,' she smiled coyly 'but Tom is so…o…o good.'

'Argh, no,' I snorted, 'too much information! But how do you keep it from Phil?'

'Well it's not easy in a small town I can tell you. It helps that Phil is away so much on business. He's in Australia now you know…'

I listened to Gloria's animated exposure of the tricks involved in getting away with an affair and how you could never really expect to be made completely happy by just the one person for the rest of your life.

'Oh Christ!' she stopped abruptly.

'What?' I said, brought back to the present, having let my mind wander off again and started to think about what was for dinner.

'I'm so sorry. I just didn't think about you … and Greg. Oh I'm sorry, it must be so painful and here I am going on about affairs. You've just been so badly hurt by him and…'

'Don't worry about it,' I said and I actually meant it. I was affair-savvy. I could handle it.

'Greg was a git and I should have split up with him long ago,' I said confidently.

'He *was* a git,' enthused Gloria, 'and you're well off without him.' And having exhausted the topic of my life, she steered the conversation back to herself again.

.

3

It was a Wednesday, and Wednesdays were still, quaintly, half days in this part of the country. Gloria's Flowers was no exception and after we had shared a hearty pub lunch lasting well into the afternoon, Gloria had slunk off to Tom's workshops in the Hall stables. Not having anything in particular to do, and politely declining the offer to join her and watch while they made eyes at each other and giggled a lot, I in turn slunk off back to Gloria's meaning to sort my washing out and work through the emails which had no doubt begun piling up in my account. A couple of hours later, having managed to put my delicates on a boil wash, crash Gloria's computer twice before finally getting to my email – deleting unread all emails from the bastard Greg – I decided it was too nice a day to be cooped up indoors and to take a walk through the town. I'd been here two and a half weeks and while I pretty much knew my way around the town I hadn't ventured out much into the countryside yet. It was a gorgeous early evening by the time I left the house, still hot and shimmery after the beautiful day; dogs panting and old people sitting in the shade, watching me wander aimlessly past them. The walk would, I reasoned, give me ample chance to get my thoughts together and work out what I was going to do with my life. I would, I reflected, return to Gloria's house that evening with a new direction and purpose.

Kings Newton is a beautiful old town, well preserved due mainly due to the fact that 350 years ago it had burnt to the ground and had to be rebuilt with fire precautions in mind. Sturdy red brick and slate cottages lining wide cobbled roads had replaced the timber and thatch houses of the original town, although one or two timber-frame houses that had survived the fire still remained on the High Street.

The site where the old town had been remained undeveloped: a memorial to the lives that had been lost in the fire. It was uneven rough ground but even though it was grassed over and covered in shrubs I could make out the dip of the old main street where it met with the present one. There were even a couple of low brick walls still standing at the far end, covered in tall grass. I stood for a moment plaiting my hair and contemplating the humps and ditches of the old town. It did seem somewhat sacrilegious that part of the land was going to be included in the redevelopment by this Lord Weston chap. According to Gloria and Tom it was this particular fact that had hardened the protestors against the landowner.

A plaque had been planted on the grassy mounds at the point where the modern high street finished and the old high street joined; a sort of urban umbilical-cord between the old and the new. Unusually, for Kings Newton, the plaque had been vandalised.

'In these fields lie the remains of the original village of King's Newton up until the fire of 1648. 67 villagers, including twelve children, tragically lost their lives in the fire, which was spread by strong winds.

'Here beneath this verdant turf,
our former township 'neath the earth
Where once our fathers lived and thrived

Now gorse and bramble there reside
But hearken! On a still night hear
Their wint'ry echoes whisper clear
Our neighbours, under nature's floor,
Slumber ye, for ever-more.

Rev. Thos Dugdale 1842.'

Someone had blacked out *'nature's floor'* and had painted in a new phrase so it read

'Our neighbours, under 58 EXECUTIVE 4 & 5 BED
DETACHED HOUSES
Slumber ye, for ever-more.'

Very witty. It made me smile.

Hoisting up my skirt I walked over the low railings towards the building site, tucked away in the far corner, which was threatening the land of the old town. It seemed to me that the building company had at least made some effort to make the development fit into its surroundings, with wrought-iron railings already in place around the site, and many of the old oaks still standing in between the pegs which, I supposed, marked out the future house plots. I'd grown up in new-housing-estate suburbia, one that was particular to the seventies, where roads were straight and the box-houses were identical to one another. A featureless, double-glazed beigetopia where the only interesting features in the cul-de-sacs were the road kill. Here at least it looked as though they were keeping the rise and fall of the land, preserving the trees and grassy verges around them as the new road twisted and turned.

A site office had already been erected against the old redbrick boundary wall of Weston Hall, partially hidden by the rampant hawthorn bushes. Great piles of building materials had already been laid by the entrance, with 'Guard Dogs, Keep Out' signs posted all around.

The picture on the hoarding showed a large detached house built of soft red brick with mock Tudor façade and a large Georgian front doorway. The architect had obviously used the buildings of

Kings Newton for inspiration, amassed all the design cues, drunk a bottle of whisky and then shoe-horned as many as would fit into one building. In front of the house on the poster a blonde-haired man was closing the front door, smiling at his wife who stood beside him on the front porch. Two impossibly clean blonde children scrambled over one another in the race to the carefully non-branded family car that stood on the drive. Very 1950s. The wife (I presumed they were married) even had a primrose-yellow flared mid-length skirt on, with carefully non-threatening high heels. Were Brydon Homes being ironic I wondered? Or had they done some research amongst their target market and found out that people today actually hanker after the 1950's lifestyle?

'Weston Hall Parkland, King's Newton: old fashioned values for the modern lifestyle,' said the slogan, 'luxury 4 and 5 bedroom houses. Phase I due for completion late spring.'

A garish red and white note was slapped across the slogan, reading, 'Phase I 100% sold. Phase II & III released soon.'

I wondered if there would be pressure to develop what would be left of the scrubland site of the old town behind me after the second and third phases were completed. I wondered how much Lord Weston had been given for the sale of the land, and what it would take for him to part with the last remains of the old town. It did seem wrong to develop on top of the old town, but such sentimentality is rather useless; I knew that. What if London hadn't been developed after the great fire, in reverence to the dead? Life goes on, people need places to live. The preacher turned poet Thomas Dugdale who had written the 'Slumber ye' poem surely didn't mean that the dead were literally buried there beneath the ground. Surely their bodies would have been taken out of the building rubble and buried in the cemetery attached to the churchyard at the edge of the Hall's boundary wall?

The poet, I reasoned, was probably trying to make a point by saying that the *memory* of the people was buried beneath the ground; the house imprints, the broken shards of pots and pans, the things that were left behind after the fire. I wondered, briefly, if that was the root of the problem, whether some people actually thought that their ancestors were quite literally buried on the site of the old town and would therefore soon have a luxury 5-bed house on top of their heads? Any substantial gardening activity might prove interesting...

The evening was closing in, how had it got so late? How had I filled my time by doing nothing at all when I had so many things to be thinking about? I headed towards the woodland that stretched down beside the development, and made my way to the well-trodden footpath. The continuous spell of hot weather had recently broken, bringing heavy rain a couple of days ago. The rich smell of the soil rose up and filled the evening air: a real treat after living in London for so long. My shoes slipped on the mud quickly getting covered in the stuff, but I walked on, holding my old long skirt above my knees when the creeping briars threatened to tear at it.

The path was becoming narrower and less well worn as I ascended and left the new development behind.

A huge bush of large-headed dog roses arched over the path and I stopped to navigate my way around it. The dusk was settling and soon I wouldn't be able to see my way through the dense trees to get back. I guessed that the path would open out onto the parkland at the top, and from there I could probably skirt along it until I picked up one of the farm tracks, and get back to the town. At least, I hoped so. I was in no hurry to get back to the house, it was still only eight o'clock and I had the entire evening to sit in the house on my own; Gloria had said she was staying over at Tom's tonight.

As I passed the rose bush, I plucked some of the flowers, just like I used to do years ago, and wound them into my hair, which, being so thick with curls and waves held them fast. I had already collected a bunch of wild flowers in the wood, intending to take them back to Gloria's to put in a vase. I took a deep breath and smelt the damp soil. I felt completely free and really happy. No more tiny terraces, crowded tubes and grey office for me! Now I could wind flowers in my hair and wander in the countryside at will. Freedom.

I turned a sharp bend in the track and saw I was right, the path did emerge from the woods, and in a moment I was out, over a stile and onto undulating parkland that stretched over the top of the hill towards Weston Hall and out into the countryside. Now that I was here, out of the protection of the huge old oak trees, I realised that it had started to spot with rain, and despite my longing to carry on exploring, I knew that I ought to go back to the house. The damp was thick in the air clinging to my clothes and my hair. I kept the woods to my left and began my descent to the town again walking quickly but finding it progressively more difficult to be sure-footed in the deepening twilight. I was amazed at how compact the town looked, nestled beside the river. It looked Christmas card quaint with its windows lit up. From high up here, I could see quite clearly the new development cut into the woodland below, looking like an open wound, its muddied surface strip-lit in rather harsh blue-white light and the tops of the diggers poking out from behind the trees.

A low hanging bough slapped me out of my thoughts. It had caught in my hair and as I was trying to unfasten it a figure shot from around the turn in the woods and collided with me. I screamed and fell to the ground, the other person skidding to a heap just past me.

A dog bounded up barking around us, circling.

'I'm so sorry,' I said, standing up unsteadily.

It was a jogger.

He turned towards me, a wave of thick black hair plastered against his handsome wet face, his cheekbones shining in the rain. However appealing he looked, in a Colin Firth in a wet shirt type way, his temper wasn't so attractive.

'What the hell do you think you were doing?' he shot out, trying to move but wincing and clutching his ankle, pushing the energetic little dog back angrily.

'I'm really, really sorry,' I felt terrible and crouched down to his level, seeing as he couldn't rise to mine, 'did I hurt you? I didn't hear you coming. I was in another world.'

'And what kind of world would that be?' He leant forward to

look at me in the growing gloom, giving me an incredulous look, taking in my mud-stained orange skirt, the now-dishevelled flowers in my hair and the snake of ivy that had stuck fast and swept down to my waist. 'Some kind of fairy world perhaps? Are you a gypsy?'

'No!' I said, hoisting myself up to the full five foot eleven that I am, pulling the dog roses out of my hair, trying to look as though I was annoyed at them being there. I was burning with shame; I could feel my face growing redder by the second.

'Oww! My ankle is killing me.' He had tried to get up again.

'Can I help?'

'I think you've done enough, don't you?'

'Well I only want to help…'

'Shit my ankle hurts. Why the hell were you lurking around here? It's gone nine o'clock.' He clumsily pulled on a scarlet jumper that had been tied round his waist.

'So?' I laughed. 'Is there a curfew in Kings Newton?'

He looked at me, surprised.

'No…' he said.

'Well then. It's only quarter past nine. And it's a nice enough night – or it was when I started out; I didn't want to be indoors. I could say the same about you,' his rudeness had made me overcome some of my embarrassment, as I realised that I had in fact done nothing wrong.

'Well you should make more noise next time,' he said, rather lamely I thought. He had given up trying to raise himself and now he was leaning back and looking up at me. He must have been tall, and was broad across the chest although his wet jumper was clinging and sagging about it giving him a dishevelled look. He couldn't have been more than thirty-five but it was getting dark and everything was in shadow. The drizzle had now turned to proper rain covering us both, his black hair dripped with water and I could feel my skirt was heavy, clinging to my legs.

'Who are you?' he said, 'I don't recognise you.'

'I'm staying with a friend in town. Look I really should try and help you because it's almost dark and the rain…'

'Yes, thank you,' he cut me short, 'but I'm not sure if I'd want some of your help. There's every chance that I'll live longer without it. It's probably just a sprain anyway.' He felt his ankle again and gave a short intake of breath. 'Jesus! Look, if you really want to help, go and fetch my dog, he ran off into your woodland home over there. I'm damned if I can go and find him in this condition.'

I was glad that I could be of at least some use to him, setting off with another apology. After a couple of steps I turned and saw him still sitting, arms propping him up, watching me with a look of bewildered amusement, which I could understand, given the way I must have looked.

'What's his name?' I called.

'Pilot.'

I turned back, laughing, probably due to some sort of madness, and ran, slipping and sliding on the wet grass, to the edge of the wood.

When I reached it, I began to realise the impossibility of searching for a black dog in a now-dark wood , but then I heard something scrabbling about in the undergrowth by the stile.

I shouted, 'Pilot,' in my best dog-calling fashion and up he came, bouncing on his well-bred paws, clearly satisfied with the small amount of exercise that he had had. He was much better behaved than the old Labrador that my parents had once owned. Pilot the dog walked close beside me, wagging his soaked-through tail as we sloshed our way back to his master, who was only just visible in the murk, sitting where I had knocked him down, talking on a mobile phone.

'… I know, I know,' he was saying as we approached, 'but I'm up at the top of Shaw's Wood. Come and get me there. By the stile. No. No. That's fine. Bring a walking stick or something with you,' he dropped his cross tone and said a few softly spoken words that suggested he was talking to a wife or girlfriend, reaching out he stroked Pilot, which was probably a mistake because his coat was sodden and giving off that wet-doggy smell that sticks in your throat.

'Well…' he snapped his mobile shut, wiped it as best he could on a dry-ish piece of his tracksuit bottoms and looked up at me again saying: 'Would you be so kind,' rather pompously, 'as to help me up and take me to the stile so at least I can sit in some kind of shelter while I await rescue.'

'I would have helped you earlier,' I said, but I could see he didn't want a stranger's help, which, I suppose, was fair enough if alternative help is nearby.

He held out his arm and somehow I managed to help him to stand. We walked slowly back over to the stile where he sat down heavily. As he leant on me I could feel that he was still hot from his jog, making me realise just how cold I had become now that the rain had soaked me and the night had fallen.

'Well I'll go home then,' I said, smoothing my skirt in a nervous action which went in some way to make my dreadful appearance seem somehow more presentable.

'Back to the woods?' he said, raising his eyebrows, a smile on his lips. 'Back to the home beneath an oak tree with your tinker friends?'

If I had jumped into a river I could not have been more soaked than I was now. I was cold and I had no idea of how to get back to Gloria's house now that there was no light.

'Look,' I said, burning with anger, 'you are just as much at fault as I am, in fact more so because you ran into me! Don't forget that I offered to help you but all I got in return is your rather pathetic sarcasm. What gives you the right to speak to me in the way you did anyway?' I stood back and straightened up, 'I'm *very sorry* that I gave you a shock, and I'm *very sorry* that you fell, but you can *shove it* if you think it's all my fault, because it's not.'

I gave him a cynical smile, or at least I hoped I did but it probably looked like nothing of the sort. I turned, striding away with my skirt slapping noisily against my raw legs, heading into the misty rain and, hopefully, back to the town.

4

Dear Mum,

I'm sorry that I haven't got round to telling you earlier but I'm sure that you understand. I've ~~finally had the strength to leave finally left~~ I have left London and Greg and the job…

Dear Mum,

I'm in Shropshire, staying with Gloria. I'm sure you understand why I ~~left~~ broke away from…

Dear Mum…

5

Gloria's assistant, Alan, was turning out to be very good company. There was no hint of the Goth about him, just a very handsome, very gay local who laughed a lot and loved making tea. True, he did wear a lot of black, but that was to do with the death of the aunt. I failed to see why Gloria had so much to moan about, because he seemed totally competent at his job in the shop, and he was very good with the customers, a skill that Gloria had not quite mastered so far as I could see. He was twenty-nine, which really surprised me because he looked so much younger, 'and because I'm still some shop boy with no responsibilities,' he said, which was harsh, but I had to admit had a ring of truth about it.

It was just four weeks now until the opening of Gloria's second florist's shop, so when she was up in the Shrewsbury store, which was often, Alan and I would go to the Blacksmith's Arms pub after the shop had shut for the day. It was odd, I thought, how I'd imagined it would have been Gloria I would have gone out with of an evening, and Gloria who I would have confided with, but it was Alan who had taken on the job. And seemed happy to do so. More than anything he made me laugh, which was something I hadn't done in a long, long time. I'd only known him a couple of weeks but already I felt at ease with him. More so, perhaps, than I did with the pre-nuptial Gloria.

It had been a long day in the shop. Alan and I had been tasked with a much belated spring clean, as well as the usual order taking, bouquet arranging and general sales of the bunches out at the front. We'd had two of the town's most prolific gossips in as well and they'd kept us talking for a good hour between them; did we know about the redevelopment, had we heard about the latest of Tom's conquests…

Gloria had pretty much stayed in constant contact that day while she was up in the Shrewsbury store making last minute preparations for the opening. I knew that Alan was more than competent to manage the shop while Gloria was away, but she wasn't much of a 'hands off' boss and kept phoning me up every hour to make sure everything was going OK. It was funny how I had forgotten that she'd always been like that, even from our school days. I remember that, come assignment time, she would always take charge and delegate jobs for me to do. Not that I minded then and not that I minded now; she was always the one to take charge. I suppose we suit each other really – the leader and the follower. Although perhaps I wasn't quite the follower these days that I had been in the past. But still, years of friendship, however vague, meant that we each knew where the other was coming from and that made it easier for us to get along. I could definitely see the situation from Alan's point of view though.

'Has the delivery arrived yet?'

'Yes Gloria.'

'And is it OK? Is everything there?'

'Yes.'

'And the gerberas… were they included?'

'Yes.'

'How many?'

'Two dozen.'

'Good. And were they…'

'…red? Yes.'

'Have you put them straight in the bucket round the back?'

'Yes.'

'And are they supported?'

'Yes.'

'What's Alan doing?'

'He's sweeping up at the front.'

'Good. Well make sure that he pulls his weight. Keep an eye on him for me…'

I think I was only able to remain calm and keep a sense of humour because she was an old friend, and because, as Alan had pointed out, I hadn't spent the last two years locked up in a confined space with her barking at me for five days a week.

Gloria must have been in a particularly testy mood that day, because when she arrived back at the house just after seven that evening, she only managed a weak 'hello' before banging her way up the stairs and into her room.

Ten minutes later she was back downstairs, going straight for the last bottle of wine in the rack.

'How are you?' I said, twisting my hair up into a knot and securing it with a pencil.

'He won't come.'

'Who?'

'Nigel Treacy! I told you on the phone today. Honestly Rosamund what planet do you live on? Nigel Treacy from the TV. The actor. I was trying to get him to open the Shrewsbury store but he won't do it. God knows who I'll get now. And I need the publicity. How on earth am I going to find a celebrity willing to trek up to the Welsh borders, to open a shop, at this late notice?'

She poured herself a glass of wine and flopped down on the sofa beside me.

'God I've wanted a drink all afternoon!' she said, 'want one hon'?'

'Love one,' I said and hunted out another glass from the

cupboard, seeing that she wasn't about to help me out herself.

'So how did you get on with Alan today?' Gloria asked, flicking aimlessly through a catalogue.

'Well,' I said, 'really well.'

'Really well? Must be a good day then! I worry about him sometimes. He keeps doing things wrong...'

'I think he just does things differently to you, that's all.'

Gloria eyed me with scepticism. 'Well if it's not how I want it to be done, it's not right. So, therefore, he's wrong. I don't know what it is about him that irritates me so much...'

'Is it because he's gay?' I ventured.

'Oh God no. No! Not at all. No. What made you say that?'

'I don't know. Just wondered.'

'Well no, not at all. I think he just … dawdles. Takes things easy too much. He needs a bit of a spark, a bit of a bite to him. Too much dope smoking I should think.'

'He doesn't smoke dope.'

'Well, if it's not drugs then there's something else about him then… You seem to know him quite well considering you've only just met him,' she turned on me suddenly.

'Yeah, well, we get on well. I like him.' I said, trying to play down the fact I really liked the object of her constant irritation, probably more than I liked her, so much so that perhaps even she'd noticed it.

'Hmm,' she eyed me suspiciously. I could see I was on the brink of losing her confidence now. She wouldn't be able to bitch to me about Alan any more.

She sighed and took a swig of wine.

'Who's cooking?' she said, knowing the answer.

'Me,' I took my cue and headed for the kitchen, diligently. Last night Gloria had attempted to cook a chicken-wrapped-in-prosciutto type meal that had gone tragically wrong. I didn't know chicken could taste so bad. But bless her for trying – I think she lived on Marks & Spencer ready meals most of the time.

Pottering around I managed to find most of the ingredients for a lasagne and I set to work. I hardly ever cooked when I lived in

London because I didn't have much equipment, and I didn't have much equipment because I hardly ever cooked. But Gloria had the works, so I set about trying to use as many gadgets as possible. In a few minutes Gloria sidled in and pulled up a stool.

'Tom's been acting strangely,' she said.

You *are* getting married to another man in just over six weeks, I couldn't help thinking. 'Oh really?' I said straining to open a jar of passata.

'Yes. There's a bit of a distance. It's bound to happen I suppose. But do you think that's the end of it?'

What?!

'I couldn't say. I don't know–'

'No, well…' she cut in, clearly not having asked for my opinion. 'It would be a real shame. I like Tom. And I can't imagine being without him really, what with Philip being away with work every other fortnight. I'd get rather lonely I should think.'

'Maybe you should go and talk to Tom about it,' I said

'Yes… maybe,' Gloria pondered for a moment while I measured out the milk. 'Do you think I should have my hair up at the wedding?' she scooped her hair up, '…Or down,' it fell to her shoulders.

There was a sudden scraping at the door, of a key finding the lock. It opened and in came Gloria's fiancé Philip.

'Surprise!' he dumped his bags down and held out his hands, 'I'm back!'

'Philip!' Gloria looked stunned, and then putting a smile on her face she walked up to him and gave him a passionate kiss, as though she hadn't just been talking about the problems with her lover. Or perhaps it was *because* she had been talking about him, and felt the need to overcompensate.

Phil wasn't supposed to be back until the weekend and on Gloria's behalf I quickly scanned the room for any signs of Tom, but I couldn't see anything.

'Hi Roz,' he came over and gave me a peck on the cheek, 'how are things? Good?' He'd obviously been informed of my arrival.

We shared out the lasagne between the three of us, while he explained how he'd called last night but no one had been home, and how he thought it would be good to surprise us anyway.

'I was out at Alan's house,' lied Gloria, finishing off her wine in a gulp.

'Oh right,' he said, never doubting her word. Poor Phil.

'So!' he turned to me, 'how has our lodger been finding Kings Newton? I trust it's pretty enough for you! Enough sweet shops and cafés to keep you entertained? How long have you been here now?'

'This will be my fourth week,' I said, surprised that it had been so little time but felt like such a long time, 'I love it. I really do.'

'Rosamund has been keeping herself busy by running into joggers up near Shaw's Wood,' Gloria cut in, laughing.

'Really?' Phil looked amused so I told him my tale and how Gloria thought it sounded like I had met a guy called Pete who worked in a nearby Garden Centre. She said he was actually a really nice chap and she'd introduce us if I was interested. As far as I was concerned the man was too rude and abrupt for my liking, however good looking he might be, but I didn't rule him out completely. After all, beggars could hardly be choosers, so I'd said that I'd think about it and left it at that. Perhaps given time he would forget about the flowers and ivy in my hair and my saggy wet skirt. How much time would that take? A fortnight? Two years?

Philip bounced around the room in a fit of excitement. He talked and talked about Australia, which was where he had been seconded for five weeks, and showed us his tan lines, and the shark-tooth necklace on a strip of leather around his neck. Gloria was not very impressed and delved into the bag he had bought her, pulling out a shell-covered box. I got a koala-bear toy with Velcro arms, which was very sweet of him.

I liked Philip. He was one of those men that you know you ought to settle down with. He had eyes that, even when being entirely serious (which he was when he was explaining, at length, the IT networking problems he had been dealing with out in

Perth) his eyes twinkled. He was so completely different to Gloria, or at least, he was completely different to the Gloria that was here and now: the girl who had grown up from the more happy-go-lucky person that I had known from way back. Now that she was developing into a hardened businesswoman, Phil probably had to make do with increasingly smaller amounts of affection. And as time went on he had likely forgotton what it had been like in the beginning. Would he have put up with so much of her attitude if he could stand back and see what was happening? Poor Philip, I couldn't help thinking, however unkindly it was to my friend, he deserved so much better.

'Whose are the shoes?' he said when he came back from the kitchen having opened one of the bottles of wine he'd brought back from Oz.

Gloria and I turned round to see a pair of Tom's trainers down by the front door. Why hadn't I spotted them earlier?

'Alan's,' Gloria lied.

'You sure are seeing a lot of Alan,' he said, pouring the wine, 'so are you getting on better with him now?'

'Not really. Well, maybe. He's still as slow as ever. But Roz likes him.'

Philip turned to me and stage whispered, 'She's not happy until everyone works as hard as she does.'

'Not true!' she looked genuinely irritated, 'You know what he's like. Well, anyway,' she settled down again, 'he's getting much better. I think it works giving him more responsibility. And he likes working with Roz so everyone's happy!'

'Any news on the protest?' he asked.

Gloria went into the news that Tom had told us, that Lord Weston had found out about the road block and ordered the diggers to the site early. They talked about who the spy in their band of protesters could be, and the next plans to demonstrate against redevelopment. Meanwhile I cleared away the dinner plates and loaded the dishwasher, managing to get lasagne all over my green wool jumper.

'I can't believe I'm going to be on my honeymoon when the big protest takes place.'

'Well we're not cancelling it,' said Philip

'No... no I don't want to cancel the honeymoon,' Gloria said without much enthusiasm, 'It's just ... I would have really liked to take part in the big protest.'

'What's going to happen in the 'big one'?' I asked. I was intrigued what could be bigger than the planned human roadblock – maybe a naked human roadblock?

'A whole group of people from the town have formed a sort of party against the development. We kept seeing the same old faces at the town meetings Richard Weston's lawyers held, and we thought why don't we team up and make a stand against it.'

'So what will you do?'

'Well *we'll* do nothing. *We'll* be in Spain... but everyone else will be putting posters and banners up around the grounds of the Hall.'

'What do the banners say?'

'Just stuff like, 'Why not develop here?' and 'Welcome to the City of Kings Newton.' We couldn't come up with anything really brilliant, but at least it will make the point.'

'Isn't it a bit late now? Haven't the builders got permission to build and the diggers are here...'

'Well Miss Optimism...' began Gloria

'Gloria!' Phil chided her

'Well ...' she wheedled, 'our worry now is that this sale of land might patch up another suite of rooms in his personal palace but what next? What happens when the gold taps in his bathroom stop working or he runs out of Camembert? I think this development will set a precedent for the sale of more land and then even more. We're going to lose the community spirit of our town before we had chance to do anything about it.'

I was beginning to wonder just where Gloria's sense of community spirit was coming from. It seemed more than a trifle strange that this busy, busy career woman wanted to devote so much of her time and energies to the good of the town when really she didn't have that much to do with it. As far as I knew she didn't sit on any local committees or business groups and she certainly wasn't a member of anything like the WI so why was she so active in the protest? Surely the building of a few more houses would be good for business in a market town? No, it was probably because Tom had fed her a never-ending torrent of information about the redevelopment and in order to keep her man she had to share his passions. Perhaps she even got a kick out of being a little bit anti-establishment, especially since she was such a serious and determined businesswoman. A bit of rebelling might be a bit of a turn on. Whatever it was that drove her into the protest Phil certainly didn't share it, I could tell by the way his eyes had glazed over and he slumped back on the sofa with a 'heard it all before' expression. He looked pale and tired.

When Gloria finally left a lull in the conversation he quickly jumped in and changed the subject, talking about the plans for the wedding. He wouldn't be out of the country again now before the big day, so I asked if I was going to be in the way but he assured me I wouldn't be. He was going to be living with friends in Ludlow for the week before the wedding.

'Absence makes the heart grow fonder,' he chimed, 'anyway, I don't want to be around when Gloria blows her top with all this stress.'

'Oh, well, thank you very much Phil,' she said indignantly. He laughed it off.

'So how are things going with *you*?' he asked me, refilling my wine glass. Was this the fourth glass? I felt bleary headed but didn't stop him.

'Oh. Fine. You know… I love working in the shop, it makes such a change from being tied to a phone and a computer.'

'I'll bet. Do you miss the City?' Phil said

'Not much.' I said after a moment's consideration, 'I miss my friends at the office, but I've got Alan to keep me company.'

Gloria snorted.

'What about Greg?' Phil asked softly.

Greg. My hands went cold around the wine glass. The bastard. I hadn't thought about him for a couple of days now. I'd refused to think about him. I hadn't let him or anything connected with him inside my head. It would be a waste of my time to spare one second of my thoughts to that git.

'Greg who?'

'Atta girl!' Phil slapped me on the back, which didn't do me any good as I now felt sick and clammy for a reason that I couldn't fathom.

'I never liked the guy much anyway. Is he…'

'…still with Rachel? I don't know.'

'You haven't asked your mum?' Gloria butted in. 'Have you still not spoken to her since it happened?'

'Hey! How come you don't know all this?' said Phil

'Well,' Gloria floundered having been exposed as having taken no real interest in my situation since I'd arrived. 'I didn't … I didn't want to bring it up because I knew Roz would be… upset'

I wasn't upset. 'I'm not upset.'

'*Have* you spoken to your mum since it happened?' Phil asked.

'No. I suppose I ought to call her but I really don't want to yet. It's just such a relief to leave everything behind and not think about it. Put some distance between me and it. Move on… you know…'

I was crying. I hadn't realised but tears had found their way down my face, my neck and onto my chest. I couldn't stop myself sobbing, which was a strange experience, almost like being outside my own body and watching me cry. I don't think I'd ever not been in control to that extent before.

'Oh honey,' Gloria came over and sitting on the arm of the sofa engulfed me in a hug. It felt good.

'I don't know… it's the wine probably,' I said, wiping the tears away with my rough sleeve.

'Yes, wine does that to me too…' Gloria began and launched into yet another gobbet of personal history…

6

Dear Mum,

I'm sure you're wondering what happened to me. ~~I've left Greg~~… I've run away. I've gone to stay with a friend until I sort myself out…

Dear Mum,

I've left everything behind! I've walked away from my flat and my job and ~~my~~ Greg and…

Dear Mum,

As you've probably already heard I've walked away from another mess in my life!!! Please support me on this because it's been ~~so hard~~ really hard it's hard to…

7

The metaphorical floodgates had been opened, and I was at an all time low. I should have spent more time coming to terms with what I'd done and planning what I was going to do with myself. Well, that wasn't true because I hadn't even spent *some* time doing it. Over the past month I'd managed to get caught up in my Kings Newton escape and had pushed thoughts of my real life to the back of my mind. And now suddenly here they were in abundance.

Since talking to Phil and Gloria I found I couldn't *not* think about why I was here. It was impossible to concentrate solely on the here and now, the florist's, the wedding, the new people in my life. Any spare moment to myself, a lull in the shop, a walk after work, and my mind would be raging. I would be stacking ribbons and I would see a flashback from in front of the fridge, or I'd see Greg, half-clothed, running after me down the street, when I had walked out with just a bag of clothes and my holdall. And then I would remember being sick at work. Crying at my desk. Urgh.

I had half thought over the past few weeks that perhaps I was a carefree woman who had broken free of her crap job and crap boyfriend, some sort of free spirit with an independent streak. But who was I kidding? My boyfriend didn't want me – he wanted my sister instead, and when I handed my notice in at work my boss had sighed and moaned about the difficulties of recruiting at this time of year, but hadn't got down on her hands and knees and begged me to stay. No-one had begged me to stay.

So here I was with a few clothes and just five pairs of pants. I must buy some more pants. I had a few pounds in the bank, increasing thanks to Gloria paying me a small sum and not charging me rent, but absolutely no direction to my life whatsoever.

And every time I tried to write to my mother and tell her that I was OK, the nagging doubts about what I had done crowded into my head and spilled out wetly onto the paper in front of me. I had stormed out of my old life and no-one, really, seemed very bothered about it – not even me, most of the time. I'm a nice person, I know I am – and it just doesn't seem fair, but there it is. Perhaps I'd built up the wrong kind of life around myself. Yes, perhaps that was it.

Gloria and Phil had started showing more affection towards me, although neither of them actually went so far as to bring up the subject of 'what I was going to do now'. They trod more softly around me, and gave me bigger plates of food, as if I needed feeding up; sort of 'never mind about the disaster that is your life, why not put two inches on your thighs'.

Was it Keats who said that it is better to wallow in misery than to go through life as one bland experience after another? Better to be desperately happy or desperately unhappy than to be middling. Beige. Suburban. I suppose I had been living a rather beige life for the past few years; certainly there was nothing very dynamic about it.

Whoever said it, I was in their camp, because in those few days I did at least *feel* more than I had done since I could remember. Every element of my body ached in a way that I couldn't begin to describe, but which made me feel physically heavy and slow as though the misery fed on my energy. But rather than do the female heroine thing; sigh, buy some new clothes and get on with my life, I decided to open myself up to the moment and revel in my gloom; to really embrace Keats' philosophy full on; I would live life to the limit, but in a tragically miserable and sad way.

I didn't really have a timescale for my depression, other than knowing that Gloria and Phil returned from their honeymoon in mid-September. So, I had around seven weeks to work out what I wanted to do and come to terms with what had happened. I wouldn't be needed in the Kings Newton shop after that, because the previous shop assistant came off maternity leave then, and I knew that she wanted her old position back. The Shrewsbury shop was already recruited for, and besides I didn't really want to be working for my old school friend in any kind of permanent capacity. That would indeed be to abandon any kind of self-respect and I hadn't sunk that low. Yet.

So I gave myself up to sheer misery and despondency and took to wandering around Kings Newton for hours and hours on end, paying only enough attention to my surroundings to prevent me from crashing in to any more joggers. I tried to focus my thoughts on what I could do with my life, but such epic choices were too much for me, so I emptied my head of just about all thoughts and resigned myself to blankly looking at the trees and the river and the cattle and pretty much kept to myself.

However, circumstances always intervene in any plan, as they did in this plan, putting a stop to my self-imposed despondency. With the upcoming wedding there were plenty of things to be doing rather than moping around on my own. There were boxes of favours to fill and place cards to write. I had been given the task of designing and printing up the orders of service, and liasing with the enormously fat and sweaty organist to ensure that he was prepared with all the music on the day. And not only that, I was co-running the Kings Newton shop while Gloria spent most of her time in Shrewsbury.

So, contrary to my Keatsian plan, I found myself being pulled out of my reveries and into the here and now, and after initially resenting it and wishing I could be on my own to mope around, I began to welcome the diversions.

Quite unexpectedly it was Alan who was the person who helped me the most during my 'dark time' as he called it. Never silent, he bobbed and fussed around me, talking endlessly about what had happened in London and what I would be doing with my life. At first it just made me realise how bad things were, not having any plan to do anything with my new freedom, and not having a burning desire to do anything or be anywhere. But he would point out that it was OK to 'go with the flow'. That it was the smart thing to do, because people who chose to go against the flow are people who are always fighting everyone else and it takes them far more effort than the smart ones who enjoy the ride.

'Look at Gloria,' he said, 'she goes against the flow at every opportunity. She opens a new store just weeks before her wedding; when she could just as well have put it back until she settles down after her honeymoon. But no, she rushes the purchase of the property so she can be in there as soon as possible. And what does it give her? Hassle. She's putting pressure on the estate agent to get the sale through quickly. She's putting pressure on the decorators to prepare it on time. She even has to recruit quickly and she's not going to get the staff she needs because she has to make do with people who are available at short notice, and they're never the best.'

'Like me,' I whined.

'I didn't say that.'

'But it's true. She needed someone to help her out in Kings Newton and I came along on very short notice indeed.'

'Oh stop moping and feeling sorry for yourself for just one minute,' he said exasperated. 'All I'm saying is, look at what it's doing to her. You keep saying how different she is from the person you used to know. She's a fighter now. A little pit bull terrier. She's had to go through her life making people give her what she wants, and it's left her with no patience, a fierce temper and a shortage of friends.'

'True…' To be honest I'd been rather surprised at Gloria since

I'd come up to Kings Newton. After the initial friendly greeting and gossipy catch up, getting to know her again I thought she'd changed almost entirely and I don't know whether she had become someone that I would actually want as a friend if I met her now. Harsh but true…

'Whereas you…' Alan continued, laying his hand on my shoulder, like a father to a daughter, 'you will never burst a blood vessel trying to get where you shouldn't be. You get on with people and you make friends easily. To be honest, I think you get on too well with people, because it sounds like this Greg fellow was clearly no good from day one, but there you are, you make the best of things.'

'Do I?' I said, surprised to learn something about myself.

'Yes. You should be more careful you know. You don't have to accept everything all the time. If you don't like someone, then it's OK not to like them – you don't have to make yourself like them just to fit in.'

'I don't do that!'

'You do. I think you take far more flack from Gloria than you should. She could walk all over you, if you let her.'

'Alan! She's been so good to me—'

'And it's in her *interest* to be good to you. You arrived on the scene at a very opportune time for her. Just stick up for yourself a bit more, that's my advice. And the next time she starts bossing you around, don't scurry away and do her bidding. Answer back.'

'But our relationship doesn't work that way.'

'But it's not the relationship you want to be in.'

'How do you know that?' I said.

'Well who would want to be in that kind of relationship?' he retorted, and I had to agree. Alan was very wise to these things. Why was he gay? He would make such a wonderful boyfriend.

Working in a small market town shop was, it turned out, a good place to meet people and I found that I was already on nodding terms with a lot of townsfolk. Besides which, with Alan as a drinking buddy I was getting to know the many pubs and restaurants in the place, so I felt at home.

Everything in my life was new, and everything was there to be learnt. The floristry business was much trickier than I would have imagined, but fortunately for me Gloria and Alan ran the place, and I was left with helping out on the more menial side of the business. Finance yes, I could tot up the day's takings and happily fill out the forms and books that were needed to log the sales. But when it came to taking orders and arranging displays, then I left it to the experts. Alan's arrangements tended to be big and bold; large palm fronds slashed into angles, stark white flowers like lilies and other flowers whose names I didn't recognise. Whereas Gloria went for more traditional bouquets of pink roses, sprays of ferny leaves and an abundance of ribbons and folded papers. The two styles didn't sit very easily together, which was another source of irritation for Gloria but amused Alan and me no end. Alan would make the chrysanthemums into 'too dynamic' a display, and she would have to cut and tweak them into something more suitable for a 'small market town in the Welsh Marches'.

'Honestly,' she would mutter under her breath, 'this isn't bloody London you know. We don't need *vibrant*, we need *beautiful*.'

However, perhaps Kings Newton did need *vibrant* because over the past week Alan had had a free reign with Gloria away in Shrewsbury and as a result a couple of restaurants in the town had started to show an interest in his bolder displays, much to Gloria's annoyance. She had been trying to initiate some corporate relationships for the past couple of years but the corporate people hadn't been interested in her homely bunches. But now that Alan was coming up with some more imaginative designs, they had placed orders and discussed the potential for weekly orders. The one-off trial displays brought in a lot of money; the potential for ongoing orders would bring in substantial amounts of money. It had bought Alan a bit more freedom and he was able to order in any flowers, up to a point, to make up his displays. This he revelled in, and spent inordinate amounts of time arranging weird and wonderful flowers and branches and leaves in enormous vases that he took down to the restaurants himself, tottering through the cobbled streets peering through the fronds.

Although they weren't to her taste, as she'd made abundantly clear, I could see that Gloria had some sort of secret respect for the flower arrangements that Alan came up with, although she would never tell him so. I caught her one day rifling through the order book next to one of his more fantastic displays, looking up some of the flowers that he had chosen, and probably making a mental note to do the same. In fact I could see that she was starting to copy his style, using more foliage and making use of the off-cuts of the twisty willow that he had bought in.

Alan enjoyed seeing the look on her face when he had arranged a particularly good display. I'm sure that it was his ability to laugh secretly at Gloria that kept him sane, and kept him working in the shop.

Whatever it was that kept him working at Gloria's Flowers I was glad. I couldn't imagine working there without him. It would be very dull indeed. But I couldn't help but wonder how long he would stick it out – especially now that he was beginning to get noticed…

9

The Swan Inn is an enormous old building situated just off the town square in Kings Newton. It's one of the few buildings to have survived the fire and has an enormous timber frame that stands out from the otherwise fairly uniform Georgian and Victorian shop fronts surrounding it. As it was Alan's favourite pub I got to know the Swan very well and we even had our own corner by the enormous inglenook fireplace, where we now sat eating crisps and drinking this month's guest cider – Old Toastie. It was foul.

The Swan was a really old fashioned pub. There were polished brasses pinned to enormous wooden pillars and old blue and white jugs arranged along mantelpieces and shelves. The bar itself was festooned with garlands of hops intertwined with tiny fairy lights that glinted on the brasses and picked up the little clouds of cigarette smoke that curled in the air. Although I suppose it was a locals' pub, as most of the pubs in Kings Newton seemed to be, I never felt an outsider there and as Alan seemed to know all and sundry there was never a dull night.

Alan had taken another swig of Old Toastie and recovering well he slapped his hand down on the table and said, 'Dammit Rosamund, I need to know the truth!'

'The truth about what?' I said, nonplussed.

'I want to know what really happened with Greg. In front of the fridge. All you talk about is the fridge, you don't talk about what went on *in front of it* and that's the interesting part.'

I took a deep breath, 'You really want to know?' I said, not really sure if I wanted to divulge the sordid details to him. I wound and unwound locks of hair in my fingers.

'Yes!'

'OK. Well I got home early—'

'Oh, it's so often the way!' Alan wailed, putting a hand on my arm as if he were Larry Grayson re-incarnate.

'Look, are you going to take the piss or do you really want to know?'

'OK, OK, I really want to know. Go on – you got home early...'

'I got home early and I thought something was up because the back door was open and I never leave it open. And I heard something in the kitchen so I walked in and there they were – Greg and my sister on the floor, naked, in front of the fridge.'

'What,' said Alan, crunching on a crisp meditatively, 'just like, naked, and sitting there?'

'No they were not just sitting there!' I said exasperated, 'They were *having sex*. Actually, Rachel was on top if you must know the gory details.'

'I must.'

'You filthmonger,' I said, but laughing and taking a swig of Old Toastie. 'Urgh, my God! This stuff is bad. Anyway, there I was in the kitchen staring at them and they were staring at me and no-one really knew what to do.'

'Did they carry on doing it?'

'No, Alan they did not! I think I must have ruined the moment or something.' This boy was unbelievable.

'Did you say anything to them?' he asked, taking another swig of cider and wincing.

'I think I said, 'Oh.'

'Is that all?'

'Well what was I supposed to say? It was a shock – I couldn't come up with a sermon about betrayal on the spot could I? I did try to think of something to say – and they looked at me, waiting for me to say something. I really cocked it up actually. I should have said something clever.'

'Never mind. So what did you do then?'

'I ran upstairs and filled a bag with clothes, and stuff from the bathroom, while they put their trousers on. I could hear them growling at each other. Then I ran out of the house.'

'And have you heard from either of them since then?'

'Ha!' I said, reaching into my pocket and pulling out my mobile. I scrolled through and came to the messages from Greg which for some unfathomable but no doubt section-able reason I hadn't deleted from the memory. Alan took the phone off me and went through them, snorting every so often.

'So why do you think he wants to talk to you?' he asked eventually, handing the phone back to me.

'I don't know. I expect he wants to apologise and get the guilt off his chest or something. But, I don't think there's much to say do you? It's not like I'm going to turn round and say, 'Oh, OK let's forgive and forget and act as if nothing happened.''

'Sounds like he doesn't realise what a big deal it is.'

'That's about right,' I said, laughing. 'He's so self-centred he probably thinks he can just apologise his way out of it and everything will be OK.'

'Do you miss him?'

I hadn't bargained on that question and I didn't know what to say. Did I miss him? No, I didn't – I felt so wonderfully free and able to be myself without him. But then I did miss my old life. A bit. You can't walk away and not regret a single thing.

'No. I don't miss him,' I said eventually and Alan nodded.

'So how come you ended up in Kings Newton then?' he stacked up his beer mats on the edge of the table and flicked them with the back of his fingers, catching them deftly.

'Well it was the most outrageous bit of good fortune,' I said, trying to copy Alan's trick and knocking two beer mats into my pint. 'I went to a café and stared out of the window a bit, then I started to make some phone calls to see if I could stay with a friend, and Gloria said yes – so here I am.'

'Did you mean to move out of London?'

'No,' I said, trying to remember how I was feeling at the time. It felt like a lifetime ago. 'To be honest I can't really remember what was going through my head. Not much I don't think. I just knew I didn't want to move back in with my mother, she thinks Greg is wonderful and would be bending my ear every five minutes wanting to know when I would be going back to him,' I laughed. 'I bet, in fact, that she'd be relieved he'd had an affair with her other daughter. It'd keep Greg in the family!'

'She's not that bad is she?'

'No,' I said. 'Well, maybe…'

'Does she know where you are?'

'I write to her,' I said, which was the absolute truth. Although I hadn't actually gone as far as completing a letter to her, or posting any of the incomplete letters, yet. It was just so hard! She had always been so critical of me; I somehow never managed to measure up to her high standards. But I ought to really try and get something posted to her, she'd worry. I did briefly think about calling her, but I couldn't have borne the inevitable grilling – what would I say about Rachel, for goodness' sake? I couldn't tell Mum it was her on top, could I. It was a lose:lose situation whichever way I looked at it.

'Do you think,' Alan cut into my thoughts, waving his pint in front of me, 'that Greg might pay you a visit, seeing as you're ignoring his calls and text messages?'

'God, no!' I said, and I really really hoped I was right. Did he know where Gloria lived? I couldn't remember whether it had ever come up, and at least I hadn't abandoned my address book in the rush to get out of the lovers' way.

10

Mainly thanks to Alan I was getting to know not just the town, but the surrounding countryside very well indeed. I had now visited most of the pubs within a five mile radius, and nearly all the restaurants, as well as the local cinema (small), and museum (very small). But there was one place that I still hadn't seen, and that was Weston Hall. It dominated the town, not the building itself, though, because you couldn't see the Hall at all from the town, it being entirely hidden behind an old redbrick wall and the enormous oak trees that grew behind it. Its dominance was more to do with the presence of its owner, who made a big impression given that he was rarely seen. But maybe that's just because I associated with his sworn enemies, and they never stopped bitching about him and his housing development.

To all intents and purposes the Hall remained distinctly detached from the town. Town and Hall didn't mix, except in the stable block where Tom had his workshop. Situated on the edge of the estate, where it met the town, the stables had been converted into craft workshops and shops, where Tom worked along with a group of craftsmen, producing woodcarvings, stained glass commissions and artwork supposedly inspired by the surrounding countryside. I hadn't visited the stables as I had been keen to avoid Tom, who was rather *keen* on female company and not necessarily discerning in his tastes. He must have thought he was God's gift to womankind. While he had the looks of a Greek statue, he had the arrogant self-confidence of a particularly repulsive car salesman. And hence wouldn't be getting my knickers in a twist.

One gorgeously sunny Friday morning, four weeks before the wedding, I got my first opportunity to visit the Hall. Gloria had been granted access to the rooms she would be hiring in order to prepare for the wedding.

I was beside myself with excitement as we headed off from the house early in the morning, arms laden with tape measures and large prints of the floor plans of Weston Hall. Gloria had been planning her wedding for the past year and a half, before Phil had even proposed to her. Although I thought that was a pretty strange turn of events, I discovered that most women do it. In particularly dull moments in the shop I had begun to wonder whether I should have some sort of a seating plan for my wedding, should I ever have one. But given the fact that I pretty much felt complete animosity to all (straight) men just now, I didn't see any need to panic and start to cut out pictures of table displays and dress designs and keep them in a scrapbook, as Gloria had been doing. I wondered, momentarily whether Greg would marry my sister? And whether I'd be invited? No. I wouldn't dwell on it.

'I don't get it,' I said to Gloria as we trudged our way down Weston Hall's enormous sweeping driveway, having negotiated the rather stern wrought iron fence in the boundary wall. I was still in a frenzy of excitement about seeing the Hall, which amused Gloria, but my excitement was gradually being tempered with concern about a possible meeting with its notorious resident. I pictured the old aristo' standing squarely on the front steps of his mansion, all offensive tweed and bristling whiskers, with a half-cocked gun over one arm, loaded and ready to kill game birds and stray locals. Surely with his beady bird-murderer's eye he would quickly mark Gloria as one of the 'locals'. The 'spy' who had leaked the news of the roadblock would no doubt have told him who was plotting the protest against him. The spy might reveal that Gloria was an active agitator against the development and then the whole wedding reception at Weston Hall situation could become quite strained.

Or perhaps he wouldn't be there and the whole thing would take place without meeting him, which seemed the best option to me.

'What don't you get?' said Gloria. 'Careful, you're trailing the measuring tape on the path!'

'Oh sorry. Can you carry this then? I think I've got too much piled on here,' Alan would have been proud of me, sticking up for myself.

'Ohh…' Gloria was exasperated and snatched a fabric book from my hands. Since when did I become her packhorse? I let it go and we carried on walking.

'So what don't you 'get'?' she repeated.

'What I don't get is this: that you hate Lord Weston…'

'Right.'

'And you hate everything he stands for…'

'Right again.'

'But you're having your wedding reception at Weston Hall?'

'Cattle grid!' Gloria called out, and we skirted around it. 'You wait until you see the place. It's truly stunning, magnificent. The National Trust have a few places nearby that I could have used for the reception, but hiring them is a really tricky business, and when you manage to book the venue then you have to accept lots of clauses that say you have to vacate the property early in the evening, you can't have drinks in some rooms and so on. I just don't think it would be much fun having to fit my wedding around a strict set of rules like that, however nice the setting. Whereas here I can pretty much do as I please. I can be in decorating the place the week before the wedding and we can party until the small hours. Richard Weston and his entourage will be in London when the wedding's on, so no one will mind. And besides, the house is *really* amazing. Some of it is five hundred years old you know.'

'But doesn't it really get to you that you're paying this Weston chap a lot of money to use his house for the day, and yet you hate him?'

'Well I'm not really thinking about it too much. It's local, it's gorgeous and it was available, so we took it. Besides, I won't have to have much, if anything, to do with Richard Weston himself. He'll be swanning around in Mayfair or somewhere like that where he has his business, and when he is up in Kings Newton he usually keeps to himself. We deal with the housekeeper and the estate manager. Saying that though, I think Richard Weston is at Weston Hall for the next few days, but I know that he's not going to be at home during the wedding, that's the important thing.'

My heart sank. He would be in the Hall. Today. I would meet him. I wasn't looking forward to the prospect of traipsing round his precious property, measuring up his rooms to help my friend prepare for her wedding. It all seemed pretty forbidding. I'd be bound to bump into some priceless *object d'art* and cause a scandal – a wedding-stopping scandal at that! Gloria would never forgive me. I'd be homeless for the second time in two months.

'So what are we doing today?' I asked in trepidation.

'God Rosamund? How many times do I have to tell you? We're—'

I snapped: 'Gloria!' She stopped and lowered her armfuls of fabrics so she could see me.

'What?'

My mind went blank; what would I say? Stop picking on me? Stop being a bad tempered old cow? Mentally, though, I congratulated myself on taking note of what Alan had said and sticking up for myself. I pushed a strand of hair from my face.

'Stop being so crabby towards me,' I said somewhat half-heartedly. Not the pick of the bunch, but not the worst thing I could have said either.

'I'm not!'

'You are!'

'Well I'm sorry if you *think* I am,' she said in a hurt voice, 'but I don't mean to come across like that.'

'Well you do.' Go on girl! Alan would be enormously proud…

'Well…' she began, 'What you don't seem to appreciate is that there's a lot going on in my life at the moment, what with the new store in Shrewsbury, and the wedding, and—'

'And there's a lot going on in *my* life too,' I retaliated, 'I've had to deal with losing my boyfriend and my sister – which I'm not that bothered about, but anyway – and my job and moving from London. And I have to come up with some grand plan about what I'm going to be doing for the rest of my life, and it's all rather scary really. It's great that you took me in to your home and you asked me to work in your shop. It's really helped. But… can't you … relax a bit? You're so edgy all the time. I find it really hard to talk to you sometimes.'

'Well that's just the way I am,' she said, softly.

'You didn't used to be like that.'

'Well people change.'

'I haven't changed,' I said defiantly.

'You're more of a prude than you used to be.'

'That's not true,' again we stopped, bundles lowered, eyes meeting,

'Well you are about Tom and me.'

'Well it's your wedding in four weeks time for God's sake. Don't you think it's just a little bit off…'

'What you have to remember,' she said, in an older sister way that took me right back to the playground, 'is that you've just come in to my life with no idea of anything beyond what you've seen in the last few weeks. You have *no* idea how Philip and I work as a couple, and no idea of what is between Tom and me. You don't know how it works, but it *does*. It works fine. It might not be your cup of tea but it suits me, thank you very much.'

It was true I had to admit. It was her business what she got up to, and as her friend I knew I should just accept it. She was, after all, being really good to me by giving me a place to stay and job to do.

'I'm not a prude,' I said after a few moments.

'You *are* a prude,' she retorted, her voice coming over the fabric bundles in front of her.

'I'm not.'

'You are.'

'Not.'

'Are. Prude. Prude. Prude.'

'Well if I'm a prude, then you are a *loose woman*.'

'Prude.'

'Tart.'

I laughed. Gloria laughed. We bumped bundles in a sort of hug, and made up. It felt good to clear the air, and Gloria seemed a lot brighter and more relaxed as we trotted down the never-ending driveway. Alan was right, it felt good to ruffle her feathers and speak my mind.

'Look! There…' she stopped and we lowered the bundles in our arms again. Weston Hall fanned out before us, a beautiful Georgian-fronted country house, its façade perfectly reflected in the oxbow lake in front of it. It was built of red brick with four enormous Bath-stone columns stuck on the front. A sweeping stone staircase led up to the enormous front door which was painted a beautiful deep green. As we walked nearer, however, the impression of grandeur was reduced, as its rather sad state of disrepair became clear. The sash windows sagged and bowed and had peeling frames and cracked panes. Even the grand stone columns had weathered badly, their ornate cornicing and coving melting down the pillars like wax down a candle.

It was the sort of slow decay that looked rotten and dirty when it happened to a normal everyday Victorian terraced house, but here somehow it didn't detract from the beauty of the place. It changed it. Perhaps it was because of the setting, or perhaps it was because ultimately Weston Hall was something that was so much more beautiful to start with.

Weston Hall was not a pristine preserved mansion but a hidden fairy tale of a house built in the heart of the town, but hidden away completely. But however grand the boundary fencing was, or how imposing the gate and driveway, the house itself was much more relaxed and had a homely look to it. If country houses were clothes, Weston Hall would be a dressing gown; comfortable and worn and not at all formal. It almost looked as though it was pressed down into the dip of the land, as though it was curtseying to us. I said as much, and Gloria just stared at me as if I had gone mad.

I don't know how I would have coped if I had been on my own. I would have had no clue how to approach the house, so I was happy to trail behind Gloria who seemed to know what to do. I knew not to go up to the main door, because that would probably be reserved for important guests and neither Gloria nor I were important enough for that. Besides, with my old green wrap dress on, and my hair fixed up with chopsticks, I didn't look like the type of person who used the front entrance of grand houses. But then, I reasoned as I plodded behind Gloria, we were not tradesmen or staff so we would not be going in through the back entrances either. Were we, in fact, side entrance people?

We were! I was pleased to find out that if left to my own devices I would probably manage OK and I knew my place.

11

Gloria knocked on a slightly shabby green door that faced towards the stables, and we waited patiently.

'Are you OK, Roz?' Gloria asked, looking at my face and frowning

'Of course!' I said, trying to effect a blasé sort of look, which basically meant pouting and raising my eyebrows a bit.

'You just look nervous, that's all.'

'No, I'm fine.'

Within a minute we could hear footsteps slowly approaching and as the door opened an elderly looking chap greeted us.

I clocked him instantly. This man was a cat kicker. I'd last seen him on one of my wanderings around the town – he had shouted after a cat in the street a few days earlier and had tried to kick it, all because it had walked in front of him as he had slowly inched his way down the High Street. Was this Lord Weston? I had guessed he would be somewhat old from what Tom and Gloria had been saying, but I hadn't expected someone quite so decrepit. This was why the family had ended with him then, with no children to continue the line. Those coke-fuelled parties must have taken place in the Thirties, because I couldn't imagine this sour faced old man drinking champagne while bouncing a girl on each knee. Gross...

Perhaps he wasn't as old as I thought he was. Perhaps his fast life had taken its toll; too long being baked in the sun while driving an open topped sports car around the village lanes at breakneck speed. His hair was a wispy steel grey, not quite white yet. Dark black-brown eyes peered at us from beneath heavy, tangled eyebrows.

Fixing a nervous smile on my face, I courageously hid behind Gloria, not an easy thing to do being considerably taller than she was, glad that I wasn't the one who had chosen to get married in this man's house.

Gloria had straightened up the minute he opened the door and bristled, no doubt with suppressed resentment at the man she hated so much. And maybe in deference to the title, although she didn't seem too bothered about it when she talked about him.

It seemed a strange thing to hate a man so much and yet involve him, through necessity, in one of the biggest days of your life. But there you go, it was her choice.

'Gloria Beaumont? Yes, yes I knew you were coming. Come in, come in. You've been speaking to the housekeeper haven't you? She told me about the booking for the wedding,' he ushered us into the hallway and on into the Hall. It was dark inside, and there was that fustiness about it that stately homes always have, but here it was mingled with floor polish and furniture wax. The floor was dark, dark brown and highly polished, our shoes clattering as we walked along following the man further into the building.

'Well you'll be wanting to measure up the rooms, am I right?' he said sharply.

'That's right,' Gloria said briskly, holding out the floor plans and explaining what she wanted to do. I glanced around me nervously, feeling as though I were trespassing in his home. It probably wasn't helped by the fact that he was such a miserable and disagreeable man. No wonder he was disliked by the people of the town, he was certainly no ambassador for the landed gentry. Gloria seemed much more at home than I was. She'd been to the Hall a couple of times before, though, once to collect the floor plan and before that to arrange the booking of her reception. So she had the advantage of knowing her way about the place and being familiar with it. And besides which, she was paying this man a lot of money for the privilege of being here so in a way she had paid her way to feeling unselfconscious about using the Hall.

'Well you're welcome to have the run of the rooms down here then,' he said, looking suspiciously at me, probably because I was the scruffier of the two of us and therefore more likely to pocket the family silver. 'Let me know if you need anything. I'll be over in the estate office, just round the back past the kitchens.'

'Thanks.' Gloria made to go.

'Oh and one other thing,' he said. 'Do you know what time you'll be leaving today?'

'Er…' Gloria looked at me for an answer, but I stared back at her blankly. Was I supposed to know this?

'I don't know,' she said, and with that he turned and left us in the corridor.

I must have had the look of a hunted animal, because Gloria put her hand on my shoulder – not an easy thing to do, given our respective heights – and reassured me that in all probability he wouldn't attack me. I laughed out loud, but was secretly relieved. The man kicked cats; he knew no humanity.

'Come on, in here,' Gloria led me into the Dining Room. It was beautiful. Pale yellow walls and misty mirrors that made the whole room an oasis of light. Long windows faced out over the gardens and drew me to them to admire the view. Above the fireplace there was an enormous oil painting of a young woman and her daughter, smiling benevolently down on us as we laid down our bundles and took stock of our surroundings.

'I can't believe how *old* he is,' I whispered after a moment.

'Well, yes,' said Gloria, 'I suppose he should have left here a while ago but I think he likes being involved in the place. He's quite a hands-on man. Miserable old bastard isn't he?'

'I'm glad he won't be around during the wedding.'

'Too right.'

And with that we set to work, carefully measuring every wall, every alcove, the position of every door and window. Gloria chatted as we went along, explaining what she'd got planned for the Dining Room, which is where she would be putting the dining tables, and the Green Room, which is where drinks would be served, and finally the Ball Room, where a disco would take place.

All the time I listened to her chatter on, I kept one ear trained on noises outside the room, hoping we would keep to ourselves and that the crotchety old landowner would not make another appearance.

After the dining room was measured up we moved on to the Green Room. It was painted a drab blue-green and had chips of paint falling from the woodwork. It looked slightly shabby but it suited the aspect of the room and the furniture, and the whole effect wouldn't have looked out of place in a *Country Living* type of magazine. There were vast wooden display cases housing plates and cups from various mismatching dinner services. And everywhere there were tarnished silver objects in need of a good polish. It was more homely than the Dining Room, certainly.

There was even a TV mounted on an inlaid cabinet in one corner, with a well worn sofa and armchairs facing it. And on a table beside the window was the most bizarre collection of cheese graters, of all things, arranged on the surface in size order. Large upright chrome graters, old fashioned flat graters and even a cast iron type of grater built into a wooden box.

'That's odd,' I said to Gloria, pointing out the collection.

'Not really. He runs a kitchenware business. Apparently he specialises in old fashioned kitchen equipment.'

'How bizarre.'

'I suppose so. But someone's got to do it.'

I shrugged and went to carry on measuring. A minute later I heard the sound of someone walking towards the room. It was an energetic sort of tip-tapping though, and it definitely sounded like a woman's walk rather than a man's stride. In a moment the door opened and in walked a very pretty, very petite woman. She must have been about my age, or maybe a bit older, nearer her mid-thirties, white blonde hair tied back in a pony tail. She was dressed immaculately in lavender dress and matching kitten-heeled shoes, looking like she'd just stepped out of the pages of a magazine.

Gloria and I hadn't been making much noise and the woman juddered to a halt, still holding on to the doorknob, looking shocked. I opened my mouth to say something but the girl squealed, 'Gloria! My God I don't believe it…'

'Sarah!' Gloria left me and the tape measures and went over to plant a kiss on *Sarah's* cheek.

'What on *earth* are *you* doing here?' the girl cried.

'It's a long story. Well, it's not really,' she considered, 'I'm getting married…'

'…to Phil?'

'That's right, still with good old Phil. So we thought we'd have the reception at the Hall, given that we're marrying in the church next door, it's so convenient.'

'Well it's a wonderful place to get married isn't it? I'd only ever want to get married in Weston Hall, it's such a beautiful setting. Oh! So when is the big day then?'

They were practicing the gushing sort of female-conversation that, like most girly skills, I completely lacked the will or skill to take part in. Sarah had stayed close to Gloria with her hand on Gloria's arm. I wondered who she was and why she was in the Hall. And how Gloria knew her. Perhaps she was a customer of Gloria's? But what was her connection with Weston Hall? I certainly hadn't seen her around town during my stay.

Up to this point I had stood smiling politely in the corner. But having no role to play in a 'but you look so beautiful/ so do you' conversation, I went back to the plans, adding up the lengths of the room. For some reason one side of the apparently squarish room was just over twenty five metres and the other seventeen metres, so I set off to re-measure.

'Oh I forgot…' Gloria chimed, 'this is Rosamund Philips. She's a friend from my school days back in Ludlow. Roz this is Sarah

Fitzwilliam.'

'Hi,' I waved feebly, but she came over and took my hand in her own dainty hand and shook it, which I thought was a nice gesture.

'Pleased to meet you. So you're up for the wedding, helping out are you?'

'Yes. I'm working in the shop while Gloria sets up the Shrewsbury shop. And of course the wedding…'

'Well you always took on so much work didn't you?' Sarah turned her attention back to Gloria which I had to admit made me more comfortable, not knowing what to say and surprised to find myself feeling quite apologetic for being around, which was odd.

'So…' began Gloria, 'are you…?'

Sarah bent her head, questioningly.

'…am I?'

'Still with Richard Weston?'

I felt my chin drop. Was she dating Richard Weston? He must be twice her age. Or more. Eugh. Yuk, imagine them kissing… it made my skin creep.

Sarah laughed a tinkly girly laugh, which bounced off the chandelier. 'Well that's just it isn't it,' she said enigmatically, moving closer to Gloria. It was quite disgusting really, I thought as I measured away silently, him cavorting about with a woman so much younger than he was. But then the magazines and papers were full of her type: miserable looking beauties in their twenties and thirties, hanging on the arm of some incredibly ugly, incredibly fat millionaire or landed gentry type who could put them up in a rambling parsonage.

'What do you mean 'that's just it'?' Gloria asked laughing.

I wondered if they still had sex together. Yuk and double yuk.

'Well,' Sarah whispered, sitting herself on the edge of a very expensive looking, highly polished table, 'as you know, we were together for a couple of years before I went off to Manhattan…'

'Oh, of course. I'd completely forgotten about that. How did it go? Didn't you open a gallery out there?'

'Gosh you have got a good memory. Well yes I did, but the Americans just weren't going to give me a break. I tell you I did everything I could to get that gallery up and running, and not one person could be credited with helping me achieve it…'

'Well that's terrible.'

'I know I know! But that's a whole different story. So… I've been in touch with Rich since I was out there, and as you know we finished pretty amicably before I left. Well I got back to the UK about a month ago, and I caught up with him and…'

'And…' Gloria was smiling, knowingly

'Well, you know… I'm working on it.'

They both laughed. I just raised my eyebrows at the mundane nature of it all and measured away. But no-one saw me, as I was behind the sofa gagging at the time.

'I really love him still,' she was saying, 'but he's just being really strange. Well stranger than he used to be, at the moment. More grumpy than ever. I don't think things are going well, he's got a lot on his plate, so I'm just going to wait for the right moment. He still loves me, I can see that, I just think it really hurt him when I left for New York and I don't think he's going to let me in again so easily.'

'Do you know if he's been seeing anyone since you left?'

'No. I don't think he has. You know what he's like though; a total recluse. If it wasn't for me then he'd just bury himself in the house and that would be that. I keep saying to him, he's got to get out there, meet the townspeople, visit people, open fêtes that sort of thing. My friend Emily Wooster lives near Cheltenham and she married a chap called Giles who was in a very similar position to Rich here, although without the aggravation of the townspeople. Anyway, Emily's out every day with some obligation or other, and it does her the world of good. And to be honest, I think after a while it would really wear me down if Rich kept to himself so much. I'd just wither away stuck in one wing of the house. I need things to be constantly happening, you know what I mean?'

'So are you living up here now then?' Gloria asked. I wondered, fleetingly, where Gloria's new found interest in other people had come from. She seemed to be very interested in Sarah's life right now. But then, it was quite an interesting set-up Sarah had going with this Lord Weston. And, I thought begrudgingly, clutching the tape measure tightly, maybe Gloria was, in fact, usually interested in other people. Maybe it was just because I was so absolutely dull and without any exciting conversation that I drove her to talk about herself non-stop. It was a depressing thought. Did I really have so little to say?

'I'm living back in London with a friend, but I try to escape to Weston Hall when I can. I think Rich really needs the company right now to be honest with you. I'm doing my best to save him from himself, I really am,' she wittered on.

Poor man. I almost felt sorry for him, being denied the pleasure of hiding himself away in his Hall by this girl with big plans.

I'd finished measuring so I went over to join them, but I didn't contribute much to their conversation. The two old friends had a lot to catch up on, so I ended up dithering in a corner, winding up the measuring tape and letting it loose before winding it up again.

We left much later, with firm assurances that Gloria and Sarah would meet up soon.

'Will you be at the Hall next Thursday? We're coming back to put up drapes and things.'

'No, we won't,' Sarah said, 'we're due to have dinner with some friends in Gloucestershire so we'll be away all weekend. Still, we could catch up another time. I'll pop over to your shop and arrange something.'

Together Gloria and I scrunched our way back up the driveway, squinting in the bright light after being indoors in the gloom for so long. I debated on whether or not to discuss the whole Sarah-and-Lord-Weston scenario, but decided that it would be best not to go there, Sarah obviously being a good friend to Gloria, and it being sure to start an argument if I riled Gloria at all.

A group of geese waddled across our path on their way to the lake.

'Oh look, aren't they cute?' said Gloria.

I changed my mind.

'Gloria, how long have you known Sarah?'

Gloria smiled to herself. She was obviously expecting the question.

'Three or four years. She used to live at the Hall with Richard Weston and she came into the shop for arrangements every week. We got on really well.'

'Oh,' I said. 'So… do you know Richard Weston quite well then?'

'No. He doesn't like getting out and about. His business keeps him holed up in the Hall anyway. I mostly saw Sarah on her own when she was living here. I saw him occasionally of course, but he's such a recluse when it comes to the town and I didn't go out of my way to see him.'

'Oh. But don't you think that…' I paused, searching for the right phrase, 'don't you think that it's a bit odd that someone like her...'

'Like her?' Gloria mimicked, 'What do you mean 'like her'? What about her?'

'Oh nothing bad,' I said quickly, 'I just mean she seems very sociable and friendly and all that. Well why is she hanging around this Richard Weston chap? I mean, you really hate him don't you. Doesn't she see what an asshole he is?'

'Apparently not,' she said, 'love is blind.'

'So is she with him for financial reasons do you think?'

'Bloody hell Roz, what's all the interest in her situation? I don't know do I?' She looked at me exasperatedly. 'Oh well' she conceded, 'I suppose she is. Her family is an old Derbyshire family, but they've not got two pennies to rub together. They live up in Eyam in a really dilapidated Hall. You think this one is bad you should see where she harks from. But there's real pride in their home, and they're determined to hang on to it. So I guess she's looking for some sort of financial security. But then who isn't?'

'But I thought you said that Richard Weston has to sell land to get money. He doesn't sound very wealthy to me.'

'Well he could be. I should think she'll work on making him

sell the place here and move up to her family house in Eyam. Groom him for being Lord of the Manor there and then put him somewhere else for a fresh start. And good luck to her, that's what I say. Anyway, you should be more accepting of people. Not everyone marries their opposite number you know. People can pursue who they like.'

I shrugged my shoulders. It still seemed pretty weird to me.

12

Another week went by in the shop. Another week of Gloria snapping and nagging at Alan and Alan sticking two fingers up at her behind her back. Another week of ordering flowers, wrapping them, cleaning the shop and trips to the Blacksmiths Arms or the Swan of an evening. Before I knew it, it was Thursday and we were due at the Hall again to carry out more wedding preparations. This time Gloria had tasked me with putting up swathes of gold fabric in the Diving Room, as well as lugging the tables and chairs into the seating plan with her.

'Roz?' Gloria asked, just as we were about to enter the house again, and that familiar sinking feeling came upon me, 'You couldn't just pop over to the stables and ask Tom if we could borrow his staple gun could you? I don't know how I'm going to get these rosettes on the fabric and I think a staple gun would be good.'

'Sure. Fine,' I agreed, secretly rejoicing at reducing the amount of time I would be in the Hall, exposed to all the strange people that lived therein. It did leave me with the tricky problem, though, of finding my own way out of and into the house again, and navigating my way back to the set of rooms Gloria had hired out.

I took a scenic – leisurely – route to the stables. They were up the hill towards the town, almost on the boundary of the town and the Hall grounds. I strolled past the lake that stretched out at the front of the house and the geese milled around me looking expectantly for bread when I passed them. I showed them my open hands to explain that I didn't have any, but they didn't understand and waddled after me as I walked by.

The main entrance to the converted stables was actually on the town side, but there was a small gate from the Hall, which I took now. Tom's shop, *Good Wood,* was behind the giant oak in the quadrangle. It was quite pleasant to walk into the stable buildings and hear the sounds of craftsmen hard at work hammering, welding, cutting and chatting to each other. A few tourists were milling round the town entrance, grouping together for solidarity before launching themselves on the shops.

I walked into Tom's workshop and came face to face with Sarah perched centimetres away from Tom who was putting a wisp of her hair back behind her ears.

'Oh,' I said, before I could stop myself and quietly sneak away. I could feel the colour rising in my cheeks as they jumped up and separated. I had a sudden flashback of the hateful fridge scene.

'Hi Rosamund, come in, come in,' said Tom, looking ruffled. I hid a smile. It was almost funny to see him caught off guard and not the smoothie he normally was. I made a mental note to tell Alan later on that evening.

'I came to ask if...' I began

'You've met Sarah have you?' Tom said hurriedly

'Oh. Er, yes,' I said

'Hi,' she gave me a little wave. 'How are the wedding plans going?'

Tom remained poker-faced at the mention of Gloria's wedding.

'Fine, fine,' I said, wishing Alan was with me. I wonder what they were doing together. Was he seeing Sarah? Certainly they had been sitting rather close to one another. 'Intimate' one might say. I wondered if Gloria knew.

'I came to ask you…'

'Sarah's here about a piece she's commissioning for a gallery,' Tom cut in.

'Oh. What?' I said, thrown off track again. So they were discussing art were they? Practically on each other's lap and gawping at each other.

'Oh absolutely,' chimed in Sarah, 'you see Rosamund, Tom makes the most divine wooden sculptures and I think they'd sell really well in my gallery. We've already worked out two pieces…'

I bet they had.

'I came to ask if…' I began again, 'we could borrow a staple gun so that Glo can hang up some rosettes or something?'

'Staple gun? Oh yes, OK,' Tom said, diving into the back room and emerging seconds later with the requisite article.

'There you go, Rosamund.' He looked deep into my eyes as he came close and gave me the gun, 'Can I ask you a favour?' He placed his hand on my arm, holding me steady. I wiggled free.

'Yeah. sure,' I said, backing away from him slightly. I was not for charming.

'Well, it's nothing to mention, really it isn't, but if you could not mention the fact that Sarah was here…'

'I mean, Gloria has just so much on her plate at the moment…' said Sarah.

'…and you know what she's like. Always so suspicious,' added Tom.

'That's fine,' I said, feigning nonchalance, 'but won't she find out from other sources? She has friends in Kings Newton who might let it slip that Sarah's *working* with you.'

'Well she doesn't hang around in the town very much these days,' said Tom, 'and as it's so close to the wedding, she's so preoccupied with the plans she doesn't have time for anybody else.'

Which must be why he was getting his kicks elsewhere, I thought.

13

Gladly leaving Tom and Sarah alone again, I approached the side door of Weston Hall and self-consciously knocked on the peeling green painted wood.

I waited for what seemed like an age, but couldn't hear anything. I was debating whether or not to knock again when from round the side a housekeeper emerged. I explained who I was and why I was there and she took me in through another door.

I followed her, clip clopping down the long dark corridor. As we walked I peered into the rooms with partially opened doors. They were half-empty, furnished with a sofa here and a table there.

'These rooms are open to the public twice a month,' the housekeeper said as we passed them, 'all the downstairs rooms are opened, but none upstairs. That's where Richard Weston keeps his private rooms and the office.'

'There must be a lot of rooms upstairs.' I said, 'The house is three stories isn't it?'

'Four if you count the cellars and the network of tunnels from the original buildings, which are over five hundred years old. But not many of the rooms are lived in now. They haven't been lived in for a few years I should think. The floorboards up in the top floor are particularly bad and none of us go beyond the first floor now. Here we are,' the housekeeper opened the double doors at the end of the corridor and the immense dining room opened up before me, bright and cheerful with its yellow walls and floor-to-ceiling windows. Gloria was beside the enormous stone fireplace that dominated one wall and had a silvered, patchy old mirror above it, covered in cherubs scrambling around the frame hauling great bunches of flowers.

'Hi!' she waved sunnily at me. 'Got the staple gun?'

'Yup,' I held it up.

'This is the old Dining Room,' said the housekeeper. 'It's actually one of the only rooms to look just like it did almost three hundred years ago. Lord Weston's had the experts in and they said that the fireplace is original, while most of the others are Victorian.'

'It's a beautiful room,' I said.

'Yes, it's one of the finest in the house. It's popular for weddings, and for filming too. *Ghost Hunter* was filmed here last year, with that Quentin Taylor chap. Most of us got walk-on parts, which was very exciting—'

'Well thanks, Hannah,' cut in Gloria, 'We'll just measure up if that's OK. Shouldn't be too long. Shall I tell you when we're done?'

'Yes,' Hannah said despondently, cut mid-flow through describing what was obviously a proud moment. I smiled as she turned to go. A sort of comrade-like 'Isn't my friend crap, eh?' smile, but she wasn't having any of it, and left us.

'God, ev-er-y time!' said Gloria. 'Every single time I get the story about the film and the leading man and the incident with the boom and the clapper loader.'

'Shhh… she can probably hear you,' I said, angry at her attitude and about to say more but then seduced by the view from the vast windows, out towards the lake. Ducks and swans were bobbing around the edges, half hidden by the huge drooping willows. These windows faced away from the town, and out to the Shropshire countryside. Open farmland in the distance, with a field of cattle on the horizon.

'What an amazing view,' I said.

'It's gorgeous isn't it?'

'I can see why you want to have your wedding reception here.'

At that Gloria smiled, and motioned me over to join her by the table, which was now covered with fabric and measuring tapes.

The tables and chairs had arrived and were stacked by the main door. They weren't excessively large or heavy and we soon got them spread out and were debating the best use of the space. Gloria had assumed her leader role, spending more time telling me where I should be putting the tables rather than helping me push them around. At one point I was on the brink of saying something to that effect when she must have read my mind, because she jumped down off the chair she was standing on and came over to help me move the top table.

I was needed at the shop in the afternoon and I must admit that I was glad that I wouldn't be staying long in the Hall because I didn't particularly want to meet the terse Richard Weston, especially now that I knew his girlfriend was going behind his back with the ever-ready Tom. It seemed like the man had few friends, and from what people had told me, and from what I'd seen, it was pretty clear why. It was surprising, in fact, just how much duplicity and general bad behaviour lurked beneath the surface of this pretty little town. Gloria had her affair with Tom to keep secret, and Sarah seemed to have a similar situation involving Tom to keep secret from Richard Weston. And then there was Tom himself who was hiding his relationship with Sarah from Gloria. What on earth had happened to honesty and integrity?

'Roz?' Gloria stopped my daydreaming. 'Can you check where the nearest plug socket to the top table is, so we can get a lamp nearby? I'm just going to the kitchens to get a tea. Do you want one?'

'OK.'

I looked around the walls but there were no sockets to be seen. How many plug sockets would a stately house have? Perhaps only one set per room – after all it must have cost an enormous amount of money to have this place wired up. Having exhausted the visible walls I began to search more earnestly, peering behind tables, bookcases and furniture. Finally I thought I'd spotted one and got down on my hands and knees to see whether it was what I thought it was. A moment later I heard a door creak open and a black dog zipped into the room, yapping. Being at ground level and hidden away, the dog hadn't seen me and almost bounded into me. It pulled up with a yelp, but edged closer, sniffing.

I recognised it instantly. How…? And then my stomach dropped. This dog was Pilot.

The door flew open with a bang and my heart leapt against my ribs. In limped the man I last saw on the stile by Shaw's Wood. Instead of t-shirt and jogging bottoms he wore a blue checked shirt, and loose tan cords.

He stopped in his tracks when he saw me, crouched on all fours behind the soft furnishing like a startled deer in the woods. Taken aback he ran a hand through his thick black hair, holding it off his forehead and staring at me with his big brown eyes.

'You!' he exclaimed. 'What on earth are *you* doing here?'

I stared up at him, dumbly, from the carpet, still on all fours and with a pencil between my teeth. I could see the ghost of a smile starting to form on his lips.

'Are you waiting to have your moment again and trip me up? Hiding behind doors and tables waiting for the opportunity to have a go at my other ankle? Well I'm on to you, you know! I see your game!'

I felt uncomfortable, and suddenly incredibly hot, torn between the shame of having damaged this man's ankle and sheer embarrassment at his evident amusement.

With as much dignity as I could muster, I slowly drew the pencil out of my mouth and said, 'Actually I'm measuring up the room for my friend's wedding reception. What are you doing here?'

'I live here.'

'You live here?' I said baffled. Was this a son I hadn't heard about? I thought Richard Weston didn't have any offspring. 'But…'

'Richard Weston, at your service.'

I could feel my mouth gaping open, and I consciously closed it and tried to compose myself. The shame of it! To have not only crippled this man, but for him to be Lord Weston. And to have confused the crotchety old man with him. And to have been so direct with Richard… Lord… Weston just now. I stayed stock still, stomach knotted in agonies.

This was Richard Weston. This was the man who owned Weston Hall and owned Kings Newton and was seeing Sarah. This man was handsome. He had beautiful cheek bones and smiley eyes and didn't look *anything* like a Lord of the Manor.

It was all slotting into place now. The man I had thought was Richard Weston was probably some sort of estate manager. Hadn't Gloria said that there was an estate manager based at Weston Hall? And unlike the nasty old estate manager, the man standing in front of me was the type of man that girls like Sarah would be only too keen on catching; mid-thirties, tall, wavy black hair, soft brown eyes that were all twinkly and smiley as he watched with amusement the dawning realisation of what had happened become clear on my face. I made a mental note to practise a poker face with Alan. It was the kind of task he would enjoy helping me with.

I scrambled up ungraciously from the carpet, mustering some pride.

'Well… pleased to meet you,' I said, poking myself in the eye as I tried to slide the pencil behind my ear.

Why was I so clumsy? I heard him muffle a laugh, and when I opened my teary eye I saw him hobble over to the table by the fireplace. Had I *broken* his ankle? A new wave of shame engulfed me.

'I did apologise before for the accident, and it was an accident…' I felt like the bumbling fool I was.

'How is it going?'

He was perched on the table close to me, and I caught his

aftershave on the air. Spicy and warm. His tousled hair seemed to be more a product of stress than any particular style, and he ran his hand through it every other minute.

I assured him that the preparations were going 'fine' and that I was 'fine'.

'Tell me,' he leant towards me and my heart beat faster although I tried to look calm and generally in-control, which was hard as my left eye was still watering from being stabbed with the pencil, 'you're an outsider to Kings Newton, what do they say about me?'

I thought for a second, contemplating his position before committing to saying anything. What do I tell him? That he's known as a wild-party giver who practically deals drugs from his breakfast room and has wild sex orgies on the patio? On close inspection he didn't appear to be the drug-crazed sex fiend that Gloria and Tom had described. I hadn't had the benefit of having met him before – at least knowingly so – so I'd just accepted what I'd been told about him. Now, though, I was beginning to question some of the 'facts'.

'What do who say about you?' I asked, cannily playing for time. Was he going to start talking about my fairy friends again?

I sincerely hoped not.

'You know who,' he said, 'The people in the town. You're involved with them now, but you're not one of them, I can tell that from the way you look at me.'

Was he making a reference to my painful weeping eye? I thought I saw the ghost of a smile on his lips but he carried on. I was probably being paranoid.

'What you are 'one of' I don't know yet, but anyway, tell me what they say about me. It's not often I have the opportunity to find out.'

I hesitated, wondering, while I was looking at him with my good eye, trying to look as poker-faced as possible. I searched for something that would be diplomatic; true but not insensitive. After all, I had no reason to dislike the man, other than the suspiciously damning reasons Tom and Gloria had given me. He was very direct, but in an open way rather than the confrontational way Gloria was. He was very informal. But perhaps that's what comes from breaking someone's bones, perhaps you bypass formality altogether? Or can you ever be truly formal with someone who you've only seen splayed across the grass in the rain, and again three weeks later, crouched on all fours on a carpet. It does break the ice I suppose. Why wasn't I more suave? Why couldn't I have met him over a cappuccino in a café somewhere? But then that wouldn't be truly me would it? Suavity was an unknown concept to me.

Not that I wanted to meet him over a cappuccino. The man was a cokehead. He seduced women in his country estate and then tore back to London when he got bored. Everyone knew that. This informal manner was probably the result of a cocktail of drugs he had just taken up in his private rooms.

'Well from what I've heard… and of course not from Gloria…' I began

'Of course,' he said, 'go on.'

'Of course. Well, from what I've *heard*, the townspeople think that you're… distant.'

'Distant?' he probed.

'Yes…' I fished for an explanation, '…that you're too aloof and don't want to take part in the town's life. I suppose they don't know you. And they don't trust what they don't know.'

'They don't *want* to know me,' he retorted, smiling at my feeling awkward and being put on the spot by him. But I wouldn't let him do that to me.

'How do you know what they feel, when you say you don't know them?' I said

'I just know. Doesn't take a genius to work it out.'

We were going round in circles, and in spite of myself I laughed.

'Well that's just ridiculous,' I said. He looked rather taken aback that I had laughed at him but seeing as he was being fairly rude and direct I didn't see that he would be someone who would take offence easily.

'No, it's not ridiculous,' he said. 'You can read it on their faces. I don't have to be told what the estate agent thinks of me when she comes round here to talk to my housekeeper about the noise from the builders. I can see it in the way she talks to her.'

'Well why don't you go and talk to her instead of letting your housekeeper deal with her?'

'Because it's more fun this way. I'm giving the public what they want, the elusive landowner tucked away in his country estate. I'm not your sporting country gent; I don't hunt foxes and I don't shoot birds. But I do hound the villagers. That is *my* chosen sport.'

'Well it's rather a feeble sport,' I said, smoothing my skirts in a rather dismissive and what I hoped was a judgmental way 'and rather a sad one at that. It's clearly your own fault that they're the way they are with you then.'

'Rubbish,' he leant towards me, a twinkle in his eyes 'it's been going on for years, decades, centuries. This thing runs deeper than you imagine.'

'I can think deep.'

'Not that deep.'

'And how do you know that? Do you know everything around here? Are you some sort omniscient god?'

'If I were an omniscient god,' he said, 'I would have caught you lurking in the bushes waiting to trip me up the other week. So I can't be omniscient. But if you want to treat me like a god then do go ahead. I won't stop you.' He turned around as Gloria walked in 'And you are most welcome in my temple, here. Hello,' Gloria looked confused, but shook the hand that was offered her.

'Well, nice to meet you…' he looked at me prompting an introduction.

'Rosamund,' I offered.

'…Rosamund! And I'm sure I'll see you floating around somewhere around the Hall. I'm on to your ways though, so don't go thinking you can trip me up that easily.'

I smiled as he strode out of the room, taking the great buzz of energy that he exuded, with him.

'Oh, and one other thing,' he poked his head back around the door, 'thanks for being so frank with me. Don't get that much here.' And with that, he was gone.

Gloria looked at me for a moment and then put the mugs of tea on the table. For some reason I couldn't properly fathom I could feel myself beaming from ear to ear. Gloria looked at me, deadpan, and I pulled myself together. She can do that to people.

'What was that all about?' she asked quietly.

'Oh… nothing… really.'

'Roz,' she hissed, 'you were *flirting* with Richard Weston…'

'No! I was not!'

'Well it looked like you were. You do know he's the biggest tosser out there.'

'Gloria! Keep you voice down,' I hissed. 'And anyway, I wasn't flirting.'

'Well good.'

'He's younger than I thought. I thought…' I was going to admit that I'd confused the old man with him, but decided to hold on to some shred of self respect. 'I thought he'd be older than he is. In his fifties from what you and Tom had told me.'

'Rosamund! You fancy him!'

'I do not. I was just saying that when I heard you had a landowner, I imagined he would be a red-faced old colonel type with side whiskers— '

'Sorry to break your heart,' she cut in, 'but he has a girlfriend, remember.'

'I know that.'

'But you admit that you were flirting with him?'

'Oh for God's sake… no I wasn't. Remember that chap I collided with? The jogger I was telling you about?'

'Yes…'

I stared at her, pointedly. Her eyes opened wide.

'No way! It was Richard Weston?'

'Yes!'

Laughter descended and we got back to our measuring.

14

Dear Mum,

How are you? I am fine.

I am staying with a friend after finding Greg and Rachel shagging in my kitchen. As you will no doubt know by now. How is Rachel – is she well?

I'm sure you're not proud of me for running away but surely you understand…

15

I woke up and lay motionless in bed. My head was pounding and I was desperate to turn away from the bright morning light that was barging its way through the flimsy curtains. It was Saturday. Friday night had seen Alan and me drinking cider at the Cross Keys pub, by the river, practising the art of being poker-faced and examining the effects of alcohol on poker-facedness. It had been a beautiful August evening with everyone out and about in the town, in no particular hurry. We'd been drinking cider since we'd shut the shop at five, and had gone on till closing time, without the benefit of food. Why was it, I asked myself, that I always ended up drinking cider with Alan? He said he hated the stuff, that it was country-yokel juice and so forth. And yet every time we went out, the drinks in front of us ended up being pints of dark yellow fizzy cider?

And, I lay there debating with myself, why did I always have the same drink as Alan? Had I really lost any shred of character, so that I couldn't even choose my own drink now?

OK, my next efforts would be focused on discovering my

preferred form of alcohol – that seemed like a good target to me, hung-over as I was.

After what must have been half an hour of debating my sad lack of drink preference I managed to heave myself down the dangerously steep stairs and into the kitchen. Not before I noticed Philip curled up asleep on the sofa.

Ah, last night. It was coming back to me now.

Desperately trying to find the front door lock with my key… Finally managing to open the door, hardly able to stand up straight, and hearing the screams and shouts from Gloria. And Phil looking like a scared little lamb on the sofa, not retaliating. And then going swiftly up to bed. Stumbling on the stairs. The smell of apples…

Oh dear.

I wandered ineffectually into the kitchen and began to go through the coffee routine. Philip sidled into the kitchen and poured himself onto one of the bar stools at the end of the counter. Poor man. His eyes were red-ringed with lack of sleep and no doubt some crying too.

I tried to look as though I didn't think anything was wrong, but that really meant avoiding eye contact, which just made me look shifty. I knew that he knew I knew. As he sat watching me make the drink, which gave me something else to focus on, I wondered whether during any part of last night's row with him, Gloria had told him about Tom.

What was the situation between them now? I presumed the fact that he was still in the house was a good thing. They were just tense with the upcoming wedding in three weeks time. Probably. The wedding that was still on…?

'Where's Gloria this morning?' I asked, making conversation. This Saturday Gloria was supposed to be in the shop with Alan, although I was sure I hadn't heard the front door close this morning.

'She's upstairs having a sleep. She's tired.'

'Tired. Right.'

There was a silence again, and Philip went back to leafing through the cookbook without actually looking at it.

'You look terrible,' he said after a moment.

'Thanks. You don't look so hot yourself.'

'Do I smell of cider?' he said.

I sniffed the air around him. 'No…'

'Well then, you're in a worse state than me.'

'God damn it,' I laughed, but then immediately regretted jolting my body.

'Roz, do you smoke?' Phil said suddenly.

'Occasionally.'

'Want a fag outside?'

'Love one.'

We sneaked out to the garden, which was a poky, winding strip that offered little place to hide from the glare of Gloria's bedroom window. Nevertheless we found a corner by a rather beautiful old sycamore tree and, like naughty school children, we lit up our cigarettes and comfortable silence took over. My mind wandered over to the Hall again, and to Richard Weston running his hands through his hair and joking about the people in the town. I wondered what he was up to this morning.

'She hates me smoking,' Phil said, after a minute or two. 'Used to refuse to kiss me if I had smoked a fag. She could always tell if I had, even if I'd chewed my way through a whole pack of gum.'

He was crying! Heavy tears were streaking down his face, which was still puffed and swollen from his last blub fest.

'I love her. I really love her, but just lately she's been so tetchy…'

He shook his head and wiped his nose on his sleeve. I didn't know what to say. I stroked his arm, which I thought was a friendly way of showing I cared and was sorry for him, but then I got to a snotty wet patch and gingerly peeled my hand away.

'I'd even begun to imagine she was having an affair. How stupid is that?' he said quietly, drawing deeply on his Marlborough Light.

Thank God! She hadn't told him about the affair with Tom. A

wave of relief flowed through me. How awful it would have been if they had called the wedding off at this late stage.

'Is she?' He was looking intently at me.

'What makes you think that?' I said, buying time, desperately not wanting to lie to him. If Kings Newton was the gossip-mongering place that Gloria had said it was, it wouldn't be long before he did find out. Probably from the check-out girl as she was scanning his weekly shopping in the supermarket. *Beep.* Hello Phil. *Beep.* So your Gloria's seeing that Tom then. *Beep, beep.* You must feel rotten about it. *Beep.* That's five pounds exactly please.

'Oh I don't know,' he said, wiping his nose on his sleeve again. 'I'm sorry. I know it's because she's under so much pressure at the moment. I know that. I suppose I've just got pre-wedding jitters or something. That's all. It's just…' he took another drag on his cigarette, 'it's just what if she never loosens the pace? What if that's it now, she opens another shop, and another. And then she's got this enormous flowery empire and all this stress and tension and angst just becomes *what she's like*. Because I think she enjoys being like this. I do, honestly!'

I couldn't help laughing at this point. 'I kind of know what you mean,' I said, 'but she's never going to have her own wedding to organise again is she? I reckon that's the real reason for all this tension – she wants it to be perfect. If she does open more shops then she'll probably get a manager in to help her out – she'll have to. Phil I'm *sure* that this is the worst it will be, after all she's got the new shop opening at the end of next week – she must be really stressed about it. I'm sure she'll go back to being the go-getting but laid-back Gloria we both know and love.'

He took a last long drag at his cigarette then stubbed it out on the sole of his shoe. 'Don't want to get a black mark on the paving slabs,' he said, before putting the butt in his pocket.

'So…' I said. I had to find out, if only because I was living in their house with them and it was going to be awkward, 'Do you think it would be best if I moved out and gave you two a bit of space?'

'No, no. I'm moving to my friend Martin's house anyway, to

get ready for the wedding, so it's no problem bringing it forward a couple of weeks. I think it'll be best, what with her being super-tense, if I get out of the way a bit. Make myself a harder target to hit.'

'I'm really sorry that I'm so in the way,' I said. 'I'll leave you in peace tonight.' Even though it obviously hadn't had the desired effect last night…

'Sometimes I wish I was more like you,' he said, 'You're such a free spirit.'

'I am?'

'Yes you are. You've upped sticks and left your job in London and you make the changes you need in your life without looking back. You've got real courage.'

'Well I wouldn't put it that way,' I said, laughing. 'It's not very courageous running away from everything.'

'No. You shouldn't write yourself off,' he went on. 'I would love to be like you are now. Doing what you want, with nothing to tie you to anything. I really admire you for that.'

'Thank you, Philip,' I said, squeezing a dry patch on his arm, 'But it's not the rosy picture that you paint. I have very little money, so I can't do all the things you do like go on holiday and buy a car. That's fine though, because I'm not really bothered about those things. I just haven't worked out what I'm going to do with my life, and it's really getting me down. Plus,' I added, 'I haven't met the love of my life and I'm not on the brink of marriage. See? You're in a great position to be in. I think things are just a bit full on for you two at the moment. They're bound to be. But don't worry, the shop opening will go well, the wedding will go well and everything will come up roses.'

'Yes, you're right,' Phil smiled and wiped the last of his tears away. 'But don't worry about your situation either. Something will come up.'

'I know! That's the problem! I just go with the flow and accept whatever comes my way. And maybe I shouldn't. Maybe I should go out there and carve a way for myself, regardless of the hand that fate deals me.'

'Rosamund,' Phil put his hand on my shoulder, reassuringly, 'don't worry about it, seriously, you have *decades* in front of you to be building a career path or whatever you plan to do. Why don't you just potter around for a while? Let it all gel?'

It seemed a plausible option put like that. 'Maybe,' I conceded, 'I could potter around a bit.'

'Come on, let's go in.'

We walked back to the house.

'I saw you both smoking,' came Gloria's somewhat terse pronouncement from above.

16

If I thought that Gloria had been rather severe with Phil and with me lately, it was nothing compared to the strained relationship she had with Alan. Theirs had never been an easy association, each having opposing characters, but Alan had told me that it was getting noticeably worse.

Alan was a carefree soul with a flirtatious nature and a fairly laid back approach to life. Gloria, as I was only too aware, was on the verge of imploding, what with the new store opening and the wedding getting ever nearer. Being in a confined florist's shop with the two of them would not be my first choice of pastime, but I had little option on how I spent my time just at the moment, wanting to keep my side of Gloria's bargain, so I kept my head down and stayed in the background as much as I could, hoping to avoid the fallout.

It was the week of the new shop opening and Gloria was virtually foaming at the mouth with stress. She seemed to take it all out on Alan, which hadn't come as much of a surprise to either him or me. She really wasn't holding back with her temper.

'Alan? *Alan?*' Gloria shouted from where she was crouched amid the window display.

'Yes?' he strolled up from his stool nonchalantly.

'Where the fuck are the cherub vases? I said I wanted them on display in the window.'

'Well I thought they looked better on the dresser at the back. They're too small to be seen by people passing in the street—'

'I'm sorry,' she said in a brittle, eye-wide tone. 'Whose shop is it? Is it your shop, Alan?'

'Look I only thought that it might be better—'

'Is it?'

'No.'

'Well, in that case, could you please put the vases where I said? OK?' She got up from the window display and as she passed me, studiously absorbed in the crossword and doing my best to pretend I wasn't there, she said, 'I wonder what I pay him for, I really do.'

'Mmm,' I said looking up. I winked at Alan and he stuck two fingers up at Gloria behind her back.

'Right then; I'm going out to see Tom,' Gloria announced, pulling her coat on a minute later. 'If you need me you can call me on this number.' She handed me one of Tom's business cards, printed on recycled, acid free, organic, gluten-free paper. 'Good Wood. Carving to order.'

'Thanks,' I said, 'Do you want us to lock up?'

'No, I'll be back in an hour or so. I just need some...' she looked at Alan pointedly, '...fresh air.'

The doorbell clanged and with a bang of the door she was gone, her heels clip-clipping down the street.

'Miserable sodding cow,' said Alan, dumping the cherub vases and joining me on the wrapping table. He pulled out a crumpled packet of cigarettes and lit one.

'You can't smoke those in here!' I said, horrified.

'I know. Want one?'

'OK.'

So we sat and smoked, filling the shop with a nicotine fug, but willing to pay the price when Gloria came back. We agreed we would tell her that a customer had been smoking and we had tried to ask them not to, but they were determined.

'Alan, why do you put up with Gloria and her temper? She's awful to you sometimes.'

'That's rich coming from you Roz! Why do *you* put up with her?'

'Because she's my friend.'

'Is she?'

I hesitated for a moment. Was she my friend? Really? Of course she was, she was my oldest friend.

'Yes she is. She's been so good to me, lately.'

'Sure. Sure. You don't have to tell me again what a saviour she is.'

'But anyway, you've ducked out of answering my question. Why do you put up with her? She's not *your* friend.'

He paused, and then leant towards me: 'Promise you won't tell,' he said, suddenly looking wide eyed and rather excited.

'Tell what?'

'Tell anyone what I'm going to tell you.'

'OK,' I said, intrigued.

'I've been working in this florist's with Gloria for over two years now, and I reckon I've pretty much learnt everything there is to know about running a floristry business. I love it, I really do. I mean, all this God-awful William Morris wallpaper and distressed oak tables and so on isn't quite my cup of tea, but I love the business and I'm…' he paused, grinning at me… 'I'm going to set up my own business.'

'No!'

'Yes! An aunt recently died and she left me a fat wad of cash and I'm going to use it to set up my own business.'

'Where? In Kings Newton?'

'God no. Although it would be quite funny wouldn't it, to set up opposite Gloria. Hee, hee! But no, it would be in Birmingham.'

'Birmingham? Really?'

'Why not? It's so cool. England's second largest city you know. Well, as I see it, London is jam-packed with trendy florist's shops.

You can't move for them down there. And they've got every other kind of florist's too. But Birmingham, well it's a bit behind the times isn't it? I don't think they've even got all the coffee shop brands up there. I know they've got Starbucks, I think they've got Coffee Republic, Café Nero, but not sure about Aroma and… Anyway, I've been spending weekends there, checking out the competition, and I must say, it's pretty bleak. You've got your run of the mill corner shop florists, and two upmarket shops in the centre, but that's pretty much it. For an entire city!'

I was so pleased for him I just sat and beamed at him.

'You're smiling again!'

'So I am,' I said, shocked that I'd remembered how to do it. 'It's great. Really. You've worked hard enough for it. So that's why you put up with Gloria, you've got plans of your own.'

'Yup. It's been pretty tough but I've always had getting my own place to focus on, so it's been manageable.'

For a moment I felt a tide of depression flood back. To be surrounded by people who know what they want to do, and work towards getting where they want to be. They don't know how lucky they are.

'I'm going to have such a sharp and fashionable shop, you would not believe it,' Alan continued. 'Of course it will be constantly changing, evolving. The place will have huge windows, polished every morning to make sure they're completely clean. All the woodwork around them will be glossy black, like the front door of 10 Downing Street; like a black mirror. Inside, the walls will be dark, dark blue. Matt walls – no gloss anywhere inside the place. I hate gloss paint inside buildings. All the tables and chairs and window ledges and everything will be brushed aluminium, with stripped wood floors and perhaps one wall with exposed brick. Very loft-esque. And I'll have exposed beams in the ceiling, with ivies cascading down like a controlled urban jungle. Very chic. As for the stock, well I won't be selling carnations.' He paused and looked thoughtful for a second, 'Well, perhaps I could in a sort of ironic-way. Retro chic. Hmm. Suburban middle class fashion. Yes, maybe sprays of peach carnations, something really naff.' I laughed and he continued. 'Anyway, besides the peach carnations I'll stock rare and exotic plants that will wake up the people of Birmingham and say 'hello twenty first century'. But I don't think that selling to the public will be too lucrative. My main income will come from businesses.' It was said in a textbook narrated fashion. He stopped and looked at me staring at him.

'Wow,' I said. 'You've really thought it all through. What will you call it?'

'I've even thought of the name. Fuschiarama. It's going to be *huge*,' he added. 'I've thought all about how I'll start if off. I'll go round the cafes and restaurants all over the city, touting my wares,' he laughed. 'And I'll have a little black shiny van that drops off the blooms every week.' He sighed. 'And an assistant. A big blonde assistant from northern Europe somewhere. Possibly Norway; or Sweden…'

'Ah but you should never mix work with pleasure,' I said

'Who the hell said that? I'll tell you who said it; it was some goddamn grey-suited middle manager from Swindon who said it. No, Fuschiarama will be all about pleasure and the surprise of something new and exotic. In my shop the pursuit of sensuality won't stop with the flowers— Hello Mrs Dawson.' He stood up in a graceful sweep and walked towards the door, where the wife of the local doctor had come in to collect her weekly bunch of yellow roses.

'Alan,' I said, when she'd bought her roses, and dished the gossip. 'What do you think of Richard Weston?'

He gave me a surprised look then said, 'Cute. But a real rascal. That man has not done himself any favours around here you know. Why do you ask?'

I related my first meeting with him, and the broken ankle. I also told him about the 'making sport with the villagers' conversation.

'Seems about right,' he said. 'He used to have pretty wild parties around here apparently although I've only heard it from other people. Lots of the London set would come up for the weekend; go riding, walking. That sort of thing. And then in the evening there would be music till God knows what hour and people living nearby got quite irritated by the whole thing, not least me because I was *never invited!*'

'Do you know him that well then?'

'No. But it would have been a nice gesture. Anyway, that's all pretty much stopped now. Calmed down a bit, they reckon. Why? Are you thinking of ensnaring an eligible bachelor?'

'No.' I laughed it off.

'Not looking for a bit of upper class totty?'

'No! I just wondered… he thanked me for being honest when I was only telling him the truth! I mean, what a thing to say. Are people dishonest around him?'

'I think people avoid him. There are a few people who work at Weston Hall; well they can hardly avoid him. They all get on really well with him. Sing his praises as much as they can do around here, which isn't much as you might expect. You're right; he'd be OK if he got out a bit more.'

'But you wouldn't push him out of bed in the morning, would you?' I said

'Christ no,' he said. 'He's quite a looker. Mind you, with the luck I've been having these past few months I wouldn't push a woman out of bed. There're poor pickings for Alan in sleepy Kings Newton, I can tell you.'

'Nice!'

'Well you did ask. Anyway, I thought you appreciated 'honesty'.'

'That was Richard Weston not me. Weren't you listening to anything I was saying?'

'Well not completely, no. Were you thinking of getting your hair cut at all? You know it's a bit on the wild side. The Victorian heroine look is all very well for oil paintings but in the twenty first century? Really?'

I slapped him.

17

Dear Mum,

    Fear not – I'm fine. I'm staying with my old school friend Gloria (you remember her, I'm sure) while I sort myself out following the scene by the fridge (ask Rachel). The picture on the front of the postcard is of Weston Hall, which is somewhere I've visited recently and even met the owner, so as you see I'm mixing in the right circles.

    Hope you're OK and I'll call you v soon.
    Roz xx

18

Working in the shop became a lot easier the next week, since Gloria was spending a few days up in Shrewsbury. The second shop opening was a success, with an oily councillor who had apparently once been suspected of tax evasion gracing the opening ceremony and cutting a ribbon. His wife was presented with the most enormous bunch of flowers: 'My arrangement,' said Alan proudly. Generally things were going pretty well for Gloria: she was busy training the Shrewsbury store staff and setting up the links with local businesses and she was out of our way for much of the final build up to the wedding. Alan and I were grateful for such small mercies.

Alan used the lull between deliveries in the morning and the preparing of orders to go through his bank loan forms, which had recently arrived. He had seen the premises he wanted, down by the canal in the heart of the fashionable area of Birmingham, and had put an offer in that had been accepted. He could hardly contain his excitement, and not even Gloria's constant nagging had put a stop to the spring in his step. I had to admire him. It would have sure dampened my mood.

'When will you get the place?' I asked.

'In about six weeks' time. I'm so excited!'

'When will you tell Glo?'

'Oh God, I don't know Roz. I only have to give a week's notice, so when she comes back from her honeymoon I guess. I can break the news then. That will bring her down to earth with a bump!' he said. 'I need the money so I'm not going to stop working here until just before I move in.'

'What's the building like? Is it the loft you had in mind?'

'It's gorgeous. Hey! You should come up and see it on Sunday with me. Yes! Come on Sunday! A whole load of old canal buildings were bought by a property developer as part of some regeneration programme thing, and they've been made into shops and offices and a few apartments.'

'Does your shop come with an apartment?'

'Yes, only a very small one right above it, but it's handy. I can do the books there because there isn't much room behind the shop itself. It's so exciting!'

I hugged him, partly to calm him down and stop him bouncing around the shop.

'Work with me,' he said suddenly. 'Come and work in my shop in Birmingham.'

Blimey! I hadn't been expecting that: 'Oh Alan... I don't know.'

'What? Why not?'

'Well I don't know if I was destined to work in a florist's shop all my life.'

'But you like it here?'

'Yes...'

'And we get on well together...'

'Yeah... it's just that... I don't know. It's not something I'd really thought about.'

'Have you thought at all about what you're going to be doing after the summer? When Gloria gets back from her honeymoon?' he said, hand on hips and sounding not unlike my mother.

'No, I haven't,' I confessed guiltily. My various rambles around the town and into the nearby countryside had only cleared my mind, not refilled it with anything more positive. I'd only got as far as putting the past behind me and coming to terms with Greg's infidelity. At least I was coming to terms with what had happened; surely I could count that as progress? But Alan was right; I had to sort something out. I still had to buy more pants… might as well start there.

'Maybe I could work in your shop for a while until I found my feet?' I ventured, 'Or would you need someone to commit for a long time?'

'Well I'd prefer it if you committed to a long time of course, but if all I can get is the promise of a few weeks or months, then so be it, it's better than nothing.'

I felt a wave of love for the boy, and gave him another hug. The surge of relief at putting off a decision was an enjoyable feeling, especially as I'd managed to suppress the guilt of once again failing to make a firm decision about my future. Perhaps Alan was right about all this 'go with the flow' business he had talked about a few days earlier. Perhaps if I went through my life taking these chances then something really good would come my way.

He went back to filling in his forms, sighing heavily as he read and reread the small print. I wound up some of the ribbons that had spun out of order below the counter.

'Would you mind if I dashed out to the bank? It's just round the corner and I really need to check some of the things on this form. This small print scares the life out of me.'

I said I didn't mind and Alan left me to it. It was a quiet day anyway, with nothing to prepare and hardly any customers.

I was sticking the prices on vases when the phone went in the back of the shop.

'Hello, Gloria's flowers,' I said, as I'd been trained to. I was always conscious that it might be Gloria on the other end, checking up on me and starting off on the wrong foot would no doubt spell disaster.

'Is that Gloria?' A male voice at the other end of the line

asked.

'No it's Rosamund. Can I help you?'

'Roz, its Greg.'

I felt sick.

'Roz?'

'Yes?' I said hesitantly. How did he know where I was? How had he traced me here? Mum! When I sent Mum the note she must have told my shagging sister who had bloody well told Greg. Aargh. Were Greg and Rachel still together? Had my sister hopped into bed with Greg saying, 'Oh, by the way, Rosamund's run off to Gloria's house in the Welsh Marches…?' My stomach was churning.

'Roz I really don't know what to say…'

I put the phone down.

Bastard. Bastard, bastard, bastard. I kicked the counter – hard. Bastard… He had no right to call me. No right at all. Why was he calling anyway? Surely he wasn't interested in me, he'd obviously preferred the company of my older sister. What could he possibly want? To talk things through? To work things out? That was just the kind of thing he would probably be wanting to do I thought. He probably didn't think of it as a very big deal, that he'd made a mistake he could grovel his way out of.

Bastard.

And Mum! She hadn't called or texted me since the whole fridge thing had taken place. Not that I was particularly surprised, we weren't hugely close and I could just picture her eyebrows hitting her hairline when she heard I'd upped sticks and run away. Talking to Greg and hoping he would make me 'see sense' and go back to London, rather than have to get involved herself, that'd be just like her.

It took me half an hour to calm down again and realise that getting worked up about it was not the same as getting over it.

I found myself wishing Alan would hurry back so I could have some company. I didn't want to be in the shop on my own right now. What kind of small print took so long to explain?

The bell over the door rang and in came wood turning, woman

stealing Tom, shooting me a confident smile and sitting on Alan's vacated stool.

'No Alan?' he said, leaning near to me and watching what I was doing.

'Hi Tom,' I said, almost happy to see him – at least it would take my mind off Greg. I tried to disguise my glee at the thought of company though, just in case he interpreted it as enthusiasm to see him in particular, which would only feed his ego and make him more conceited than he already was.

'Alan's just popped out for a moment.'

Tom nodded and then went on to make small talk, asking how I was handling working in the shop, and what I thought of Kings Newton, given I'd now spent a couple of months here. It was easy enough talking to him, but I did find his constant intense look rather off-putting. He was very keen on keeping eye contact, and was one of these people who would invade your space every other minute with the touch of an uninvited hand.

I went into a sort of automaton mode and served a couple of customers while he talked away about the 'filthy' redevelopment and the 'bastard' Richard Weston. As soon as I heard the name my ears pricked up and I tuned in to what Tom had to say, although I dipped back out the more passionate he got. 'Kings Newton will just be a suburb of Ludlow soon. Like all the villages and small towns that used to be around Ludlow once were. They've been swallowed into the main town and the only reason they've kept their names is to make it easier to understand the bus routes. I can't believe the planners actually let Richard Weston get away with it. I wonder how much they paid him for the rights to develop here. Wankers.'

Tom's talking at me was beginning to wear rather thin, especially his disregard for my opinion, which was never asked for but assumed to be the same as his. Men, right now, were standing pretty low in my estimation and I didn't particularly want to sit and listen to this one whinge about his particular gripes.

'Kings Newton hasn't had much development though has it?' I said, the devil's advocate in me itching for a fight. 'I mean, there have been very few houses built in the past 50 years. It's almost strange how it's survived like this up till now. Preserved. Pickled, almost.' The idea of a pickled town tickled me, but clearly not Tom.

'But that's no reason for us to give it all away now, is it? It survived because old Thomas Weston, Richard's father, actually had *pride* in the town and wanted to preserve it as it was.'

'Like a museum?'

'Like the *community* it is.'

'But the Westons have run out of money haven't they?' I reasoned. 'That's why the house is in the state it is. And that's why people like Gloria can have their wedding reception there. Surely he's selling the land for the money he needs, not just money he wants.'

Tom looked incredulously at me as though I had given birth to a goldfish on the shop floor, and then he lightly smacked my hand, which irritated me enough to make me leave my stool and pointlessly rearrange a display, just to put some serious physical distance between the two of us.

'I *like* you,' he said, coming over, unperturbed. 'You've got a passionate spirit in there.' He sidled up close, and looked as if he was going to put his arms around me at any minute. 'You question things, you don't just accept what people tell you, do you Rosamund. I like that. You're a free spirit.'

What was I supposed to do? Thank him? As irate and generally not-in-the-mood as I was, I found myself thinking that I could see what Gloria found so attractive. He was very good looking and had a gorgeous body, which must come from whittling the huge logs in his workshop I supposed. But I just couldn't get past the overriding sense of self worth. He was attractive but boy did he know it. He was the Kings Newton Romeo, stalking man-hungry women and injecting a little spurious excitement into their lives. I wondered whether Sarah was his latest conquest, or whether she was just leading him on in order to get her own way? After a few ciders in the Blacksmiths' Arms one night Alan had told me that just about everyone knew about Gloria and Tom's affair, but no one bothered to gossip, preferring to talk about people who they at least cared enough about to dislike. I wondered how Gloria would have felt if she knew that she wasn't 'worth' the gossip, or that Sarah and Tom were possibly an item. Knowledge is power, and the tales made me feel just a little superior to Gloria who was woefully out of touch with the town, spending so much time out of it these days.

Before I knew what was happening Tom had his hand on my shoulder and had bent his head to kiss me.

'Stop it!' I pulled away and leaped back over to my stool, putting the wrapping bench in-between us. My heart was beating hard, not from any kind of passion but blistering anger at him thinking he could just leap in any old how.

'Tom, I am really not interested!' I spat at him, banging my hands down on the table. 'Do you hear the phone ringing in the back office?'

'Yes,' he looked perplexed.

'Well that is in all probability my ex, Greg, calling me, as he did a few minutes before you came in. I just cannot come to terms with that situation right now so if you can just *back off* and leave me alone—'

'Hey, Rosamund, I'm sorry…' a ruffled Tom said, coming over and standing opposite me, the workbench still between us, 'I thought you liked me.'

'I'm sorry, Tom, but you're such a self important wanker, that the only person you could ever hope to have any sort of meaningful relationship with is yourself.' Is what I should have said. However, what I did say was: 'Sorry Tom, but I don't think I'm really your type.'

'No, *I'm* sorry,' he said, making a grab for my hand, which was rapidly withdrawn from the table top. 'Gloria told me that you'd recently split up with someone. It must really have hurt.'

'Not particularly,' I lied. It wasn't something I was in any hurry to talk about with lounge lizard Tom.

He looked nonplussed, 'I thought you were engaged to him?'

Had she told everyone?

'I was. However, he is an idiot and I should have broken up with him long ago.' Why was I telling him this? I hadn't even told Gloria how I felt, probably because the subject never arose. She'd still not asked me much beyond 'how are you coping' or 'how are you feeling today'. Apart from that time on the walk up to Weston Hall. I wondered how Tom and Gloria had managed to get it together, both being talkers rather than listeners. I bet their conversations would have made interesting listening. If they had conversations… Maybe that was how it worked – maybe they just had hot sex. Eugh. Thoughts of Greg and my sister beside the fridge swam before my eyes. Would I ever have a healthy attitude towards sex again? Would I ever look at a refrigerator in the same way again, for that matter?

'What happened?' Tom persisted, seeing I had drifted miles away.

'He was sh…seeing my sister. It was horrible.' I shook my head. Tom nodded understandingly but fortunately didn't leap over the table and hug me.

'Anyway,' I brightened up, pushing the thoughts behind me, 'what about you and Gloria? You're seeing my friend —'

'Who's getting married in eleven days time,' he added.

'So is that the end for you two?' It was only fair that I should be as direct with him as he was with me. It was a great opportunity to understand a bit more about their relationship, which Gloria had accused me of not understanding. Of course I'd never ask her that personal a question, but seeing as Tom had set the mood I didn't see any reason to stop now.

'Well…' Tom shrugged his shoulders in a caddish sort of way, 'Never say never is what I say.'

'Yes, I bet you do,' I whispered to myself, dipping behind the counter to pick up another bundle of tangled ribbons.

The doorbell jangled and in came Alan, giving me a secret 'thumbs up' which I took to be about the forms, before diving into the back office to make a cup of tea.

'Well, anytime you want a friend to talk to, Rosamund, I'll be there for you,' said Tom, with Hollywood style deep sincerity. 'You can come round and see me any time.'

Would nothing dent this man's ego? Would no rejection be taken seriously? 'Thanks,' I said weakly.

Alan came out of the back, 'Do you want a cup of tea, Tom?'

No. No he doesn't want a cup of tea. He's going. I glared at Alan, hoping he would retract the offer.

'Yes, that'd be great,' Tom said, and then turned back to me. 'So, you've been up to Weston Hall – is that right? Did you meet Richard Weston when you were there?'

'Yes. I've met him a couple of times now,' I replied, enjoying the sudden awkward look that appeared on his face.

'Oh. Really. And what did you think of him Rosamund? Did you like him? Apparently he's handsome. A bit of a one for the ladies.'

I snorted with laughter. To imagine that Tom, the smoothest of smooth, might recognise the qualities of such a person but not relate them to himself.

'Yes, I think he's very attractive actually,' I said, recovering, 'and no, I wouldn't say he's one for the ladies, as you put it. Just…' I searched for the right description. It was difficult, what *was* he? '…playful.'

'Playful?'

'Well, something like that. Not how I imagined him anyway.'

'Pff,' sneered Tom, 'the guy doesn't even do a hard day's work. He used to bring his London totty up to the Hall and entertain at weekends. It was quite well-known hereabouts a few years ago. Awful scandal about a group of them being caught naked in the gardens, playing some sex game or other, off their heads with drugs. They were spotted by one of the locals out walking the dog. That soon put an end to it.'

'The dog?'

I heard Alan's laugh echoing from the kitchen.

Tom wasn't amused.

Even though I didn't want to pay any attention to what Tom had to say on the subject, his comments couldn't but help take some of the shine off what I felt for the man at the Hall. Richard

Weston didn't look like the sort of person who would open up his house to wild parties, but then had I ever, I wondered, looked like the kind of person who worked in an international head office in the City of London? Probably not.

So many people couldn't be wrong could they? There must be some element of truth about the parties and the women. But perhaps they were just exaggerated a bit. Perhaps the people were only *partially* naked. Or only on really soft drugs. I wondered how long ago it was, if it was at all.

Tom broke my train of thought, 'A lot of people like him when they first meet him you know. You ought to be wary of people like him… All boarding school charm and the glamour of wealth. Put them in a semi-detached suburban house and the shine would wear off quickly enough. All girls like to dream of the man with the title in the big house. It's the Cinderella complex.'

'Yes, thank you Tom,' I said, furious that he was possibly classing me as one of 'those girls'. 'I don't think I'll be tripping over to see him in any social capacity soon, so you don't have to persuade me of just what a rogue he is. I can pretty much make up my own mind on the subject.'

Privately I wondered if I could, in fact, make up my mind about that subject, being woefully inadequate at making any sorts of decisions in my life, even down to alcoholic beverage preferences. Still, I could at least try to *appear* to be someone who knew their own mind.

Irritatingly, my impassioned speech seemed to spur him on, all winking eyes and leaning close.

'Listen,' he said, moving closer to me, so far as it was possible what with the table and a mound of ribbons separating us. He was practically clawing his way over the workbench. 'A couple of days after Gloria's wedding, there's a few of us from the town that are going to protest up at Weston Hall. Do you remember us talking about it a few weeks ago? Well it's nothing too terrible, we just want to make the bastard stop and think before he sells off any more of our land. Now I know Gloria feels the same way as I do, although of course she won't be coming because she'll be off on her honeymoon to Spain. So why don't you come along and help ruffle a few feathers? I'll stick by you and make sure you don't get lost.'

I bet you will, I thought, I'll be looking out for any bushes or bike sheds mind…

'Yes, Gloria's mentioned it,' I said, 'she wanted me to go.'

'Great. So you'll be coming then?'

God it was exasperating. Did no one think I had my own mind and might be capable of independent thought? 'No Tom. I don't know if I'll go. I don't really do… that kind of thing.'

'Oh don't worry, it's nothing strenuous or illegal or anything. It's just fifteen or twenty of us are going up to the hall in the evening to put up banners, walk around a bit, kick up a fuss, get ourselves noticed. We want to make him recognise that we're just not going to tolerate his big schemes any more, and that he has to listen to us.'

'Nothing illegal? It sounds like breaking and entering, or at least trespass.'

'It's only in the grounds.'

'It's still his property.'

'But he opens it up to the public sometimes.'

'Yes, but not at midnight. Anyway, how do you know he'll be at home?'

'He's due back from London on the Monday after Gloria's wedding and he'll be staying for a fortnight. I spoke to Sarah.

Ah yes. Sarah. Passing on the information to Richard Weston thereafter, no doubt. Was she the spy Gloria had been talking about? Surely Tom wasn't so stupid as to trust her with his secrets? She must be the one who had let Richard Weston know about the protest.

'I don't know,' I said after some time thinking about it, 'it's not that I don't want to help you Tom, but I really know very little about all this, I'm just not sure.'

'Oh come on, I had you down as a bit of a free spirit, girl,' he said, looking at my rather hippie skirt. 'Come on, you've shaken off the shackles of capitalism once before…'

'No. I just left my job in the City. It wasn't for any political reason. And just because I don't wear the jeans and T-shirt uniform doesn't mean I'm any different to someone who does. I'm no hippie.'

'OK. Hey relax, I didn't mean to upset you or anything. I think you look great. You should learn to accept a compliment graciously.' He held his hands in the air, which infuriated me, but I let it pass. His face was close to mine again and for a split second as I looked I thought I saw make-up. Was he wearing concealer? Was he that up himself? Here, in the country?

'Well, I know that Kings Newton already means a lot to you,' he was saying. 'Talk more to Gloria about the protest if you like. See what she thinks about you taking part. It would just be really nice if you came along with us, joined in,' he smiled and squeezed my arm. 'I'd really like you to take part Rosamund. It would mean a lot to me.' He gave me another one of his intense looks. 'You're really beautiful, you know that? When you get cross you frown too much though. And you have lovely hair, you should never get it cut, I love long hair on a woman it's very sexy.'

The man was practically begging for a slap. I didn't rise to it though. He was Gloria's friend and I don't think he meant to offend me. Besides, I'm a nice person and don't go around slapping people, unless it's Alan but then he generally deserves it.

The phone was ringing and I heard Alan pick it up. I almost hoped that it would be Greg again, so I could get rid of Tom.

'It's for you!' Alan called from the back.

What on earth was I going to say to Greg? I didn't have any time to prepare, so I just apologised to Tom and he nodded and drained his tea. 'See you around,' he said. 'Come and see me.'

'Sure. Yes.' Whatever... I backed off and picked up the phone, 'Hello?'

'Hi. It's me!'

'Who?' I said. It wasn't Greg this time but I recognised the voice.

'Alan!'

I looked up; he was on his mobile.

'I thought you might need rescuing from the creep,' he said into the phone.

I laughed, 'Thank you. But you offered to make him a tea.'

'Well he's cute. What can I do? Mixed messages!'

19

Dear Mum

Another postcard – this is a picture of the old market cross, which is near to Gloria's house where I'm staying. Thanks for your letter and sorry to hear about Auntie Mary's dog.

I'm starting to move on and things are going ~~well~~ OK here. Gloria is ~~a bit testy~~ ~~a complete fucking cow actually~~ nervous about the wedding as there's still so much work to be done. I've met the local Lord of the Manor (honestly!) who is ~~very nice~~ ~~who is nice~~ ~~who~~ ~~The local landowner is really...~~

20

Weston Hall was only open to visitors on a few days each year and, since this was one of them, Gloria said that I really ought to go and explore. I leapt at the chance, not just so that I could have a proper poke around the fabulous home of the enigmatic Richard Weston, but to escape from the tension back at the house and the shop.

Gloria seemed to have cloaked herself in a perpetually foul mood, as all the parts of her life came together for a few time-consuming days. She knew no mid-point, no half measures. My easy-going ways were beginning to rankle with her, and I think she was starting to lump me in with Alan, which didn't do me any favours in her eyes. I could see her looking at the pair of us whispering together, seeing how we were turning away from her, and it only made her temper worse. I wasn't going to talk to her about it though, as she had a thousand and one other things to deal with rather than some soft relationship matters. Besides, there was an element of truth to it. Alan and I were good friends and if it had to be at the expense of my friendship with her, then that would be Gloria's decision and not mine.

Alan was still managing to keep the shop in Birmingham a secret, although Gloria must have been starting to think something was up. He was volunteering to work more weekends which was rare for him, but it gave him time mid-week to visit the shop and meet the developers who were putting the finishing touches to the place. This was combined with an unquashable high-spiritedness that she couldn't break with her usual well-practiced anger. I could see her itching to ask him what he was doing with his time off, but without being seen to ask outright. So eventually she asked me instead.

I played ignorant, which I think I passed off rather well. Alan and I had agreed to stick to our plan to tell Gloria when she came back from her honeymoon, any earlier and she would probably fret about it on the beach; it would ruin her holiday. Alan had somehow roped me in to being with him when he broke the news, but I suppose it was in my interest too – I was after all going to be helping him out with the shop, so at some point I would have to break that news to Gloria, so why not do it all together?

'If you would make a small donation,' the tour guide said as we stood in the main reception hall of Weston Hall, pointing to the donation box on the table, 'it would be very welcome. I'm sure many of you are aware of the problems we've got here…'

It was ten o'clock and there was a large group assembled, waiting for the tour to start. The entrance hall looked positively homely – painted a vibrant yellow that shone in the sun. Everything seemed quite higgledy-piggledy with an umbrella stand crammed full of walking sticks and umbrellas, two maple wood tables displaying stuffed birds in enormous glass cases and pictures and paintings covering the walls.

'Well, now we're all here, let's get underway,' she began and one by one we followed her into a narrow hallway to the right of the sweeping staircase.

With a rather wheezy intake of breath our guide, Rose, launched into her narrative. We first passed through the set of rooms in the west wing of the house, all Georgian high ceilings with large windows that looked out onto the gardens and down to the lake below.

Rose shuffled her small plump frame around the furniture, picking out the interesting pieces; here an armchair, there a painting. All combined with an anecdote. The couple beside me was particularly vocal throughout the tour, 'mmm'ing and 'ahh'ing in agreement at whatever Rose said, and nodding their heads. They were middle aged and garishly dressed in matching lemon yellow trousers and zipped up jackets, with the words 'Hi Adventure! Casual Sportswear' embroidered on the back in magenta.

They struck me as professional house-visitors. I had been dragged around enough country houses in my time to be able to recognise the breed. Tucked up in their (genuine) leather wallets, which were probably also matching, would be well-used membership cards for the National Trust and English Heritage.

'This glass ceiling,' Rose pointed above our head, 'was installed by the fifth Lord Weston of Kings Newton who wanted more light between here and the library – as you can see it would have been a dark corridor otherwise. I think it's a nice feature. Quite unusual.'

'Well yes,' said the female yellow tracksuit, gazing upwards with critical eye, 'they have one quite similar in Sunbury, although they've really let theirs get into a terrible state of disrepair.'

'Well that's not unusual you know. We have the renovators round quite a lot,' Rose said, 'there's always something past its sell by date round here. Last month it was repairs to the chimney in the dining room. The fireplace alone cost in excess of four thousand pounds.'

Rose led us round the ground floor, explaining in her steadily paced tour-guide voice the history of the hall and the collection of furniture and paintings in it. None of it, not one stick of furniture or hanging tapestry seemed to reflect the man who lived here now. I suppose it was because the furnishings were all inherited with the house, and why buy a new table when you have three perfectly good Georgian tables already? It just seemed odd that I couldn't make out much modern influence on the house at all. It was lived in and more homely than most stately houses but it wasn't *Richard Weston's*. Not that I'd particularly know what *his* was.

But then we came upon a room that most definitely was *his*. The library was at the far end of the building and in the oldest part of the house. The door frame was lower than the previous rooms and much, much wider. The room had old lattice windows with glass that bubbled and swirled and hardly showed the view outside at all. There was a huge stone fireplace carved with two fish-tailed men holding up the lintel and an enormous grate, still filled with the remains of a fire waiting to be swept up.

Beside the fire were a couple of fairly modern leather armchairs and on one was a copy of Autocar magazine and a Mars Bar wrapper. The other was covered in scratches that suggested it must be Pilot's preferred resting place. The room was dark and pokey, painted a deep cherry red and contained six huge mahogany book shelves all crammed with the usual leather-bound almanacs and atlases.

I wandered around while Rose narrated some anecdote. There was a small writing desk in front of the window, piled high with correspondence. All bills I noticed.

The cleaners may have done their best to eradicate all trace of Richard Weston, but they must have finished cleaning last night and this had been left from the morning. A cold mug of coffee sat on the windowsill.

'Goodness me, what's that,' said the male yellow tracksuit, pointing behind a side table.

Rose bent down to examine it. 'Ahh. That,' she said, 'is a slice of toast. With marmalade on one side. As you can see, Weston Hall is very much a home and not just a show piece like some other stately houses.'

The people on the tour looked impressed; it made a refreshing difference to see that even meticulously cleaned stately homes couldn't escape everyday accidents.

We visited the now-familiar rooms that were being decorated for Gloria's wedding and I felt a misplaced touch of pride at being involved in the Hall in some small way. The dining room was only glanced at through the glass French doors because it was so crammed with chairs and tables. Likewise the Green Room was seen but not entered, the bar having been set up in one corner and the furniture removed.

The tour was over fairly quickly, since only a few of the ground floor rooms were open to the public. As we filed out down the hallway and into the main entrance hall I had a last look up at the stairway. It stopped me in my tracks. Richard Weston was sitting halfway up, watching our tour party file out through the front doors. He had a hunched, dishevelled look about him and dressed in muted colours he almost seemed to fade into the worn stair-carpet, which meant that very few of the people on the tour probably noticed anyone sitting on the stairs. And the ones that did see him would probably have dismissed him as a cleaner or some other contractor, he certainly didn't give off an aura of the Lord of the Manor.

He waved at me and I raised my hand tentatively to wave back.

He beckoned me over and so I turned round and went to where he was sitting.

'Hello,' he said, not getting up.

'Hello,' I smiled back at him, 'do you always watch the tour?'

'No. Just today. Was it interesting?'

'Yes,' I felt rather awkward at having gone round his house to look at his belongings. It didn't seem quite right, not when you sort of know the person.

'Come upstairs, I'll show you the study.' He saw the look on my face and added, 'That's if you've got time.'

'Yes. Absolutely,' and with that we went up the large staircase that snaked up to the first floor.

I felt very small and insignificant in the tall, imposing hallway. On either side, dark panelled wood encased me, and huge oil portraits of Weston's ancestors looked down at me with pompous expressions. It was darker here than in the rest of the house, and had a musty, unaired scent that I knew I'd smell on my clothes when I left.

With my big clumsy feet clattering on the old floorboards, I followed Richard Weston down to the other end of the corridor. The study was the last door on the left.

The difference between the old panelled corridor and the study couldn't have been greater. The room was strip lit with a neon light, making me blink as my eyes became accustomed to the stark brightness. The plaster walls were a dirty white, with a large Formica table in front of the French window that looked out over the stables. A mishmash of tables and chairs, boxes and shelves were laden with papers and parcels. Unopened letters were scattered on the floor in a mess of brown and white. Coffee mugs sat abandoned on various shelves while a computer hummed away in the corner. I could not imagine a room more at odds with the rest of the house. It was as if it had been cleansed of all its character – it felt more like the characterless City office in which I used to work than the house I had just been round.

'Come in, come in,' said Richard Weston, crouching on the floor, amassing some papers under a large leather box. 'You'll have to excuse the mess.'

'I would never have expected a room like this,' I said, walking into it carefully and taking a seat by the window.

The room smelt of him. Warm and musky.

He laid the papers on the desk and took a seat near me.

'Well it's practical I suppose. Plenty of light and all that.'

We sat a moment, looking at each other.

'Well my ankle is better.'

'Oh of course!' I'd completely forgotten, 'Well that's good isn't it?'

'I think so.' He smiled at me, waiting for me to say something else, like offer another apology I supposed. But I wouldn't stoop so low.

'It's quite a home you have here. Your guide really loves it,' I said, to break the silence.

'Rose? She's been doing the tour for years,' he said. 'She's been here longer than I have as a matter of fact.'

'Rose was saying that there's a lot of work to be done on the house,' I said, keen to find out more but at the same time wondering if perhaps I shouldn't mention it. He didn't seem to mind my question, and he gave me a long and detailed account of the subsidence of the Georgian front, the damp in the kitchen, and the dry rot in the back rooms.

'And to crown it all,' he went on, 'the Heritage Trust has very specific demands which, if I want its money, which I do, I have no choice but to accept. My hands are tied. I tell you,' he said, pointing a finger at me, 'should you ever have the misfortune to acquire some important property and the Heritage Trust want to help you out with it, read the small print. I didn't. Now I'm in this position. It's ludicrous.'

'Rose did say something about the Heritage Trust trying to get more rooms in the hall opened up, and longer opening times,' I said.

'Quite. Well that's all very good for Court Abbey and the like. I mean, have you seen those houses? They're huge! Old Harrington-Crow was given an entire wing to live in when they opened up his house to the public. The rooms were far away from the tourists and completely private. But you see you can't do that here. There's no self-contained apartment within Weston Hall and I need to use at least one of each of the kitchens and the bathrooms. It's far too small to work like that but they don't see it from my perspective. They expect me to turf out one of the tenants from the lodges and live there, which isn't an option as far as I'm concerned.'

'That's very noble of you not wanting to turf your tenants out.'

'Well, that and the fact that the lodges are in a worse state than this place; I wouldn't live in one of them if you paid me to.'

'Ah,' I said, not sure whether to smile at what might have been a joke or to be appalled at how he treated his tenants.

'Anyway, they not only bring in a bit of income, but I've got an arrangement with a few of my tenants' wives to clean Weston Hall regularly in exchange for a lower rent on their cottages. I get cleaners and they get cheaper accommodation – perfect!'

'Well,' I changed the subject, 'you don't often come to Kings

Newton do you?'

'Talking to your townsfolk chums again? Well, I come here once a month at least. I would want to come more if it wasn't for the HT and the paying guests. It's just…' he struggled to find the right words, playing with the envelopes on the desk, 'it's just that I have to come to terms with the rather gritty fact that I'm probably going to be the member of the family who gives the old ancestral home up, and I didn't imagine I would be. It's tough. I'm just glad my parents aren't alive to see it. Five hundred years…'

I sat in silence; there was nothing I could think of saying so I looked out of the window. I felt that, for some reason I really couldn't fathom, he wanted to talk to me about the problems he faced with the house. That much was clear because I hadn't needed to do much prompting, but I didn't know whether he now regretted what he'd said, especially as we were virtual strangers, give or take a sprained ankle.

'Well, anyway,' he said, 'what I particularly don't like is the way the Heritage Trust dictate how my house should look. *My* house. I don't have any say in it at all! I have to apply for permission before I do so much as install a toaster. And even when I do ask for permission they hardly ever grant it me anyway. They expect me to live like a bloody Victorian.'

I smiled and he held up his hands, 'I'm sorry,' he said, 'it must be very tedious for you to listen to, it's just that I'm *so* frustrated by them. I've had them on the phone for the last half hour or so and it always gets to me, so I'm afraid you're seeing the effects of that. At the moment I've got a problem with rainwater coming into one of the guest rooms. It's damaged a lot of hideous Victorian wallpaper which, to be honest, was my intention because it is truly hideous. That's why I left it so long before I mentioned it to them. When I took the opportunity to request that I redecorate and make something presentable out of it, something I could actually live with, they told me that the wallpaper is some God-be-damned rare stuff and costs an arm and a leg. Regardless of what I or anyone else thinks about it, I have to leave the undamaged bits and pay a small fortune for someone to make more of the rotten stuff to put

113

up when the ceiling's repaired.' He gave a short laugh and stared out of the window in silence. His hair was tousled; he had been running his hands through it throughout our conversation. He looked tired and I felt sorry for him. He sighed and looked back at me, smiling sadly.

'Is that why the music room is painted turquoise?' I said, remembering the brutal colour that Rose had had rather a lot to say about.

'Oh no,' he laughed, 'that's not 'turquoise', that's 'Regency Aquamarine'. They had it specially mixed. It is, would you believe it, a rare example of that particular Georgian paint colour.'

'And therefore unalterable…?'

'You understand! I mean, how could someone spend more than ten minutes in a room that's painted that colour? The honorable ancestor who chose the colour was as mad as a ferret anyway. She thought she was a fairy and used to dance around the gardens in specially designed costumes. Totally bonkers.'

I laughed. It was strange how relaxed I felt in his company, I was in a crumbling mansion, with a latterday lord and not at all in my usual comfort zone. There was, though, a tension in the air. He had an undeniable presence that would usually have had me in awe. As it was, I felt more alive in his company, and every sense seemed somehow intensified. He had this animated way about him that was catching. But suddenly the lost look was back and he was staring absently out of the window. When I followed his gaze, I saw he couldn't have been focusing on anything. He looked down onto the table pushing envelopes absentmindedly across its surface.

'What do you think of Kings Newton?' he said, looking into my eyes.

'Wow…'

'What?'

'That must be one of the few times since I got to this town that someone actually asked me for my opinion.'

'Really?'

'Yes. The people I'm staying with…'

'…Gloria?'

'Yes, Gloria, and her friends, all talk *at* me. Hardly anyone knows what I think, or feel.'

'That's probably because you don't get… to… the… point.'

'Oh, right!' I laughed. "What do I think of Kings Newton?' I think it's strange,' I said. 'You'd expect new people to have come and settled in the town, but it's almost as if it hasn't altered for centuries. The place hasn't been touched by progress. The same families live in the same streets and nothing moves on.'

'Exactly! You see – you come from outside the town and you see exactly what it's like. That's what's good about the new development. No place can be so stuck in the past and still survive. It's such a pretty town that people want to live here. The development can do nothing but good. OK, it's sad that some of the old town will be built over, but the county archeologists have done their report and there's nothing particularly interesting down there.'

The room was silent, except for the buzz of the pc monitor in the background, and a faint squawking of geese around the lake.

'I go away and I miss the place. Then when I come back, I remember how stagnant it is and I hate it. Sometimes I feel that I don't belong anywhere.'

'I'm sorry,' I said, wanting to put my hand on his and comfort him in some way, but remembering the horrors of Tom's over-friendliness I restrained myself.

'Don't be.' He looked up at me quickly. 'But don't say anything to them will you?'

'No – of course not,' I said. 'Isn't there any other way that you could break down some of the barriers between you and the town? Why don't you go to the fair next week?'

He mumbled something.

'What was that?'

'I've got a friend who says exactly the same thing.'

A *friend*?

'It's not Sarah is it?'

'You've met her then? Wanting me to go out there and shake some hands every five minutes… She doesn't realise what it's like here, she just sees what she wants to see.'

'What *does* she want to see?'

He smiled at me: 'Herself as lady of the manor and general venerable type, opening fêtes and so on.'

I laughed.

'No seriously,' he said, 'the girl's on a mission.'

'Well why don't you ask her to stop?' I said, candidly.

'It's not worth it. There are too many other difficult things going on in my life without causing ructions in that particular… friendship. Better just to let it lie.'

I was wondering whether that was the most sensible course of action, given the fact that Sarah hadn't picked up the signals. But maybe this was all talk and really he cared for her and wanted to keep the peace with her out of genuine affection. What did I know? His familiarity with me, although I loved it, was catching me off my guard, making me feel like I knew him better than I actually did.

He was sitting back, looking at me, 'You're not at all fazed by it are you?'

'By what?'

'The 'Lord' thing.'

'Not really. Should I be? Should I curtsey or something?'

'Oh God no!' he laughed. 'Most people are that's all. So I just find it quite refreshing… nice… that you're not like that.'

'Oh. Well thank you,' I said. 'Glad to be 'nice'.'

'The people down in my part of London see it as an achievement, to get into the circles that I do, but that's pretty much where it ends, there are a lot bigger fish than me out there. Up here it's the opposite. It's not so much curtseying and bowing, but there's a definite reserve, as well as downright rudeness. But you, you're a bit of a wild one aren't you? Unfettered and all that.'

'I get that a lot,' I said, shaking my head, 'But really, what is unfettered? I'm not a natural wanderer. People think that leaving the City of London behind means I reject what it stands for and—'

'You used to work in the City?'

The phone went. For a moment he looked as though he was going to answer it, but he pushed a button and diverted it.

'You used to work in the City?' he repeated.

'Yes, just some dead-end job in a dull office. Very uninteresting,' I said dolefully.

'What made you leave?'

'A relationship break-up made me leave London. And the realisation that I wasn't where I wanted to be means I've no urge to go back.'

'Where do you want to be?'

'I don't know. That's the trouble. A friend has given me the opportunity to work with him in a florist's shop in Birmingham in a few weeks time, when I'm no longer needed in Kings Newton.'

'Are you going to take it?'

'Probably. I can't stay here, and I don't have any other plans…'

'Do you work in the florist's here?'

I told him where I was staying, and where I was working. I was so grateful to have found someone who listened, other than the lovely but preoccupied Alan, of course, that I told him all about Gloria and the forthcoming wedding. I even told him about her affair with Tom, which given the fact that he knew Sarah so well was perhaps, on reflection, a bad idea. But he was easy to talk to and I enjoyed talking to him and it slipped out without me having time to think twice. Oops…

'Wow, well you are at a crossroads aren't you,' he said, leaning back in his chair after listening to me chattering rapidly for the last ten minutes. 'Well it's a good job that your friendly lord of the manor is here to listen to your woes. The rest of your so-called friends sound like a pretty rum lot.'

The thought suddenly dawned on me that Gloria had told me Richard Weston should have been in London until after the wedding. Did his being here now mean he would be at the Hall during the wedding?

'What?' he said, sensing the question hovering about my lips.

'Well I was wondering… I thought you were in London. Gloria's getting married at the end of next week and I was sure she said that you were going to be out of the Hall during the two weeks leading up to the wedding. And on the wedding day itself.'

'Well I was going to be in London. A friend has got a gallery opening and I was supposed to be going, but to be honest I just can't be bothered. It's a gallery devoted to modern art and apparently the first show is by an installation artist who makes sculptures out of old cutlery. Frankly, if you gave me a spoon I'd rather tuck into my own arm than spend a couple of hours discussing how a pickle-fork sculpture 'talks' to me. Do you think your friend will mind if I stay here? I'll closet myself away in the back of the house, I promise! You won't know I'm here.'

I giggled. But as soon as I had, I regretted it. It was sad that he had to become a stranger in his own house by necessity. And I believed he really would hide himself away in the back and let the party go on in his dining room.

'Do you often hide in the back when you've got guests?'

'Occasionally. Mostly I get myself off to London so I can avoid it. The rooms always smell bad the morning after, what with the drink, food and cigarettes, and the caterers usually spend the Sunday cleaning, which I try to steer clear of because they always make so much noise and clatter.'

I asked him what took him to London, and it thankfully took us off the subject of him hiding away from Gloria's wedding. He was starting up his own kitchenware business, and spent a lot of time promoting it in the capital. He was basically trading off his title he admitted, but why the hell not? Might as well put it to good use…

'Will it pay for you to keep the Hall?'

'Maybe, one day. If it goes well. But then no-one knows what's around the corner. Another wing could suddenly subside into the clay and I'd never be able to cover the cost of that.'

The door opened and Sarah entered, knocking loudly.

'Hi,' she said, uncertainly at me, 'I could hear voices.'

She whispered something in his ear. I was clearly in the way. I got up, pushing back my chair but with more vigour than I thought I had, and it crashed to the floor. Face burning, I apologised and stooped to pick it up. Where was my City girl panache when I needed it?

'I'll be off,' I said.

'Oh I didn't mean to interrupt,' said Sarah, meaningfully, pulling the dainty cardigan that was perched on her shoulders more tightly around her. 'I simply wanted to ask Rich's opinion on something I'm working on.'

'No, no, I've got to go,' I said, and stumbled out clumsily, saying a hasty goodbye to... Lord Weston? Richard?

I hurried out, clomping quickly down the corridor, down the staircase and out through the open door at the front.

I wished more than anything at that point that I could be more like Sarah: dainty and pretty and small and fragile. Someone a man would want to fling his arms around and shield from the slings and arrows of outrageous fortune – or Gloria and the fridge thing, at least. I wished I was the sort of person who could perch on the edge of a desk without looking like a roosting giraffe. Ah well, at least I had better hair than Sarah...

I hummed all the way back to Gloria's house. I wasn't completely sure why, but I was happy, nevertheless.

21

It was the Tuesday before the wedding; just four days to go until the big day. Since Phil's departure from Gloria's, the place had been transformed into a wedding warehouse. Her dress was hanging from the study door, her shoes were out of their box and displayed atop the TV and all around us were fabrics, wrapping paper, expensive underwear, make up, orders of service and *bonbonierre*.

One of her town friends had been round the past couple of nights to give her advice on party organising, and promised to be 'there for her' on the big day. 'And of course the hen night too,' she'd added. Before she left she had surreptitiously handed me a feathery pink headband to wear on the hen night. 'And one for Alan too,' she said. I smiled to myself – he'd love it.

Today was another day of decorating the Hall; in fact it was the last day of decorating the Hall. I wondered whether I'd meet Richard Weston again, and what Gloria would say when she saw me chatting familiarly to him. I could see her now, eyes popping out of their sockets, hand clutching tightly her wedding plans.

With a light heart I sailed down the sweeping driveway to the house, Gloria by my side. I hadn't been able to get Richard Weston out of my head for the past few days. But then, perhaps it wasn't such a surprising thing, given that he was inadvertently the centre of the world I had become involved in. His home was the venue for my friend's big day, and the business with the development was the reason why a protest would take place – my first protest, if I could pluck up the courage to actually attend. So, really, it was completely understandable why I should be thinking so much about him, he was going to be a big a part of my life for the next couple of weeks. And yes, perhaps, if I'm really being honest because he was so incredibly attractive. Stop it, Roz… it really is getting out of hand. Urgh! The protest… The sudden remembrance of it filled me with a dread that took the edge off my good mood. Gloria and Tom had been talking more and more about the details of the 'big night', and Gloria was bitterly disappointed that she wasn't going to be there to take part in the demonstration. I was desperate not to take part in the thing, and had managed not to commit to anything up to this point, but the pressure from Tom and Gloria was definitely mounting. Gloria saw it as a sort of pay-back for having put me up, and that regardless of how I felt about the redevelopment thought that I would take part for her sake alone. Tom seemed to think that I was some kind of hippie anti-establishment type who would just leap on board any sort of scheme like this. Alan said that the time was ripe for me to get my hair cut and wear some smart casual clothes like most of the population did, but I resisted stoically. Actually I told him to shut it. But I had another card up my sleeve – the knowledge that Richard Weston would be *at the Hall* during the protest. I knew they hadn't bargained on that fact, and no doubt it would up the stakes considerably knowing they could well be caught mid-protest. It would, in fact, probably scupper their plan completely, thus neatly preventing me having to take part.

I decided that the moment was ripe for the taking and broke the news to Gloria just as we were reaching the top of the hill and the large wrought iron gates to Weston Hall came into view.

'I think he's going to be there you know,' I said.

'Who?' said Gloria, disinterestedly.

'Richard Weston.'

'What do you mean 'he's going to be there'?'

'I think he's going to be in Weston Hall when your wedding reception's on.'

'How do you know that? Who told you?'

'He did,' I said. 'Well… he said something about *possibly* being at the house during the time the wedding reception's on…'

'Oh great. So I should invite him to the wedding shouldn't I…'

'No. I don't think so,' I said. I told her that from what I'd understood he had seemed pretty resigned to being locked away in the upstairs rooms and that it was normal practice for him to do so anyway. I thought it was rather sad that he hadn't had an invite, even out of politeness. Surely the presence of a Lord milling around the drinks reception would impress some elderly aunts and uncles…

'Well I can't very well be seen to know he's at home and not invite him… that would be awful. And I'd have to invite Sarah too. I was sure that she told me she wasn't going to be around on the Saturday. Why would she lie to me? Eugh! I really don't want the miserable so-and-so to be there on my wedding day.'

'Gloria,' I said, 'you are paying Richard Weston *how much* to use his house?'

She looked at me with a surprised expression before saying, 'Three thousand pounds.'

'Three thousand pounds… to use his house. For one day. Therefore I think you have a right to choose not to invite him if you don't want to. And besides, you can plead ignorance and pretend that you didn't know he would be in the house. You hate the guy anyway.'

'I suppose so…' she said.

We crunched down the gravel driveway in silence for a few minutes, until we reached the bend in the road that would reveal the Hall and the lake. It was so beautiful, every time I saw it I thought so. I looked over to see if Gloria was as entranced with it as I was but she was staring resolutely at the driveway, probably deep in thought about the wedding and not about the protest so I pushed the conversation on a bit more.

'It means that Richard Weston will be at the Hall during the protest, too.'

'Oh,' she said and looked up from her thoughts, 'I hadn't thought of that.'

'Do you think you'll maybe have to call it a day? You know, not do it… That sort of thing?' I bumbled.

'Christ, I hope not. We've put hours into the thing. Tom and I have spent so much time and effort sorting it out. It's taken months just to find a date when most people are free to take part. No way, we should still do it but I guess we'll have to be more careful than we originally thought. Remind me to go and see Tom when we've got set up today. I'm glad you're thinking about the protest, too,' she added. 'I'm glad that you're taking part. It means a lot to me.'

I smiled wanly and let my hair fall around my face so I could scowl unseen the rest of the way to the side door.

The weather was due to hold for the next few days, which meant that the plans for the party to spill out onto the terrace beside the lake could go ahead. Today our task was arranging the urns and hanging strings of white lights in the large horse chestnut trees that flanked the back entrance.

'Right,' said Gloria, 'We have to get these…' she held out the lights to me, '…up there,' indicating the tree.

I looked at her and she looked at me. 'You're asking *me* to put them in the tree aren't you?'

She smiled and raised her eyebrows pleadingly.

'Oh come on, Gloria! I can hardly scale a tree in this dress, can I?' I said. It was an old blue wool wrap dress that reached down almost to my ankles. It did, as Gloria and Alan had both pointed out, have a few small holes in the fabric but really it was a classic piece and I was really fond of it. It did truly amazing things for my cleavage.

'Well I'm so short I could never do it,' she whined. 'I could get a ladder maybe...'

'There is no way I'm balancing a ladder against a tree and doing that job,' I said firmly. 'OK, I like a challenge, give me the lights and I'll climb up.'

I took the string of lights and hoisted myself up to the first low branch and began the graceless, not to say reckless, business of climbing a tree in a frock.

'You have checked with Richard Weston that it's OK to climb his trees and put lights up?' I called from a low branch.

'He'll be fine with it.'

'That's not what I asked.'

'I'm fine with it.'

We turned to see Richard Weston walking towards us, Pilot bouncing along behind him and not in the least bit fazed about what was going on in his garden.

'Hi,' he said, peering up the tree at me. 'At home with the fairies again? Ready to leap out on me and squash me flat? Foiled again... I told you I'd find out where you were hiding!'

Embarrassed and amused, a heady mix, I sat on my branch and burnt with shame. The dress had ridden up to above my knees and I tried to tug down the hem in an effort to become a mite more respectable, but I didn't manage it.

Gloria, so far ignored, introduced herself into the conversation, 'I'm *so* sorry but you don't mind if we put these lights up do you?'

'Not at all. Here, let me help you,' and he stripped off his jumper to expose an old t-shirt. He hoisted himself effortlessly up to my level, annoyingly quickly and easily. Pilot barked excitedly down below.

'Hello,' he said, beaming at me from an opposite branch.

I grinned back, my heart beating fit to bust – and it wasn't the effort of getting up the tree.

Gloria, caught off-guard by the situation, nervously passed a string of lights up and together Richard Weston and I crept around the tree, threading the strings of bulbs around the branches. We took them quite far up, and at one point I looked down to the gravel drive and caught my breath.

'High isn't it?'

'Yes,' I held on a little tighter to my branch.

'Roz, I'm going into the house to plug it in OK?' Gloria called up and scrunched indoors.

Richard Weston and I remained on our perch. Looking down to the ground, I sneaked a look over at him, but caught him looking at me. I smiled, embarrassed, and looked away.

'Bit bossy isn't she?' he said after a moment.

'Yes, she is. She didn't used to be, she used to be quite a laugh a few years ago.'

'What happened?'

'She got a couple of businesses and a wedding to arrange.'

'Ri–ich, why are you up in a tree honey?' a voice wafted up from the ground below. We peered down through the foliage and there was Sarah standing directly below me. 'Oh hi Rosamund,' she said, seeing me above and giving a little wave with her tiny, tiny hand.

'Why not?'

'Seriously Rich…'

'Putting lights up.' Surely it was obvious. He shot me a look to say as much.

'Well I'm ready to go to town when you are,' came back the terse reply, and she flounced off.

'She's a bit fragile isn't she?' I suddenly ventured, mimicking what he'd said about my friend. For a moment I thought I'd misjudged him and had overstepped the mark.

'She is,' he said, 'but I think she likes me.'

'Yes,' I smiled, 'I think she does too.'

He was looking straight at me, nodding to himself.

'Have you known her long?' I asked.

'All my life. Her lot are friends of the family.'

There was another pause in our tree top conversation. A soft wind whispered through the branches, lifting the leaves up and smoothing them down again.

'Er… Rosamund,' There was another voice from down below, this time it was Gloria. I leant over and looked down to where she

was standing… with Greg.

My heart plummeted to meet him. I could see Richard Weston looking at me, and then down to where Greg was standing. It must have taken the slightest moment, but to me it felt like an enormous amount of time, all four of us eyeing each other up; two up a tree, two on the ground.

'Hello, Rosamund,' Greg half-waved at me.

I said nothing, my hands clamped like claws around the branch.

I could feel everyone looking at me. Waiting for me to say something.

'Er… could you come down from there?' Greg called up.

I didn't know whether that would be physically possible. I couldn't feel my body; my legs and arms were numb. I was milliseconds from tears and to top it off I felt horribly like being sick. I really, really didn't want to do that though. It would make a hell of a mess on the way down.

I said nothing but stared down at Greg, dumbly.

'Who is he?' came a whisper from the opposite branch.

I could feel hot tears that I dearly didn't want to shed running down my face.

'Ex-boyfriend,' I said hoarsely.

'Nice chap is he?' he whispered back.

'Utter bastard…' I was glad to be half hidden in the tree with Richard, it felt a lot further away from Greg than it actually was.

Lord Weston nodded thoughtfully.

'Look, Roz,' Greg was shouting from below, 'I drove up from London this morning. I took a day's holiday to come up here. I really want to talk to you…'

'I caught him with my older sister,' I whispered. I don't know what made me say it, but I knew I wanted to, 'I walked in on them. They were in front of the fridge. It was horrible.'

'Crikey!' Richard Weston looked suitably shocked.

'Roz, I really would like to talk things over!' shouted the voice from below. 'I'm really really sorry about everything. I'm worried about you. We all are. Your mum said you were here so I thought

I ought to come…'

'Do you want to talk to him?' Richard Weston asked, 'I can help you down if you want. Or you could just fall on his head…'

I smiled desperately and tried to stop my nose from running but my hands weren't operating properly. This was the least sophisticated I had ever been, and at a time when I could really have done with putting on a bit of a show. Perhaps the way to do it would be to imagine how someone like Sarah would cope with such a situation and then act in that way. But it was too late for that – Sarah would never have hoisted her skirts up and climbed a tree in the first place.

'I think…' I said to Richard Weston, 'I think that I'd like to stay up here for a bit.'

'And not speak to him?'

'Yes.'

'Hello there?' Richard Weston called to Greg, who looked as if he was actually contemplating scaling the tree himself. The man who never climbed trees. Never played sports. Ironed his jeans.

Greg looked up.

'Yes, hello… I don't think that Rosamund really wants to come down right now.'

'Rosamund, who's the idiot in the tree with you?' Greg responded.

I could see Gloria down beside Greg. Her mouth fell open and she looked absolutely mortified, busying herself with checking the plug to the string of lights. At any other time it would have amused me enormously, but as it was I just felt rather embarrassed to have been at all associated with the moron.

I looked over at Richard Weston who seemed unflustered by the comment. He was probably used to that kind of rebuke, considering what he'd told me of his experience with the townspeople over the last few years.

'Oh, I'm so sorry, I didn't introduce myself,' Richard called down to Greg. 'I'm Lord Weston. Of Weston Hall. *This* Weston Hall.' And he did a broad sort of sweep of the house and grounds.

Greg was suitably reduced to silence, staring up at us in the tree, his mouth gaping open like a fish. He quickly recovered though and turned to me and shouted up.

'Rosamund, we really need to talk you know.'

'Look I'm sorry… er… Greg, but I really don't think that she wants to talk to you right now.'

Even from up here I could see that Greg was torn between swearing at Richard and reverence for his title, so he just stood there clenching and unclenching his fists.

I could feel the initial shock of Greg being here, in my safe haven in Shropshire, wearing away. How *dare* he come here and pollute my life – my temporary life – with his being here. How *dare* he think that I wanted to see him and that we had something to talk about? The anger started to burn and thawed out my icy hands that were still dug into the bark.

Of all the things I could have shouted down to him, of all the clever put-downs and offensive insults, the only thing that I could summon up was: 'Just go Greg. Go back to London.'

'But Roz you can't just run away from everything. You've got a life back in London and you can't just leave it and hide yourself away up here forever. That's stupid.'

'No it's not! Sod off Greg. There is absolutely nothing that I want to say to you, and I don't want to hear your voice ever again. In my life. Ever. Don't phone me, don't write to me and don't come and see me.'

'Well we were worried.'

'We?'

'Your mum. And Rachel…'

'Oh, Rachel's worried is she?' I snorted. 'Worried she might have upset me a little, eh?'

'Oh come on Roz. She feels awful about it. We both do.'

'We? *We*? Do you sit and talk about it then? How do you have time to sit and talk about me when you've got all that *shagging* to be getting on with?'

'Ro-oz… it was a stupid, stupid mistake and I'm really sorry. Rachel means nothing to me, I don't know how it happened…'

'But it *did* happen, you pathetic shagging bastard,' I shouted back, not knowing where it really came from, but liking it all the same.

Richard Weston had been taking in the slanging match as a silent observer, but at this point he leant forward and looking at Greg said: 'Right, Grant, or whatever your name is, I've had just about enough of you and I don't want you trespassing on my private land any more. You either leave *right now* of your own accord or I'll make you leave,' and with that he let out a whistle which brought Pilot crashing through the rhododendron bushes and towards the tree.

It seemed to have the desired effect.

I could make out Greg's expression far below me, trying to work out what else he should say without having the wit to think it up. Dejected and cautioned by my horse chestnut hero he looked up and said, 'Well, you've got my number...' and sloped off.

Gloria must have walked him back to his car. We were left alone in our eyrie.

You've got my number... Like I would ever want to call him again after what had happened. Like I would be grateful that he still wanted to talk to me. Arrogant, arrogant bastard.

'Urgh!' I lay back, slowly, on my branch, staring up into the canopy. I managed to balance myself so my arms and legs hung down below me like dead weights. A huge sense of relief was tempered by dying anger. I was pleased he had gone, but somewhat mortified that he hadn't put up more of a fight, especially in front of Richard Weston. Surely I was worth a bit more than that? He could have pounded the tree trunk or shouted a bit more passionately. Shed a remorseful tear maybe? Clearly not. No, clearly from Greg's wet, ineffectual pleas I was someone who is OK but not worth too huge an effort. I was someone who could be let go. I lay there watching the dappled sunlight through the leaves, feeling the soft breeze and feeling very grateful that I was up a large tree.

'I'm sorry you had to listen to that,' I said after a while, perhaps to no one because from where I was lying I couldn't see whether Richard Weston was still in the tree.

'Not at all. You must feel pretty low,' came a voice from opposite the trunk.

'Well. No. I've had over a month to come to terms with it.'

There was a moment's silence.

'So he's the chap you were talking about? When you said you were changing your life?'

'Yes. I'm a fugitive from my old life.'

'I see.'

I lifted my head up from the branch and looked across at where he was lying on his branch. Looking into the canopy. I leant back, comfortable, swinging my arms and my legs below me again, my back resting along the thick branch.

'I think you beat yourself up too much about what you did,' he said after a moment's silence had settled in the canopy.

'What do you mean?' I asked, looking over at him.

'I mean that you're probably lying there now thinking why did I throw in my job as well as my boyfriend and walk away from it all? But really, I think you're very brave to know when your time's up and you should move on. Seriously, it's a gift.'

'Really?' I sat up, 'You really think I did the right thing?'

'Well I don't know all the details…' he sat up too, 'but what else could you do? You made a choice to change your life completely, and you did it.'

'I guess so…'

'And aren't you happy here in your new life?'

'Yes I am… mostly.'

'Well then. Wipe your nose and let's climb down. I have whisky in the house.'

'Whisky! Lovely.' I said and managed to slither and slump my way down the tree and onto the ground below without showing too much leg or getting too horribly caught up in my unsuitable skirts.

22

DEAR MUM

~~DEAR MUM~~

~~Mum~~

~~I can't believe you told Greg where I was staying!!~~

Mum

I was ~~rather~~ very upset that you told Greg where I was staying. He came up, as you know, and made an ~~arse~~ exhibition of himself. As I said before, I'm really not interested in seeing him again. After what happened. ~~Surely you understand?~~

Anyway, please don't tell him any more about me, I'd prefer it if he didn't know.

Apart from seeing Greg things are going very well over here. ~~My friend Alan has offered to let me use his car~~ A friend has offered to let me use their car so perhaps I can pop over for the day and see you?

Roz x

23

Gloria's wedding preparations were in full gear, and nearly all our time was spent servicing the big event at the end of the week. Added to that, Alan was increasingly excited about his new business (ad)venture and had to be forcibly silenced for fear of making his plans known and upsetting Gloria before her wedding.

And then there was Tom, ejected from Gloria's life temporarily by her impending marriage. He had been sulking round the shop, dropping loaded comments about Gloria's new life and how she was never around any more. He muttered things like 'Gloria expecting me to be at her beck and call' and 'she shouldn't be surprised if I moved on from her', not, I think, because he wanted to share his thoughts with me, but because he wanted me to relate them to my friend… which I declined to do. The girl would rip me limb from limb if I passed on such messages from Tom – she was completely unacquainted with the phrase *don't shoot the messenger*.

With so much activity buzzing on around me, I was glad to get out and about on my solitary rambles. It was such a beautiful time of year and I was so happy to be out in the countryside and not cooped up in the City. I was still managing to avoid spending much of my time thinking over what I would be doing with myself, which was very irresponsible, I knew, as time was running out on my Kings Newton interlude. Gloria and Phil would be married and back from their honeymoon in just over two weeks' time and I was not going to be welcome in their house then. I tried, I really did, to come up with some plans but it was far more interesting to turn my mind to the things that were happening here and now in Kings Newton. The most pressing problem that I had turned my attention to was dealing with the threat of the anti-development, midnight protest. The protest that I had to take part in or else seriously let down my long-time pal and benevolent host.

I'd spent a good portion of my walk one afternoon trying to think of what I could do about the protest when, out of the blue, the solution presented itself. One minute I was nervously skirting a field full of aggressive looking cows and the next I had mounted the stile, was admiring the view when *wham* it hit me. A plan *extraordinaire*.

I strolled confidently back down to town mulling over the details and feeling pretty smug. I just knew it was a goer. I decided to run through it with Alan as soon as possible, to see if he agreed with me. He must do – it truly was outstanding.

I broached the subject of the protest with Alan during an illicit car journey to Birmingham, on our last free day before the wedding. Not being what you'd call a *safe* driver or, perhaps, what you'd call a *driver* at all judging by some of his moves, I left off talking to him until we'd cleared the A-roads and were on the relatively straightforward motorway section of the trip.

'Alan, I have a cunning plan for the night of the protest!' I announced.

'Well good,' he said, slipping into the outside lane. 'I don't know what the hell he flashed his lights at me for. Honestly, some drivers. Well then ... what's the cunning plan? Is it devilish clever?'

'I don't know about that. But it's good. Basically— LORRY!'

'OK, OK, I saw it. Don't worry. Gosh you're really tense. Are you OK? You're sweating!'

'Yes I'm fine. Fine. OK then... er... basically I *have* to go to the protest —'

'Why?' he cut in.

'Because Gloria really, really wants me to go and I don't want to let her down. She's given me food and shelter— '

'Yah-de-yah-de-yah...' Alan cut me off again.

'Yes well she *has*. Whatever you say... And she's my oldest friend and I'm very fond of her, despite everything, so I don't want to be the kind of person who says 'thanks very much for all the help you've given me, and I know we've been pals for nearly two decades but I'm really not interested in helping you out with your big project.' It would just be mean.'

'Well what about helping out at the shop or the wedding? Those are big projects. Why aren't they enough?'

'I don't know Alan. I just know that if I said I wouldn't take part in the protest then she'd be really upset about it.'

'Fine.'

'And,' I added, 'it's so much easier if I go to the protest – I won't have to listen to Tom sounding off about it all the time and trying to convince me to go.'

'Well, yes that's true. He does go on and on about it. But what about Richard Weston?'

'What about him?' I shot a glance at Alan who was concentrating on the road, fortunately.

'Well excu-use me for noticing,' he laughed, 'but every time his name comes up in the pub of an evening you go all starry-eyed.'

'I do not!'

'Yes, you bloody do. 'Oh Richard Weston mew mew mew',' he turned to me all doe-eyed with lips pursed in a kiss.

'Watch the road Alan!'

'Well, what about lover boy anyway. Going on the protest isn't going to help him is it?'

'Well actually, Mister I-Think-I'm-So-Smart, my master plan

is going to do exactly that. I shall turn up and be counted by the protesters. I shall break into the grounds along with all the other ruffians and then I'll lurk around an exit point and, when everyone is busy breaking the law, I'll set off my rape alarm! Everyone will scarper, minimum damage will be done and—'

'Everyone's a winner!'

'Exactly. Genius isn't it?'

Alan contemplated this while cutting up an Audi in the middle lane. 'It's not bad. You have an alarm then?'

'Yep. And I think I pretty much know the grounds now, so I won't get lost. I just have to make sure I don't get caught in the act. But everyone should be pretty much busy and it will be dark so ... it can't fail can it?'

'Well if that's what you want to do, then good for you,' he sighed. 'Personally I think you should stand firm and say no to Gloria, but I understand where you're coming from. I'm having nothing to do with it though. You're on your own.'

Having safely negotiated the outskirts of Brum we eventually found our way to the canalside area and managed to locate a parking space. Alan's shop was just as he had said; right on the waterfront, and in the heart of a trendy new area that had emerged in the past few years. Beautiful cherry trees filled the squares, and a network of artistic water channels was cut into the pavement; beautiful but potentially lethal to those who were short-sighted or too preoccupied to look where they were going.

'Here we are!' Alan said as we turned a corner past some very chi-chi looking bars and a restaurant. '*Maison* Alan. Shame about your shoes do you think they'll dry out?'

'Not soon enough…' I said, looking down at my surely-ruined green suede pumps, 'What kind of stupid architect *does* that kind of thing?'

'Well they were round the sides of the pavement. And surely your enormous feet should have spanned their width. Look!'

He unlocked the large glass door and in we went. The building had originally been an old wharf house sitting on the canal, but it had been opened up and was easily accessible from the main town and the café area we had come from.

My pulse raced as I crossed the threshold. I could only imagine how exciting this would be if it was my own business. No wonder Alan had been so wild-eyed with excitement recently. It was amazing. Our footsteps clattered (well mine squished, actually) on the huge expanse of floor, and echoed off the sandblasted walls. Brushed metal shelves had already been erected along one side, with a large, imposing preparation table in the same material standing in front of them.

Alan flipped a switch and the room was illuminated by dozens of spotlights arranged on thin wires along the ceiling and running down the near wall.

'Wow…'

'It's amazing isn't it?' he said, 'Amazing that I could actually own this, and work from here.'

'It's huge. It's a cavern. How on earth are you going to fill it all?'

'I was thinking that I could get some sofas and a couple of tables in this bit here, and make it like a coffee bar area. For friends to hang out in. After all, we're not frantically busy all the time, so it would be handy if people came round to ours for a chat sometimes.'

'Ours?'

'Yeah! Yours and mine Roz! You are still on for working here aren't you?' His face fell.

'Sure. Yes. For a while. Until I sort myself out.'

'Great. For a moment there I thought you didn't sound too keen. Come and look through here, into the kitchen,' and with that I got the full grand tour. He was a more passionate guide than Weston Hall's Rose. Alan drew my attention to every piece of carpentry, every detail of the renovation, all of which had captured his heart. Nothing was forgotten.

However exciting it was for Alan, it wasn't quite so enthralling for me, and almost an hour and ninety-nine individually specified rivets later I pleaded with him to stop, and we went round the corner to a chic little bistro called 'Le Brum'.

'To Fuschiarama,' I toasted and as Alan and I chinked glasses, 'may your business bloom!'

'Why thank you!' Alan beamed and took a swig. 'Ooh this sure beats cider...' he carried on but I tuned out, having just seen someone familiar walk into the restaurant. It was in the blink of an eye, as they walked across the bar area; they must have moved behind one of the enormous cast iron pillars so I couldn't be sure it was who I thought it was.

'What are you looking at?' Alan bent round to see.

'I could have sworn I saw someone from Kings Newton...'

'Really?'

'Mmm...'

'Who?'

'It is!' They'd come into view again. It was Richard Weston's girlfriend, Sarah, with *another* man on her arm (so it wasn't just Tom, the minx). This one was definitely the ugly duckling compared to the other men in her life. He was rather lanky with scruffy brown hair and an 'arty' look about him, which came, I suppose, from the ruffled old shirt and necktie that he wore.

'What should we do?' I hissed at Alan but it was too late, we'd been spotted.

'Hello there!' Sarah waved, tip-tapping in her petite shoes over to where we were sitting. 'What an absolute coincidence, bumping into you two in Birmingham. My god, it's a small world isn't it? Move up move up, there's room for two more small ones in this booth isn't there?'

And with that they joined our table.

'I'm sure we've met before…' she said, looking at Alan, 'but I can't think where.'

'Alan,' he said, shaking her outstretched mitt, 'I work in Kings Newton. You used to order flowers from the florist's shop where I work.'

'Ah that's it. I remember now. Well … isn't this nice? Oh! Rosamund, Alan, this is Pierre. Pierre this is Rosamund and Alan, from the little town I was telling you about, the one that Rich owns. Gosh what a surprise to see you here of all places. So why are you here?'

Alan was on the brink of launching straight into the Fuschia-rama saga – I could see his face take on that familiar wide-eyed look. I kicked him sharply under the table – there was no way he could go blabbing about it yet, especially not to a friend and sometime customer of Gloria's.

'Ow!' he shot me a cross look

'Sorry Alan. I was trying to find some room under the table for my feet. So, Sarah, have you been out with *Gloria* since we saw you last?'

Sarah started answering as I glanced across at Alan. At the mention of Gloria he'd realised what he'd been about to do and gave me a surreptitious thumbs up from across the table. Silly boy. It wouldn't have mattered too much I suppose, because it's not as if Gloria had any spare time to sit gossiping with friends right now. But better, surely, to be safe than sorry…

'… but she's just so busy with everything. Anyway, is the place decorated for the wedding now?' Sarah broke into my thoughts.

'Yes. All finished. I can't believe it's so soon…' and we launched into wedding chit chat. Alan was getting on very well with Pierre. I couldn't tell what they were talking about, but he looked remarkably animated. Pierre, I noticed, was leaning in towards Alan, who was, in turn, leaning in close to Pierre.

'So what brings you to Birmingham?' I asked

'Ah well Pierre works in the jewellery quarter just north of here. He's helping me out on a commission I was given a few days ago. I don't have all the equipment to hand so he's setting some of the gems for me.'

I still didn't take to the girl much, I couldn't help it. I suppose it was because I knew she had her self-serving claws into Richard Weston and because she was very likely going behind Gloria's back and seeing Tom, too. But all the same it was a pleasant enough lunch and we all got on well together. Pierre and Alan, I noticed, had even exchanged phone numbers and I overheard Pierre say at some point 'when we meet up', so things had obviously gone swimmingly on that side of the table.

The coffees had been drunk and the bill paid. We got up and headed for the door.

'I'll see you at the fair then?' Sarah said.

'Oh. Are you going to Gloria's hen do?' I asked. I hadn't even thought about the hen night and I had a sudden panic that there was something I should have been doing about it.

'Yes. She invited me the other day. I thought I might try to persuade Rich to come along. I know men strictly aren't allowed at a hen do, but I'm sure Gloria won't mind. It would get him out of the house.'

'I thought he didn't do things like that. He doesn't like things like that does he?' I babbled. He absolutely could not go – he could not see me in the pigtails and teenage make-up Gloria was insisting were *de rigueur* for the night. Besides which with all the drink flowing I was sure to make a complete arse of myself. Still, after the shouting match from the tree tops and, in fact, most of the times I'd met him, I don't think there were many more depths I could sink to in his eyes.

'Well, yes, I know it's not Rich's cup of tea,' Sarah was saying, 'but as you know, I'm working on him!'

I nodded and sipped my wine, wondering what 'working on him' entailed exactly.

'Isn't he a babe?' said Alan as we headed back to the car.

'Who? Pierre? No. He's an anti-babe, he's scruffy. Eugh.'

'Seriously? You don't think so?'

'No I don't. He's … thin and straggly.'

'But I think he's beautiful. Pierre. Pierre …'

'Is he from France?'

'No. I asked him. He's from Hull. But his dad was French. Well he thinks his dad was French. He's never met him. Hmm… Pierre …'

'So he knows you're moving to Birmingham, then?'

'Yes. Well I told him about the shop and…'

'You did *what*? Alan!' I stopped in my tracks, hands up in the air. Had he got no sense?

'Well I told him to not pass it on to Sarah, obviously…' he said sullenly.

'And after the full forty five minutes or so that you've known him, you trust him to do what you asked?'

'OK… you can stop shouting, *Mum*. Of course he won't tell her.'

'Alan you're a bit too trusting aren't you? Supposing he tells Sarah and Sarah tells her pal Gloria. That's going to be—'

'Oh calm down you big stress monster. I'm going to be telling Gloria myself in a couple of weeks' time. It's hardly a big deal.'

'Fine. Fine. I'm calm. It's not what I would have done…'

'Obviously …'

'Obviously … but I'm sure you're right.'

'Richard Weston could be going to the hen party, then?' said Alan. 'That should be fun…'

'He won't go. She thinks she has more power over him than she does. You'll see.'

But I wished, deep down, that he would. I wished very much. Despite the plaits and the hens.

24

Since Tuesday, the market place had been closed to all traffic except the lorries and caravans that formed, according to posters that were now pasted up over the entire town, 'Alex Thornton's Fair – Shropshire's premier travelling attraction'. It had become more and more difficult to get in and out of the house, with people milling about outside, setting up the rides and stalls right up to the front door of Gloria's house. The small cobbled square was now full of machinery, with only narrow walkways in between the rides that the townspeople squeezed through.

Gloria sighed and moaned about it, but was nevertheless excited, especially as her hen night was going to involve going on as many of the rides as was possible. At least we wouldn't have far to crawl home.

At seven o'clock we could hear the music start up and the bass came thumping through the windows. We opened them up as we dashed around the house getting ready. Sleek hair was backcombed, make-up applied in layers and risqué clothing pulled on, pulled off again, and then put on again after a couple of drinks.

I had divided my hair into two long plaits and had applied rouge and lipstick in the same way a ten year old would. I still looked pretty much pre-Raphaelite though, I guess there was no escaping it. Only now I looked more like a pre-Raphaelite muse going for a clown's job. What if Richard Weston did turn up? What would he think of me looking like this? Ah well, who cares, he was going to be with Sarah anyway…

At about eight o'clock a gaggle of Gloria's friends arrived at the house. They too were well overdressed and wearing fluffy pink hair bands and pink net veils trailing down their backs. The house buzzed as we opened bottles of champagne and toasted Gloria, pinning the necessary 'L' plate to her back and putting on the band and veil.

Relaxed and at last completely dismissing the notion of work, Gloria came alive and was more like the old Gloria than at any time I'd seen her since my stay. She pranced around the room and laughed and was generally 'up for a good night out'.

Alan arrived a little after the girls, bearing bottles of Farmer Jacob's Best Monmouthshire Cider.

'It's not mine,' he said, opening the bottles up for us. 'It's a friend's and she hates the stuff. Her parents are organic farmers in some hippy commune and she gets crates of this stuff. We're doing her an enormous favour by drinking it.'

'Ugh Alan…' it was foul. Bitter and bubbly – and so much of it.

Nevertheless, we managed to work our way through the entire bag before we set off, at a quarter to nine, smelling strongly of fermented apples. Farmer Jacob's cider improved remarkably after the first empty bottle.

Outside, people were everywhere. Each ride had its own music, pounding away in competition with the ride immediately beside it. Added to that there was the continuous rumble of truck engines, chugging out diesel, but nobody seemed to mind. There was a rather old-looking wooden helter-skelter outside Gloria's, and she had kept the curtains to her bedroom closed since Wednesday in order to preserve some small shred of privacy.

The dodgems hugged what remained of the castle wall, next to them stood a giant big wheel, all spindly steel and rickety carriages turning slowly.

'Holy cow,' said one of Gloria's friends as we walked past a ride called the 'Star Searcher'.

'I am no way going on that.'

'Oh come on!' Gloria interrupted, 'We're *all* going on *every* ride.'

I didn't bother to argue with her, but there was no way I would be riding the 'Star Searcher'. I had heard enough horror stories about touring fairs to know that there was a distinct likelihood that I would end my life on one of these rides. Alan had helpfully reminded me that there had been cases of women with long hair having their necks broken when their hair became caught in the ride's machinery. I tentatively felt my plaits and wondered if they were long enough to catch in machinery. Scary.

The 'Star Searcher' and the 'Demon' were the two loudest, brightest, fastest rides; the first spinning screaming people round and round, undulating faster and faster. The 'Demon' was a sort of spidery ride with four spinning carriages on each of six spinning arms. There were hordes of rowdy teenage boys accompanied by heavily made up girls hanging around the rides, some taking hasty sips from double strength cider cans before passing them on in exchange for a puff of Silk Cut. Parents with young children stood around the old market cross, where rides like the 'Tea Cups' and the 'House of Fun' were providing toddler thrills. Everywhere was noise and lights. The strobes from the 'Star Searcher' lit up the crowds around it, flashing neon strips around the 'Demon' pulsated to the dance track coming out of the giant battered speakers.

Making my way slowly through the crowd, I tried to take in everyone, looking for Richard Weston in the crowd. Would he come? I didn't really think so, but I hoped so – fool that I am.

Operating in a tightly bound pack, the hen-nighters pushed Gloria onto as many rides as we could, one after another. Fortunately Farmer Jacob's cider had taken the edge off our fear, and as we soared and dived over the remains of the old castle walls it didn't seem as frightening as it should do. Alan loved it. When we dived seemingly into the crowd he leant out of the car and screamed at the schoolgirls, who screamed back over the throb of the music.

I didn't fancy the dodgems and neither did Gloria so we stood watching the girls smack into each other and en-masse chase Alan around the circuit. Alan, I noticed, was driving in exactly the same way that he had done on the motorway a couple of days ago.

'Don't look now but your new friend's watching you,' Gloria said, her eyes not leaving the dodgems.

'Who?' my eyes darted through the crowds, and then from across the other side of the dodgems I saw Richard Weston looking at me, Sarah by his side. I was so ecstatic to see him that for a moment I couldn't hear or see the fair; it was a bright moving mess around us and the only things that were constant were Richard Weston and I, staring at each other from opposite sides of the ride.

He waved.

I waved back, and as I did he stepped back into the crowd and disappeared from view.

'I said… what's going on between you two?' Gloria asked. I hadn't heard her the first time.

'Nothing,' I said, my breath coming in jitters.

'You're leading him on aren't you? Right in front of his girlfriend.'

'Pardon?' I said, eyes wide staring at her.

'Flirting. In front of Sarah. Don't you think that's a rather… cheap thing to be doing?'

'Gloria!' I said, feeling my temper rise. How could she say that when she was on the very brink of getting married and yet still she was prepared to continue her relationship with Tom? How could some harmless flirting, which I was in denial about anyway, be any worse than that? I began to say as much but was cut short by the hens coming off the dodgems.

Gloria leant over to me and whispered in my ear, 'Just don't spoil my wedding. That's all I ask… I don't want to be left without a reception venue because of trouble between Weston and— Oh, hello!'

He was beside us, Sarah smiling and fingering Gloria's faux veil.

'Fantastic get up,' she said. 'Congratulations to the hen,' and she gave Gloria a kiss on the cheek. 'You don't mind if Rich tags along as well do you? I didn't want to leave him alone in that big old place while I came down here.'

'Well it's a *hen party…*' Richard Weston said. 'I don't want to crash it or anything, but Sarah wouldn't let me stay in the house alone…'

'No, that's fine. The more the merrier,' said Gloria through tight lips with a plastic smile painted on her face.

Richard, clearly uncomfortable at being dragged out on a girls' night, stood a little apart from the group. He looked amazing, just in a dark wool polo neck and old worn jeans. I started to move over to him, regardless of what Gloria cared to think, when Alan stepped up to me and leant in.

'What did Gloria say?' he whispered, 'You went puce when you were talking to her.'

I told him, briefly. Gloria was too busy talking to Sarah to notice I was confiding in Alan.

'She's just protecting her own interests as per usual,' he said, 'and to be honest it shouldn't come as a shock to you that she said as much. You shouldn't let it bother you, just let it go.' He patted my shoulder in comradeship, 'Whatever you choose to get up to is no concern of hers. Go for it. They're not married, are they…'

'Pardon?' I said, looking straight at Richard Weston while Alan whispered to me.

'Go on. Grab him. His so-called girlfriend's a real dishcloth. If you want him, make it clear to him. I think he fancies you and I don't think an offer would be turned down.'

I stared at Alan, the little devil on my shoulder. I was absolutely elated by what he was saying, but at the same time shocked. Had I actually told anyone how I felt? Was it so obvious?

'Look,' he gripped my arm, 'you've been hurt in love right?

Your boyfriend having it away with your sister—'

'Alan!' I hissed. 'Keep your bloody voice down!'

'Well it's true,' he lowered his voice, 'and you said yourself that in the past you've had a couple of boyfriends on the go at the same time.'

'Oh come on…'

'And what about what Gloria's doing with Tom and Phil? Now that's seriously playing with fire.'

I stared at him dumbfounded, waiting to hear what his point might be.

'So what makes you think,' he began, 'that you have to play fair when everyone around you doesn't play by the rules? Why do you have to?'

'Alan it's not my style…'

'Well I think you should do something about it. They're not engaged, you're not with anyone. The night is young. Oh come on, Roz. What's the worst that could happen?'

'But I don't know that he even fancies me.'

'He hasn't stopped looking at you.'

'Oh!' I could hear my heart beating. 'So are you saying,' I began, feeling my face go red after his last comment, 'that I should put myself forward as some sort of 'bit on the side' in addition to Sarah? Is that your point?'

'No. Stupid.' He comedy-knocked on my forehead: 'Hello? Is anyone at home in there? What I'm saying is… *be* his bloody girlfriend. Supplant her. Replace her. Step into her goddamn shoes.'

'That last one's a real impossibility.' I looked down dolefully at my enormous shoes.

Without warning the aforementioned girlfriend was by my side, and Alan melted into the background, grinning at me. Sarah linked my arm and conspiratorially whispered, 'Come on Roz,' steering me towards the shooting gallery, chattering about Gloria's plans for the rest of the evening. I itched to pull my arm lose; I wasn't someone who enjoyed being hugged or handholding with other girls like some do. I knew that I ought to feel pretty ashamed of the fact that I had had that conversation with Alan, and the fact that I didn't want to talk to her and did want to talk to her boyfriend. But, on the other hand, Alan's pep talk had ignited something inside me, and had made me realise that, yes, I did like this man, and perhaps, if what Alan had said was true, he liked me. And besides, Sarah had said she was *working* on him. So she obviously didn't reckon she'd actually *got* him yet: all's fair in love and war...

Alan emerged again from behind us with a bag chinking full of bottles of beer, and began offering them around, 'Sarah?' She shook her head. 'Ah – Lord Lovely, you'll have one won't you?' he gave me a huge smile and a beer to the awkward looking Richard Weston, who took it, looking amused – or was it bemused? It was hard to tell in the flashing lights of the fairground.

'You know,' said Sarah, 'Richard is a very good marksman. Aren't you? I really think we should see what you can do on the shooting gallery.'

As Richard obediently sought the right money from his pocket, Sarah examined one of the rifles. 'You know, I used to be quite a markswoman myself when I lived in North Derbyshire.'

'Well why not have a go against Richard!' chimed Gloria.

'No I couldn't,' Sarah looked all disappointment. Alan and I made faces at each other and cracked open more bottles of beer. The girl was so transparent.

'Roz is a good shot!' Alan suddenly piped up. I stopped, mid-swig from my bottle and stared at my betrayer. 'Go on Roz. Why don't you have a pop at the target?'

I could have killed him.

Everyone turned back to look at us, a slight frown forming on Sarah's face now that we weren't persuading her to have a go.

'Come on then,' said Weston, picking up the second rifle and putting it in my hands. I gave my bottle, and a cross look, to Alan and paid my money.

We stood together, side by side in front of the counter, and the old woman who owned the stall set up the ten metal ducks, 'Three out of three wins the toys on the first shelf, six out of six you can go to the second shelf, nine wins the Pooh Bear.'

We both paid our pound for three shots, and I went first. The hens were silent and huddled around us. I aimed my heavy rifle and pulled the trigger. Ting – a duck went down. Everyone cheered and Alan proffered me a swig of beer and a 'huzzah!'.

Richard Weston leant the butt of the gun into his shoulder and aimed. Ting – a duck went down.

'Come on Ros-a-muuuuund,' shouted Alan from the back. I aimed and hit. Down the duck went.

Again, Richard aimed and hit.

For the third time, I pointed the rifle and pulled the trigger. A duck went down. Attention turned to Richard Weston who steadily aimed and fired. Three out of three.

'Again!' clapped the hens: 'Come on Roz.' By now a small crowd had gathered – to watch Richard Weston, no doubt. As we paid the owner and she reset the ducks I glanced back at the throng.

'He practises with foxes,' I heard one of them mutter, clearly knowing it to be loud enough for him to hear. 'Foxes and commoners,' said the other one and they sniggered. Richard was examining the rifle intently, waiting for the go-ahead and patently ignoring what was being said.

We aimed and hit the first round. My second round first duck bounced back but the woman on the stall let me count it as a hit, which made the crowd cheer. Richard Weston aimed and, slowly, squeezed the trigger. The end duck fell. So far we were equal.

I took a deep breath, put the rifle up to my shoulder again and took aim. This time I went for a middle duck and, squeezing the trigger, I shot it down – six out of six. I lost my cool and jumped up and down.

I turned to Richard Weston and, putting down my rifle, folded my arms across my chest and watched him take aim, my eyes never leaving his face. He steadied his hand, and leant back slightly. Perfecting his aim. His eyes flicked sideways at me and caught me watching him.

'You're putting me off,' he whispered.

I leant forward and whispered, 'Putting you off what?' my face close to his. He turned and looked at me, and gave me the most devilish smile, which completely took my breath away.

'Quite…' he said.

He looked forward again and, concentrating, pulled the trigger. He missed. The crowd behind us cheered and clapped, and Alan knocked me hard on the back. 'Way to go Roz,' he shouted.

Sarah stepped in-between us as soon as Richard had fired and clung to his arm, her back to me. 'Did you hear what they were saying?' she said. 'The people in the crowd?'

'What would you like?' the old lady beamed at me.

'They said you'd shoot at anything that came on your land, even if it was a villager,' Sarah muttered at Richard.

'Anything on the second shelf!' The old lady said. I paused for a moment before choosing a plump Welsh dragon with a friendly face.

She handed it to me and I held it proudly like the trophy it was, a bottle of beer in the other hand.

'To the pub!' I declared, buoyed up with the elation of winning, and with Richard Weston appearing to have taken the bait…

'To the pub!' echoed Alan, and we all wound our way out of the crowds and down to the Blacksmith's Arms.

We found a table in the corner by the huge inglenook fireplace, and sat around it. We made a lively party although we didn't fit in too well, our hen night regalia marking us out from the regular Friday-nighters and fair-goers. Sarah had got my headdress on and Richard Weston was wearing Alan's. I sat and listened to the conversation, and all the time Richard Weston's presence opposite me at the table filled my thoughts.

Sarah was talking about her jewellery designs and something about profit sharing being the way forward.

'You must be doing very well,' she said to Gloria. 'Do you supply many shops around here?'

'Two,' Gloria said, always happy to talk about her business, 'with another in a couple of months. It's been a real sacrifice to my personal life to get it off the ground but it's starting to pay off now.'

Sarah agreed and started talking about the sacrifices she had made to get her business going.

'Well I think you have to dive right in there,' she said. 'It's no good messing around because you never get a second chance do you? Someone once said to me that you have to push, push, push when you're under 30 because it's so much easier to make something of yourself when you've got youth on your side. Really, after that, you're just washed up.'

'I don't think so,' I cut in, not so much wanting to get involved in their conversation, but disagreeing strongly with what they were saying, and having the courage of drink inside me. 'When I worked in London I had a couple of friends who were obsessed by achieving everything by the time they hit 30 and it drove them mad. They worked all hours and had no life whatsoever outside of work, and those that didn't make it ended up feeling like a complete failure even though they'd achieved loads. I mean,' I carried on, having to add something now everyone was looking at me, 'no-one really thinks about just how long you're around in this life. I don't think people fully appreciate that after your twenties, you've got your thirties to build your career. Then your forties, and fifties. Some people live as though life tails off after 35. All those people who've reached their pinnacle by the time they're 30... what do they do after that? What keeps them going a decade later, or a decade after that? Life can be a really long time when you think about it.'

'Well I'm sure that's a very good point,' said Gloria, heatedly, 'but what Sarah was saying is that it's easier for people when they're under 30. People have lower expectations of what you can achieve, so it's easier to impress them when you do achieve. And you don't have the bind of having a family dragging after you. You're free to do what you want.'

'But—' I started to say.

'Well you would obviously feel different,' chimed in Gloria, 'because you're a bit of a…' she searched for the right word and then obviously couldn't find it '…drifter. You float from career to career and then you drop out of the system. Did you burn out?'

How dare she? How dare she be so downright rude to my face? This was probably thanks to the Richard Weston talk she'd given me earlier. I could see Alan bristle at her comments but I shot him a look to stop him from saying anything. Gloria was probably irritated that I was 'flirting' with Richard Weston, and this was her way of getting back at me. I wasn't going to rise to it.

'No,' I said, trying to keep my voice sounding calm while seething underneath, 'I didn't burn out, but I realised that what I was doing wasn't making me happy. And I was honest with myself and I had the courage to jack it all in. That takes courage as well as the will to succeed.'

I sat there wishing I hadn't piped up in the first place. I felt like a complete idiot and I busied myself with my pint and folding little pleats into my skirt. Thankfully the conversation moved on so I sat and listened in, determined not to speak again.

Neither Richard Weston nor I said much after this exchange, but everyone else clamoured to speak so there was no opportunity for anyone to notice our inattention.

By the end of the evening it looked as though everyone had pretty much had their fill of Gloria. They were ignoring her signals when she wanted to butt into the conversation and glazing over when she did manage it. It was sad really, it was her big night, but then she had been a bit much. Alan was quite pissed, which had come as no great surprise, and had given up on our party to take a seat at the bar. He was busy chatting up the barmaid who looked like she was rather flattered, but ultimately in for a disappointment. I looked over to where he was sitting and smiled as he pulled the barmaid's hand towards him, mopped it with a sodden bar cloth, and started to pretend to read her palm, hopelessly drunk and slurred. She leant close to him and laughed a lot.

I felt something beside my leg and glancing down at the table I saw Richard Weston had stretched out his legs and they were now right up against mine, *touching* mine. He didn't move them away. I looked at him and he was looking at me. It was as if the pub went silent. The people were only half-there, the music had turned itself off, my heart was knocking against my ribs.

I was on fire. Neither of us said anything, nor even looked at each other again, but just sat letting the conversations wash over us. At one point I remember Sarah asking me how I liked being a florist or something, and I managed to string something semi-coherent together. I felt a twinge of guilt, since she was still sitting beside her would-be boyfriend presumably unaware of the fact that his legs were against mine, enclosing mine. What if she noticed?

I don't know how long we were sitting there, our legs intimate with each other, but when it came time for us to leave I lagged behind the group, hoping to say something, anything, to Richard Weston. Sarah, however, her edge not dulled from the very many vodka and oranges, quickly fastened on to him, and they headed off towards Weston Hall. I heard them go. 'You see,' she was saying, 'you should get out and get involved with the town more. They love you, and it's such a good PR exercise.' He turned to look back but he didn't see me – I was propping up Alan. Everybody walked on, leaving me once again to take Alan home.

We turned the corner and headed down Shaw Lane, picking our way through the discarded burgers and paper cups. I was back down to earth with a bang. It had all happened so quickly; people standing up, our legs quickly snatched back and then we were out of the door and into the cool night.

'Rosamund!'

I turned and saw Richard Weston running towards me. He stopped and glanced quickly at Alan, who was clearly no longer of this world.

He stood in front of me looking awkward.

'Is she your girlfriend?' I asked plainly.

He paused, looking straight into my eyes. 'No. She used to be when we were at university, but she isn't now. She wants to be, and I have lapsed recently. But not since I met you…'

'Aaaah assss nice inssnit. Sslovely,' Alan slurred, pointing

152

roughly in Richard's direction.

'Rich!' Sarah was calling him, 'I'm cold!'

'I have to…' he fished around for a word, 'go. Shall I bump into you at the wedding maybe? You could pop into the kitchens or something.'

'That would be great,' I said, all a-flame with something that felt very good indeed.

'See you there then.'

I stood in the middle of the litter-filled street, watching him go, realising that the flames probably meant I was falling in love with him.

'Yous shouldda kished im,' said Alan, stumbling off, having given up waiting for my supporting arm. 'Don't choo mind me. I'm going hhome now.'

Drunken sod.

25

I heard ringing. Very far off.

I ignored it.

It was still ringing. Continuous, and then in shorter bursts. Brrrrrrrrrrr. Rrrrrrr. Rrrrrrr.

Then I opened my eyes. Oh God. The pain. In fact, it wasn't pain, it was Pain. And nausea.

I pulled myself up into a sitting position. I couldn't work out why my hair was standing up above my head. I reached up and patted it.

'Oh God,' I'd been sick. In my hair…

Brrrrrrrr! Brrrrrrrrr! Brrrrrrrrr!

It was the doorbell.

Where was Gloria?

Shit! Oh holy fuck.

I inched out of bed, fell to the floor and staggered up again. It was Saturday. It was the wedding.

Brrrrrrrrrrrrrrrrrrrrrrrrrrrrrrrrrrrrrrrrrr.

By holding on to the banister the way an old lady holds on to her bag-on-wheels I managed to manoeuvre my way down the stairs.

Brrrrr. Brrrrrrr. Brrrrrrrr went the doorbell.

Bling-bling. Bling-bling went the phone.

'Jesus Christ,' which one should I get? The doorbell had been ringing for longer. Hadn't it?

I opened the door, using it for support as I did so, swinging with it as it rocked backwards and forwards.

Two very well dressed, very *rigid* people, stood on the doorstep.

'Well!' said the female one. 'We were beginning to think there was no-one in…' She snapped her phone closed and Gloria's phone stopped ringing. Beautiful silence.

Still hanging from the door, I let Gloria's parents in.

'Sorry, Barbara, Peter. How are you?' I managed, slowly closing the front door.

'Better than you I think Rosamund,' Peter said, giving me an air kiss on the cheek. I hid the patch of dried sick on my hair but I think the smell must have been a giveaway. I couldn't tell. My nose hadn't woken up yet.

'And where is the bride?' said Barbara, scanning the downstairs rooms.

Shit. It was the wedding day.

Hazily, dreamily, the events of the night before came back to me. Richard Weston. The table. His legs enclosing mine beneath the table. Alan being so drunk he couldn't stand unsupported. Getting back to the house. The girls finding more of Farmer Jacob's Cider. Eugh. Cider. My stomach did a back flip at the very thought.

'Is that…' Barbara had spotted a leg in the living room. Peering behind the sofa she saw it belonged to one of the hens who was intended to be a bridesmaid in a few short hours, '… Angela Patterson?'

'Mmm,' I nodded.

'Where's Gloria? Where's my child?' Barbara turned and fled up the stairs in a panic. Peter raised his eyebrows at me and followed his wife up the stairs. I examined the wreckage in the living room, which was indeed Angela.

I shuffled off to get some coffee. A minute at a time I managed to get everything together to make said drink. Up to this point in my life I hadn't realised just how complex making coffee is; you need a kettle, some water, coffee, sugar, milk, a mug, a spoon. I arranged everything I needed in a line on the work surface and then set about using them in order. I heard Barbara's dismayed half-scream as she found Gloria in some ghastly state or other.

'She OK?' I shouted up.

Peter put his head over the banisters. 'What were you girls drinking last night?'

'Cider,' I said, apologetically and went back to the coffee.

I took up a tray of coffees and some water to Gloria's bedroom where Barbara and Peter were sitting on her bed; Gloria lay slumped against the headboard looking very ill.

'Well thank you Rosamund,' clipped Barbara, 'at least someone doesn't appear to have drunk themselves into a stupor.' Gloria was resolutely focusing all of her attention on the embroidered pattern on the duvet. A sure sign that she was holding vomit at bay, I thought. I left them to it and headed back downstairs to wake up Angela.

To be honest I don't know how we did it, but we did. The wedding was at 1pm and by 11am we were up and about, feeling rather delicate but other than that OK. The other bridesmaids, who had gone home earlier the night before, all arrived at just after eleven and the house was filled with frenzied chatter.

I wasn't a bridesmaid. The chosen few had all been selected over a year ago and even though I was Gloria's oldest friend, her new friends were much closer to her than I had been at the point of bridesmaid-selection. I was glad of it, not having to wear the powder-blue disasters that she'd dressed them in and not having to be at her beck and call on the day. Once again I felt the lack of my 'girly' skills and found the chatter in the bedrooms too much to bear. I hobbled downstairs and joined Peter in the garden for a cigarette.

I was the first to leave the house; the others would be arriving at church in the limousines, even though it was only a few streets away. It was a beautiful day to get married on. There wasn't a cloud in the sky, and everyone I passed in the street seemed to be more cheery than usual.

I had decided to wear a rather gorgeous pea-green dress, which clung to me in all the right places, and showed off an amount of cleavage appropriate for the occasion. I'd managed to find a pair of plum, kitten-heeled, pointy slip-on shoes. They had been a real cause for celebration for me, having wide size nine feet that weren't exactly well-catered for in the shoe shops. A thin, wispy plum shrug completed the outfit, covering up my old-lady upper arms.

Phil was looking nervous, standing by the church door smiling tightly at everyone.

'Good luck,' I said, giving him a peck on the cheek.

'Thanks Roz. How did she look when you left her?'

I had a flashback to Gloria slumped in bed looking vomitous with her hair frizzed around her green face and big black bags under her eyes.

'Beautiful. Beautiful. Don't worry, she'll do you proud,' I lied.

He nodded nervously.

'God I'm dying for a fag. I don't suppose you've got any have you Roz?'

'I might well have actually,' I dug around in my handbag. I was right; I thought I remembered buying a pack last night on the way back from the fair.

The two of us dashed round to the side of the church leaving the best man in charge. We stood for a minute, enjoying the nicotine rush.

'I bet you're looking forward to having the house to yourself,' he said, 'a bit of peace and quiet.'

'Yes and no. It'll be lonely without you both about.'

'Well we'll miss you. Do you have any plans for what you'll be doing when we get back?' he said, wanting to talk about something that wasn't connected to the wedding. Understandable really, judging by how nervous he was.

'Mmm,' I said, cigarette in mouth, 'that's a conversation we can save for when you come back from your honeymoon.'

'Quite right, quite right. God I'm nervous.'

'Here, have a mint.'

'Oh, thanks.'

Inside the church I found Alan texting furiously on his mobile phone.

'Mind if I join you?' I asked.

'Not at all. Ooh…you look nice. You know, Roz, you should make more of an effort with yourself; you look quite presentable today. Nice boobs by the way.'

'Oh can you see too much of them?' I glanced down horrified, trying to pull the sides of the dress higher up my chest.

'No they're fine. Leave it, *leave it!*' he said, pulling my hands free of my dress. 'You look great.'

'Oh, well, thanks a lot.'

'So, how did it go after I left you last night?'

'What, with Richard Weston?'

'Of course.'

'Well it didn't.'

Alan looked crestfallen. 'Did I mess things up for you?' he said, affecting doe eyes.

'No. Not at all. There was nothing to mess up. 'Who are you texting?'

'Pierre,' he grinned.

'Oh,' I nodded. 'Hey, we were really ill this morning after all that cider. You were lucky to get away so early. When we got back to the house we found the other bag of it and finished it off. Angela was really sick this morning.'

'How was Gloria?'

'Pretty green when I first saw her. Bit ropey to be honest, but I'm sure she'll pull herself together.'

'And what's the dress like?'

'Awful,' I whispered. 'It has lace.'

'No!'

'Yes! Acres of the stuff.. And bows on the back.'

'You're kidding…'

'Seriously. It's horrid.'

'Poor girl. She has absolutely no taste when it comes to clothes. Anyway, is it true that Lord Lovely is going to be at the house when the reception's taking place?'

'Yes. But he's going to keep to the upper rooms and the kitchen, so we won't know he's there.'

'You could go and see him then.'

'Alan!'

'Well you *could*. You need to chase him a bit more. Stick those things in front of his face,' he pointed to my chest.

I laughed.

'Well I am going to, as a matter of fact,' I said.

'Ah ha! I wondered why you'd made such an effort with yourself.'

'You bastard!'

'Sshhhhhh,' an enormously fat woman turned round to us and glowered. The wedding was about to begin.

It was a good one, as weddings go. Everything was present and correct: the big dress, the nervous bridegroom, fat ugly relatives in pastel coloured hats and the usual selection of tired old hymns chosen so that everyone has a good chance of knowing them: 'All things bright and beautiful' – why?

Although I looked out for him, I didn't see Tom at the service. I finally caught up with him on our way to the Hall, which was a leisurely stroll away. He was watching while the photographer set up his equipment down by the lake. He was deep in conversation with one of Gloria's friends from the town, her children milling around them excitedly, spinning around in their expensive dresses.

Weston Hall was beautiful. The huge front doors had been thrown open and the guests standing in the hallway transformed it into something that looked like the setting of a Jane Austen novel.

I looked up the staircase to see if Richard Weston was peering at us through the banisters, but I couldn't see anyone. Pilot, likewise, was not around.

It had been a hard slog decorating the three rooms that Gloria was hiring but it was well worth it. They were an excellent backdrop for all the wedding drapery that now hung around them. The guests seemed impressed, and the reception was going as well as a wedding reception can go. Gloria looked radiantly happy up on the top table, beaming a smile at anyone who looked her way.

Tom hadn't cheered up much from when I'd seen him earlier. Alan and I were sitting at the same table as he was, but had hardly spoken to him. At present he was concentrating hard on the business of cutting up his food. I didn't particularly want to talk to him, so I left him to it, happy to have Alan for company.

'There are a lot of chubby, mean-faced women on Gloria's side of the family,' murmured Alan.

'Shhhhhhhhhh,' I said, but laughing all the same. 'So do you think she'll turn into one of them?'

'It's already happening. Look at Phil, does he seem scared to you?'

I looked and couldn't help agreeing with him. A group of particularly nasty bulldog-faced women were huddled round him, smoothing his hair and feeling the lapels on his jacket doing that 'isn't he a big strong man' thing that some older women do so well.

After the meal we wandered onto the lawns and sat around the lake, Alan and I found a cousin of Phil's who was quite good fun so we went on a tour of the grounds with him and his girlfriend.

A band arrived just after seven and started to set up in the ballroom. The Hall staff had cleared away all the ornaments and display cabinets earlier that week, so we weren't in danger of doing too much damage. Still there was no sign of Richard Weston. Where had he hidden himself? Was he waiting in the kitchens as he said he would?

'You're looking a whole lot better than the last time I saw you.'

My heart leapt and I turned round. It was Peter, Gloria's father.

'Oh thanks,' I said, trying to hide my disappointment. 'Yes, the hangover has finally gone. Last time I drink cider.'

'Awful stuff. Still, not to worry. Are you having fun? Marvellous venue isn't it?'

I agreed, and while Alan excused himself to go and get drinks, Peter and I walked over to the ballroom where the bride and groom were preparing to take the first dance.

It was about nine o'clock and I still hadn't seen Richard Weston. I was wondering whether I should venture towards the kitchens when I saw Sarah making her way over to Gloria and Phil, a small present in her hands. I couldn't see Richard anywhere, although I craned this way and that to see if he was lurking in the background.

'Sarah!' Gloria had spotted her, 'How lovely to see you!'

'What a beautiful dress! I hope I'm not interrupting right now but I just wanted to give you this,' she presented a tiny gift box to her.

'Oh,' Gloria pounced on it, 'thank you.'

She unwrapped it and gasped, and then seeing me looking over she called out, 'Roz, come and see what Sarah has given me.'

I had to admit it was beautiful; a delicate silver necklace with confetti-style pendants hanging from it on tiny silver chains.

'I made it especially for you,' said Sarah. 'Well, I designed it and my friend Pierre made it up. It *is* lovely isn't it?'

'Lovely,' I cooed doing my best impression of a girly girl.

'Is his lordship about?' asked Alan on my behalf, bless him. He'd just sidled up with the drinks.

'Oh hello, Alan,' said Sarah. 'I don't know, I've only just arrived from London. I guess he's around though. How are you by the way? Has your shop opened yet?'

My heart stopped.

26

I looked over at Alan whose eyes were slowly opening up wide with horror. Gloria was still fiddling with the necklace, trying to fasten it around her neck.

'What shop?' she asked vaguely.

Thank God. It hadn't registered.

This was awful.

I looked at Alan and he looked at me.

'…the florist's shop,' said Sarah babbling on. 'He's opening a florist's shop in Birmingham. I bumped into Alan and Roz the other day when they were having a look round. I thought you said it was opening in a couple of weeks. Isn't that about now?'

Nobody said anything.

And then it sank in. Not awful, worse. There was no escape.

The necklace fell from Gloria's hands and slithered down her neck, coming to a rest on the rim of her décolletage.

'Er… did I say something?' Sarah looked at our faces. I felt as though mine was burning up and all of a sudden I had begun to feel jittery and sick. What an awful way for Gloria to find out.

'What shop?' Gloria repeated loudly. I could feel people turn to our direction.

'Everything all right over here?' The groom had casually wandered over to his smouldering bride, and handed her a glass of champagne, for a moment blissfully unaware of the lion's den he was entering.

'What's up?' he said.

'Alan,' Gloria said, 'is opening up a shop. Apparently. A florist's shop.'

'Great. I mean oh, really,' he managed to turn his smile into a grimace, 'right.'

'Sorry,' mumbled Alan.

'How could you *do* this to me?' she said, loudly and trembling. The ballroom started to quieten. Although some people were still talking you could feel that everyone's ears were pointing in our direction.

'I didn't do anything to you,' ventured Alan slowly, 'I'm doing it *for* me.'

'It's opening *now*? So just *when* were you going to tell me about it?'

Alan was lost for words. He stood facing her with his mouth open.

'After you came back from your honeymoon,' I cut in, 'so you wouldn't have to worry about it beforehand. We were thinking of you. We didn't want to upset you.'

'And *you knew* about it?' she turned on me. 'As a friend don't you think you ought to have told me that he was going to be leaving me in the lurch the minute I got back from my honeymoon? That he would be stealing the secrets of my business to start up his own copy of it.'

It's her wedding day. It's her wedding day.

'Gloria, please, don't overreact,' I said, 'it's not as bad as you think, and you really don't get on all that well with Alan so it's a great opportunity for you to—'

'That is not the point Rosamund!' she shouted, staccato. By this time the room had fallen completely silent with all pretence at over-hearing now forgotten. There was no hope of anyone not noticing this now. Sarah stood where she had been standing, frozen to the spot with a plastic smile on her face and horror in her eyes.

'Traitors!' Gloria spat out. 'To do this to me, on my *wedding* day. On the one day of my life…'

Why didn't Sarah step in and say that it was her fault that Gloria was getting to know about it on this day, in this way? Why didn't Sarah break free from the ditsy, waify blonde stereotype that she had slotted herself into, and say something to defend us? I looked over at her and it was clear she wasn't going to be able to say anything; she was completely useless. There was nothing I could do because that would start a full-blown argument with the bride, and that was not an option. I stood there, resolute. I would take what was coming.

Barbara and Peter steamed over and put their arms around their daughter who was crying by this time.

'I just feel so let down!' she wailed to them.

Alan and I stood frozen to the spot, watching the bows on her dress quiver when she sobbed.

While Barbara simpered and fussed over her and Phil stood by with hankies at the ready, Peter winked at me and whispered, 'Maybe you ought to disappear for a little while. Don't leave though,' he added, 'she'll come and apologise in a while, I'm sure of it. It's an emotional day for her and I think that after the events of last night everything has rather taken its toll.'

I nodded and backed off, leaving Sarah still standing in the position she had been when she'd delivered the news, and Phil beside her in not much better a state. Poor Phil.

The long walk through the room to the French doors was one of the hardest walks I have ever taken. A hundred and thirty pairs of eyes watched us leave, all of them narrowed and accusing. It must feel like that when you are the 'Weakest Link'. Sort of… It flitted through my mind that I could turn round to the captive audience and defend Alan and myself, but what good would that do anyone? The blessing was that I would never see the majority of these people again. Still, my cheeks were on fire with the shame of what people must think of us. As far as I could, I tried to walk normally: not head-bowed-in-shame, which would be proof of guilt, and not overly confident and above it all, which would have gone down pretty badly. I focused on my goal of the door and walked straight to it, Alan pattering beside me like a nervous dog.

As soon as we turned into the corridor we heard the room come alive again with the buzz of conversation. We kept on walking. Not talking or even looking at each other, just keen on putting some distance between us and the room full of wedding guests. We walked down a long corridor, turned into a wider flagged floored corridor and then Alan stopped and looked up at me.

'Oh. My. God. That was awfuuull,' he said. He had tears in his eyes and he'd gone as white as a sheet.

'Oh Alan,' I wrapped my arms around him. Suddenly he seemed very vulnerable and sad, 'Don't worry. It's not your fault. You did everything you could do, and if it wasn't for Sarah then you would have been fine. You've done nothing wrong. You of all people know what Gloria is like; you didn't expect her to be happy for you did you?'

'No,' he managed a wet smile, 'but… but what a *bitch…* that Sarah.'

'I know. Here do you want my handkerchief?'

'Thanks,' he blew his nose loudly into my handkerchief and offered it back to me. I declined.

'Hello.' Richard Weston was standing in the doorway of the kitchen. I hadn't realised that Alan and I had walked in this direction, we had been keener on distance than trying to find a particular place. A wave of happiness challenged my all-consuming misery.

'Hi,' I said, trying to think of something to add, but failing. Alan, too, was noticeably lost for words, but managed to blow his nose loudly into my hanky again.

'What's happened?' he asked, 'Come in here and take a seat.'

'Thanks,' we went in, and he closed the door behind us; some meagre protection from the bulldog women in pastel hats.

I'd never been in the kitchen at Weston Hall, but now that I was, I thought it was one of the most inviting rooms in the whole building. It must have been in one of the oldest parts of the original building, because it had thick walls and tiny recessed leaded windows that didn't let much light in. The floor had large dark flagstones. An enormous fireplace now housed a shiny cherry coloured Aga, and all around the room, in the dim light, I could make out the shape of copper saucepans hanging from hooks in the wall. We were seated round a huge old scrubbed pine table that was cluttered with kitchen implements, which Richard was no doubt collecting for his business. An old Welsh dresser stood opposite, laden with crackled blue and white china. Somewhere in the room I could hear the low tick-tock of a clock but I couldn't see where. It was so dark that the edges of the room seemed to fade into blackness. It was a million miles away from the glitzy lit ballroom where the wedding from hell was taking place.

While Richard uncorked a bottle of wine and Alan sniffed into the hanky, I explained what had happened and how we'd come to be fugitives from the ballroom.

'Crikey,' he said after I'd finished. 'Full marks to Sarah for that one. Where is she now?'

'She was in the ballroom when I last saw her. Do you think you should go and rescue her?' I asked.

'God no. She got herself into this mess and she can deal with the outcome.'

'Well, to be fair, she didn't mean to do it,' I said. 'She had no idea that Alan's shop was a secret.'

'True, but it sounds like she didn't defend you when your friend was claiming that you'd announced it deliberately.'

'Well she was probably shocked,' I said. Why was I defending Sarah? I didn't want him to go and get her. This was reasonableness beyond the call of duty. What was I thinking?

'I'd better go and check on her then,' he said and got up. Damn! Why did I have to sound so convincing? Alan poured out the wine and pushed it towards me.

'Drink!' he said, and showed me how it was done. I managed a smile and downed half the glass.

Richard was back in under a minute.

'Sarah's fine. She's comforting your friend and generally being loved by everyone, so no need to worry. She excels at fussing round people so I should think she's in her element.'

He sat back down and took a swig of wine. He had a very crisp white shirt on, the kind with proper cuffs but without cufflinks, which meant that the sleeves flopped over his hand in a rather sexy way. Honestly, noticing things like that at a time like this, what am I like?

'So what does this mean about you staying at her place?' he asked me quietly.

Oh God. I hadn't thought about that. I'd completely blown it with her – what if she wanted me out?

'I don't know,' I said grimacing. 'Well at least they leave for their honeymoon today. I can get into the house and get my stuff together.' I couldn't bear having to have my wardrobe even further reduced by leaving another place in unseemly haste.

'You can stay with me of course,' Alan chipped in. 'It's a two-bedroomed house and besides, I won't be around much now I've got no reason to stay. I've got the place for three more weeks and by then you'll have moved up to Birmingham anyway. So if you want to stay in Kings Newton then you can stay at mine.'

'You're going in a couple of weeks then?' Richard Weston looked up at me as he spoke, and was it my imagination or did he look a little sad? *Why? Did he want me to stay in Kings Newton?* My heart beat that bit quicker.

'Yes. Well, that's the plan,' I said.

But then he changed the subject and started asking Alan about his florist's shop in Birmingham, which cheered Alan up no end. I'd heard it all before so I drank my wine in silence, content to look around the enormous room and, as my eyes became accustomed to the dark, see what was lurking in the corners. In particular I sought out the kitchenware, which was arranged on the scrubbed table by the window. They were beautiful things, I could see that, whisks with porcelain handles and smoothly arched ladles and spoons. The colanders had holes punched out in the shapes of stars and moons while the sieves had little wire flowers twined round the edges.

'How is *your* business going?' Alan said when he had exhausted himself talking about Fuschiarama.

'Really well... We just got another commission to supply a London store so things are definitely on the up. I have a few staff down in London but I can see I'm going to need more very soon. I should be down there more often. I should give this place up sooner rather than later I know. It's keeping me back…'

'So… if you don't mind me asking…?' ventured Alan

'Go ahead,' Richard said.

'Well … if it's doing so well, how come you have to sell off land here to property developers?'

'Ahhh!' he sighed.

'Sorry… I—'

'No, don't worry about it. It's the bane of my life this house, it really is.' He shook his head, his shiny black hair swishing over his ears. 'Well, I've already told Rosamund a lot about it,' he began and my heart missed a beat as I heard him say my name. Honestly, it was like being at school and having a crush on a sixth former!

'The house has wet rot and dry rot, infestations…' he began

"Ewww!' butted in Alan, dropping his olive

'…in the roof timbers.'

'Ah.'

'And a whole host of other things. There are six roofs, three of which leak. The house has leaky walls and leaky windows as well as leaky pipes and leaky gutters. And that's just the leaks. It's knackered really.'

'How has it got so bad?' I asked, luxuriating in the sound of his half-posh accent and only semi-listening to what he was actually saying. I was getting the gist of what he was talking about, but I was more interested in the rise and fall of his voice as he listed the Hall's problems.

'Because…' he paused, 'because my father was a dreamer. He

loved this place, he really did, but he loved it in a romantic way. I'm different, I'm more practical. Well, I'd like to think so anyway. And now all the repairs and maintenance that he put off, because he didn't see he needed to do anything, just thought the decay gave the place more character, I have inherited tenfold. A few tiles missing off the roof ten years ago now means that entire ceilings need replacing in three of the guest bedrooms. The plaster has become soaked and is collapsing. A wall of penetrating damp twenty years ago is now a wing of penetrating damp. And so on.

'Hasn't the land sale raised enough money to fix things up?' I asked, quietly

'No. Nowhere near.'

There was a silence, filled by the tick-tocking of the clock and the distant sound of the band in the ballroom on the other side of the house.

Alan and I were looking at Richard Weston, leaning back in his large wooden chair, swirling the wine in his enormous wineglass.

The door opened. All three of us sat up swiftly from our lounging positions as Gloria, enormous and white in her beruffled wedding dress, tip-toed into the room.

'Roz? Alan?' she said into the gloom.

We owned up to being present and she came over to our corner of the kitchen.

'I should go,' Richard started to get up, his chair scraping on the flag floor.

'No. Stay,' I said boldly. I'd lost ground already and wanted to make sure that my selfish friend didn't lose him for me for good.

'I just came to apologise,' Gloria muttered, thoroughly downcast.

We sat in silence, more not knowing what to say than in anger or sympathy.

'Well…' she said, 'that's it really. I shouldn't have shouted at you.'

Alan was mute as ever, so I thought I ought to say something to her. 'Thank you,' I said. 'We know you've had a really hard few days, and you have to believe us when we say that we were going to tell you about Alan's shop, but only when you got back from your honeymoon so that it didn't worry you and spoil your holiday. I can stay on in the shop until you get back and your old assistant comes back off maternity leave. Just as we agreed I would when I arrived…' I petered out.

'Yes,' she said, smoothing her skirt, 'but I'll need more than just Deborah there – I need cover until I can replace Alan. You can stay on until I do that can't you?'

I winced, caught between wanting to help Gloria out and already having promised to help Alan out in Birmingham. It would have been really good at that moment to have been able to tell Gloria I could help her out, but that would be to go back on what I'd promised Alan. And Alan had been so much better a friend to me than Gloria had been, certainly for the last couple of weeks, at least…

So I said, 'No. I can't be there because Alan needs an assistant and he's already asked me. I'm sorry…'

I could feel Richard Weston smiling at me from the gloom opposite. Alan put his hand on my knee.

'Oh,' she said, icily. 'Oh. Well, if you've told *Alan* that then…'

'But I will have done everything you wanted me to do for you, when we discussed it first,' I said. 'I helped out in the shop and I helped prepare for today, so I haven't let you down. We originally agreed that I'd leave after you came back off your honeymoon, and that's when I plan to go.'

'But circumstances change…' she began.

'As have mine.'

Gloria stood still for a moment. Examining the flagged floor intently.

'Fine. Fine then,' she said.

I sat there, mutely looking at her and feeling completely pants. But then that was the desired effect! I just needed to sit firm.

'Well Alan you are free to go now. I'll arrange for you to be paid for today but that's it.'

'Fine,' he said, feigning disinterest by deliberating over which savory snack he would eat next.

'And Rosamund, can you call Deborah first thing Monday. Her number is on the back wall of the office. Tell her I know she's due to come back to work when I get back from my honeymoon but she'll probably be able to come back early. She'll help you in the shop. She's *flexible*.'

I got the dig but didn't respond.

'Fine,' I said. 'I'll stay over at your place tonight if that's OK and I'll move out tomorrow.'

'Fine by me.'

I wanted to add something but there was nothing to be said…

'We're leaving tonight and going straight to our hotel, so I guess I'll see you in a fortnight,' Gloria said finally.

'OK then.'

She nodded vaguely and turned round and went back to her party. Totally sour-faced. Poor Phil with a such a crotchety old bride. What a nightmare.

After she'd gone, I got up and closed the door behind her, sealing us off from any more interruptions. Richard went to get more wine and the conversation eventually picked up again. We talked about florists and potato peelers and what on earth I would be doing with my life.

It was very late when Alan got up to go to the toilet, leaving Richard Weston and I alone, lit only by the light above the Aga and a couple of dripping candles on the side-board. Four empty bottles of wine with expensive looking labels stood before us, as did the wreckage of a couple of food platters that one of the caterers had thoughtfully offered having heard voices. In the background someone had put on Joy Division, and the heavy songs wafted down the corridor. I looked up at Richard and caught him looking at me. I was too drunk to say anything, so I just looked back, deep into his big brown eyes. I could almost hear my heart beating as I held his gaze, not knowing what to do. He leant towards me slowly.

'I've been sick,' Alan emerged in the doorway, staggering and holding on to the work surface to steady himself. He looked up and added, 'In the toilet. It's OK.' He went to get his coat, 'I'm so sorry.'

'It's OK,' Richard got up.

'I'd better go home with Alan; make sure he gets home OK. Thank you so much for the food and the wine and the entertainment…'

'No, thank you,' he said, and then he became serious for a moment and came up to me. 'Will you come round again? I'm out tomorrow and Monday during the day but I'm around in the evening.'

My heart leapt and I was about to say yes when I remembered about the protest. I blearily tried to remember why I was going, when I'd appeared to have fallen out of favour with Gloria and her pals anyway. And then I remembered about my excellent alarm plan and saving Richard Weston from the vandals.

'I can't. Busy, sorry.'

'Tuesday then?'

'OK. What about Sarah though?'

'I'll talk to her. It's bad of me, I know, but I haven't properly laid out the ground between us, and I could never think of a way to despatch her kindly, before. But having seen the way you two 'tell it as it is', I think I've learnt more than enough to let her down at least partially gently,' he smiled roguishly.

'C'mon Rozzie you're well pissed you are.' The forgotten Alan tugged drunkenly at my hand and pulled me out into the night. I drew my shrug around me and looked back at Richard, now silhouetted against the doorway, watching us go.

'Bye,' I said quietly. So quietly I wondered whether he heard.

'Good night.'

We wandered up the road back to the town. Alan leant heavily against me and kept telling me how 'damn nice' Richard Weston was, and how 'damn nice' Pierre was and how he wondered whether either of them would be at all interested in a joint business venture in Birmingham.

I walked him to his house, and he ran the key all over the front door until he found the lock.

'Ssso, are you living here then eh?' he said, slumping against the doorframe.

'I'll call you in the morning,' I said and he winced. 'OK, in the afternoon then!'

'Ssshure. Night then.'

I hugged him goodbye and closed the door behind him.

27

Peeling open the curtains on Sunday morning, I looked out over a heavily symbolic prospect. Rain was pelting down and in the street I could see people scurrying from shop doorway to shop doorway, desperate not to get drenched. The slate roofs were washed to black, the usually cheery red brick of the buildings was soaked to a dark brown, and above the scene a dark grey sky filled with bubbling rain clouds completed the picture. Was this the breaking of summer? Were we into autumn already?

And not half a mile away there would be Weston Hall, still beautiful in the rain, but trampled down and dirty. The main rooms downstairs would be littered with wedding debris, crushed cake in the rugs, empty wine glasses, beer cans, cutlery and confetti. The windows would be opened and the doors left ajar and the cleaners would be walking in, shaking their heads at the task ahead.

And upstairs, hidden away from the public rooms, Richard Weston would have woken up and when he did, had he thought of me, I wondered. I also wondered where Sarah would be waking up this morning, and where she had been waking up over the past few weeks. From what I understood from both of them, it sounded as though she was in a guest room, but then maybe not…

I pushed that thought out of mind.

The situation with Gloria had turned into a complete mess. As I turned back to my bed, I wished that things had been different. What had gone wrong exactly? When did things start to turn bad?

It was such a dreary grey Sunday that I didn't feel like doing much, so I packed up my meagre belongings in preparation for the move to Alan's, and I moped around Gloria's house smoking the remaining cigarettes in the pack I'd bought on Friday. Initially I went outside to smoke but it was so drizzly and grey that I stood in the doorway wafting the smoke outside. There were a hundred and one questions I had to answer, such as where was I going to live in Birmingham, but I just couldn't be bothered to think about it.

It felt odd being in Gloria's house after we'd had such a falling out. I felt like a burglar who had set up house. Well, at least I would leave Kings Newton knowing I had done as much as I could for my friend, however much circumstances had transpired to make her feel let down. I would work in her shop right up until she came back, and I'd show my face at the protest tomorrow night and make sure she and Tom knew I'd still supported their cause even after what had happened. They didn't have to know that I was on a mission to jeopardise it.

God I hoped it worked. I must be due good luck some time soon, and what better opportunity than this? To turn up at Weston Hall the day after the protest, sit back in an old leather armchair and say, 'Yes, Richard, it was me who stopped those dirty protestors from desecrating your estate. And I thought only of you…' Or perhaps I should stress the dangerous part a bit more.

'They forced me into taking part but I betrayed them. I betrayed them all ha ha ha ha, ha ha ha!'

Hmm. I needed to work on my speech a bit. Something sincere and heartwarming. Less of the Pink Panther…

Richard Weston. Lord Weston. Richard… From the minute I had opened my eyes that morning I had been thinking about him, and thinking about last night. I wondered what he was doing right now? Out jogging I supposed, looking much as he had done when I'd first met him, what seemed like months and months ago: soaked to the skin, his hair all shiny and soft around his face. Pilot lolloping behind him enthusiastically.

I held on to this image of him, adoring every detail.

But reality gradually seeped in and ruined it. In a couple of weeks I was due to be in Birmingham, working in Alan's shop. I knew that I had to start working again more or less straight away, as my funds were still low and I wouldn't be able to afford to live without working.

So would anything happen between Richard Weston and me? No, it wouldn't, it couldn't. I felt awful admitting it to myself, but I had to be realistic. That wouldn't stop me going to see him on Tuesday evening though and I could certainly enjoy the freedom of the couple of weeks I was still in Kings Newton while Gloria and Phil were away. Why not make the most of it? *Why not?*

Who was I kidding?

I *wanted* to be a carefree spirited thing, but deep down it didn't fit. A couple of weeks of fun just wouldn't cut it. But what would? What did I expect? Urgh.

28

The Victorian terraced house that Alan rented had to be the smallest house I had ever seen. Situated in the conservation area opposite the church it was an absolutely gorgeous place, especially so since the owners had recently renovated it and filled it with brand new mini sofas, a mini kitchen table, mini chairs and even a fully equipped kitchen in miniature. It even had a mini-bar, which Alan pointed out. It was stocked with, would you believe it, cider. The tiny garden to the rear consisted of a patio with room for an outdoor table and two chairs and a few terracotta pots, which Alan had filled with flowers and trailing ivies.

My room overlooked the garden and I wearily dumped my suitcase on the single bed before descending to the kitchen for a chat.

He cheered me up no end, being completely dismissive of the whole Gloria episode now that he had actually cut his ties to Kings Newton.

'Oh come on Roz, stop moping! You tell me one thing you've done wrong in your relationship with Gloria. Nothing!'

'You're right, I know you're right,' I said, stirring my tea and then stirring it some more, 'I just feel sad about it, that's all. It's a bit like breaking up with a boyfriend isn't it? Being close to someone and then having nothing to do with them. Makes you re-evaluate friendships doesn't it?'

'You're all Mrs Maudlin and just because Lord Lovely didn't kiss you last night!'

'Yes, well whose fault is that, Mr I've-Been-Sick-In-Your-Toilet.'

'I'm sorry about that. I guess it did ruin the moment a little.'

'A little…!' I laughed. 'So, Alan, if I'm getting over my friendship to Gloria and I'm pursuing Richard Weston then do you think I'm on the rebound?'

'Quite possibly. When's the big night then?'

'Tuesday. And Monday's the protest…'

'I can't believe you're going ahead with that whole rape alarm thing. You don't have to take part you know, you could just call up the titled one and tell him about it and he could arrange for the police to be hiding in the hedges.'

'No, I want to make Gloria think that I was at the protest. And then I've acted completely blamelessly towards her haven't I? I can leave Kings Newton knowing I did absolutely everything she asked of me.'

'I guess so. Still seems fraught with the potential for a complete cock-up. Well you must phone and tell me what happens. I want a blow-by-blow account of the night you know, no brief outline. I'm off to Birmingham this afternoon and won't be back for a while so you'll have the run of the place. Make sure you water all my plants won't you.'

'Of course!' I said, having been forced to memorise watering instructions from the minute I walked in through the front door. Honestly, he was getting as bad as Gloria.

'So do you think you might become a Lady then…'

'Alan!'

'Well, I bet you've thought about it!'

'Alan! It's only dinner on Tuesday! Besides, I don't really think of him as a *Lord*.'

'That's crap. And you know it.'

It was crap. I had thought about it. I'd even wondered, in a moment of real weakness, whether there was a family tiara I would inherit. Diamonds maybe…

'Anyway,' I said, pulling myself together, 'what does it matter what I like about him, it's hardly going to be a permanent thing is it? I mean, it's the sort of situation that will never work out, and,' I paused, 'I wouldn't want it to.'

'Well … noooo…'

'I *wouldn't*.'

'I believe you. You are *oozing* sincerity Rosamund.'

'God you can be irritating when you're being cynical.'

'And you can be so blind.'

'What?'

'Roz, you *really* like this guy. It's obvious. And he *really* likes you too. I know, I'm good at this sort of thing, honest.' He paused and looked at me, and I just looked down sheepishly at the mug in my hand.

'You just can't see it can you? Whenever you're with him, he's always looking at you, and the tension between you two positively vibrates. I tell you, I felt pretty in the way the other night in his kitchen.'

'Well why didn't you go then? You could have gone home, or back to the wedding party!'

'Yeah, like that was an option!' he laughed. 'Well, I enjoyed being there, and the wine was great and the food wasn't bad either, so I put up with feeling in the way. I can bear some hardships in a good cause.'

'You're very good.'

'I know.' He raised his eyes, piously. 'Aah, it's just so romantic isn't it…' he began, 'two lovers on the brink of a wonderful relationship, and what better way for her to demonstrate her love for him than breaking into the grounds of his house and setting off a rape alarm in front of half the town. It's just so romantic—'

'It's a good plan, Alan. You mark my words!'

'I don't deny it's a *good plan,*' he said, 'It's a good plan to get him to think you need some kind of psychiatric help. Just how many people are going to be there?'

'About forty.'

'Jesus. I thought it was supposed to be a small scale thing.' He looked surprised.

'Surely you know Kings Newton better than that now? Richard Weston is loathed here.'

'Poor man.'

'I know! Hence the rape alarm plan… I will single handedly stop them defiling his property and save him from the humiliation of having banners put up and graffiti sprayed.'

'You know, I'm really sorry I'm going to be missing you in action Roz. I could really do with a good laugh.'

29

It was a quandary, and I was in it up to my neck.

What I should wear to protest in?

On the bed in front of me were almost all the items of my sad wardrobe and I was trying to come up with the most suitable outfit. I cast my mind back to when I was throwing my belongings into the bag at Greg's flat. Why hadn't I thrown in my decent clothes, some sensible country stuff?

Clearly the overriding need of the night was going to be *concealment*, so anything in a bright colour or anything that rustled would have to be abandoned. Back into the wardrobe went my hippy skirt with tiny bells on the drawstring, and my red silk blouse. My primrose yellow jumper and my stripey cardigan went with them.

But, I reasoned, not only did I need to be dressed in dark and noiseless clothing, I also needed to be waterproof. It was raining outside and it looked as though the weather was all set for the night. I'd brought with me my orange waterproof mac, which would have been excellent at keeping off the rain, but on the downside: a. it was a vibrant colour, b. it was expensive and c. it creaked when I walked in it. So that was out too. At this rate I would be protesting naked. Christ, I'd have to beat Tom off with a big stick.

A guilty rummage through Alan's wardrobe revealed a rather large dark blue mac that would be ideal, so I borrowed that for the night.

Eventually I decided that my darkest blue jeans would be fit for the job, and I had a black polo neck jumper that would do. It was the shoes that really stumped me though. I really had managed to pick up the most inappropriate of my shoe collection from Greg's place. The plum suede kitten-heeled shoes (great for the wedding), black pumps (ruined on my first encounter with Richard Weston in the rain), orange flats (which I'd worn nearly every day working at Gloria's shop) and a pair of slippers. Nothing. *Nada*. I knew that back at Greg's there was the most perfect pair of hiking boots just sitting on the shelf waiting for me to reclaim them, but I had neither the time nor the inclination to revisit Greg's place. I still had the key to the front door though – maybe I could sneak back one day soon when I knew for sure he'd be out (and not secretly shagging anyone by the kitchen appliances) and retrieve all my belongings.

The thought left me cold and I knew I'd never go back: stuff could always be bought, peace of mind hardly ever.

There seemed to be no option but to go for the ruined black pumps. The leather had gone all crispy since the drenching all those nights ago and I didn't have any polish to sort them out so they'd shrivelled up. Plus they had absolutely no grip and given the poor forecast I'd need to be careful tonight. There was no way I was ruining any more shoes though, and the slippers were right out.

The doorbell went. I raced downstairs, which took a matter of seconds given they were so tiny and I took two at a time.

'Hi there Ros-a-mund.'

It was Tom; smooth, slick and leaning against the front door in an overly familiar way. He was dressed in black with only his light blond wavy hair and his pale face shining out from the gloaming.

'Nice action at the wedding. Really made the evening for me.'

I smiled tightly.

'Turned out to be a corker of a night, shame you dashed off like that.'

I certainly wasn't going to tell him I'd stayed in the house and taken solace in the kitchens with Arch Enemy Number 1.

'Well aren't you going to let me in? It's pissing it down out here.'

If I must. 'Yes,' I said, standing back and letting him walk wet footprints all over Alan's carpet. 'How did you know I was here?'

'Well where else would you be? I did try Gloria's first but I suspected you'd have moved out. Hey, you're looking like some cool protester in that getup. I like your polo neck. Very... well fitting.'

Eugh. I made myself think about the utter confusion I was going to bestow at the protest and managed to not rise to his smarm. Oh to see him running away in fright! Priceless.

Tom, once he had installed himself in the living room was quite content to yak away at me about the wedding and Alan's 'comic timing'. In the past I would have listened and probably begun to feel rather embarrassed about what had happened, or at least want to explain it from my point of view, but I couldn't be bothered. He could believe what he wanted and when I believed that, then he wouldn't be able to touch me. I busied myself clearing away my clutter around him while he happily talked to himself moving on to preach about the development again. I was on the brink of offering to make tea, which seemed like the kind of thing I should do, when Tom saw me filling the kettle and bounded over.

'How about something a bit stronger?'

'Coffee?'

'Stronger.'

'Hot Bovril?'

'No,' he didn't laugh. 'Has Alan got whisky?'

I hesitated. Did he have whisky? 'Yes, probably, if it's made with fermented apples,' I said.

'Well, Rosamund, shall we check?' he said, trying to lead me by the hand to the living room but I wriggled free and scowled at him. His hands were rough from the woodworking. I went over to the sofa, quickly hiding some brochures on apartments in Birmingham. I didn't want him interrogating me about them.

'…so he really might be doing it,' he was saying, turning round to me with two very large glasses.

'Crikey, that's a lot of whisky,' I said, accepting mine but doubting whether I could manage it all. On reflection though, Farmer Jacob's finest cider had probably pickled my stomach and I would never be overly affected by alcohol again. 'What might *he* be doing, who's 'he'?' I asked.

'Lord Weston.'

'Oh, what?' I said, suddenly keen for Tom's inane gossip and bitter ramblings.

'Selling up.'

'No!' I was shocked. I gulped down a large sip of whisky and felt it burn its way through my body.

'Yes, it's a definite possibility. You know Sarah…'

I gave him a pointed look which he ignored.

'… well she told me that Richard Weston has had some conservation body round to assess taking the place off his hands and the implications of it. I bet he does it you know. I bet he makes a mint out of the sale of the place. Apparently he can't officially put it up for sale because he's accepted benefits from the conservation company, so they have the first refusal, and they're definitely interested because they don't have many properties up here in Shropshire.'

'You're joking?' I said, incredulously, the wind taken out of my sails. 'He didn't say anything about it to me.'

As soon as the words left my lips I regretted saying them. Tom took a slow sip of his quarter pint of whisky, eyeing me above the rim of his glass.

'Oh?' he said, into the silence that had followed my remark. 'Oh.'

What could I say to that? Should I come out with the truth

and tell him just how I felt about Richard Weston? Tell him that over the past few weeks I'd seen rather a lot of the man, and the more I got to know him the more I liked him? Should I tell him I couldn't think of anything but Richard Weston since I'd bumped into him? That I often thought back to the times that I had met him, and was aching for tomorrow when I was due for dinner at seven thirty in the great hall. By candlelight... The hall that my friend had paid thousands of pounds to hire for the night, and I would be there with the Lord of the Manor himself, eating his food, under the watchful gaze of five hundred years' of his ancestors.

No. I could not say that. I took another gulp of whisky and stared at the carpet.

'You seem to know him quite well,' said Tom, filling in for my silence.

'Not really.'

'Come to think of it…' he said, emptying his glass, 'Gloria mentioned that there was something going on between you.'

'No,' I said, a bit too quickly, 'Gloria thought we did, but she was absolutely wrong. Besides he has a girlfriend, as you know, Sarah.'

Tom snorted derisively. I ignored him. He certainly had his metaphorical finger in a lot of metaphorical pies around Kings Newton.

'I just happen to have met him quite often. When I was helping Gloria out with the decorations,' I explained.

'Oh yes. And the rather nasty jogging accident.' He snorted with laughter.

God I hated him. Arrogant self-obsessed git. I swallowed my whisky silently. He deserved what was coming to him…

'Well this protest could be just what the old landlord needs. The final push. I tell you Rosamund, it couldn't have come at a better time. I think he's down on his knees and this will be the last kicking before he falls over. Bastard.'

He was testing me, I realised. He wanted me to rise to his taunting and defend Richard Weston. No doubt he would find it hugely amusing that he had managed to manipulate me, just as he manipulated so many other women in Kings Newton. Tom's problem, though, was that he had the subtlety of a Piccadilly Circus billboard.

I smiled and nodded, 'You could be right. I wonder what the Heritage Trust will do with the house once it's theirs?'

Tom raised his eyebrows at me, and went over to pour himself another whisky.

'I mean,' I continued, 'when the Heritage Trust opened Suddersly Hall in Staffordshire, I heard that it caused enormous problems for the nearby village. Apparently a bypass had to be built just to keep the tourist traffic out of the middle of the village. And the fields nearby were turned into car parks to accommodate all the cars. Not only that, but because Suddersley was part of the tourist trail, it became *the* new attraction in the neighbourhood and house prices rocketed. And once the houses were snapped up by moneyed commuters, the whole character of the town changed. Suddenly it was quite a chic place to be, and everybody wanted to live there. In the end there was so much demand for housing that they had to build on the outskirts, just like you've got here, although there it was on a much greater scale and—'

'You're talking bollocks Rosamund.'

'No I'm not.'

'You just are. It's crap. It won't happen here.'

'Why not?'

'Because we won't let it.'

'Jesus Christ Tom, you can't spend your life fighting against every change that happens to the town you know.'

'Excuse me,' he said, 'aren't you supposed to be supporting *us* tonight?'

'Yes. And you can see that I'm prepared to,' I indicated my clothes, 'but what I'm saying is that you have to draw the line somewhere. You have to accept some things that don't fit exactly with what you want.'

'No I don't.'

'Well what do you want to happen to the Hall? If you manage

to push Richard Weston out, what or who do you want to take his place?'

'I want it to be open to the public of course. But it's hardly the size or importance of Suddersly Hall. What you were saying about Suddersly village just isn't going to happen here in Kings Newton. You'll see. We'll attract a small number of people, probably localish, the craft centres in the stables will benefit and the town will grow prosperous – *yes I admit it* – but not to the detriment of the people that live here.'

'But,' I said, 'Richard Weston might not sell his house to the Heritage Trust. After all, it's just a rumour.'

'He will. If we do our job tonight he will.'

It sounded ominous.

'Come on Ros-a-mund. Are you ready? We have work to do.' He patted my leg and stood up in front of me, 'What are you getting up to now Alan's away in Birmingham? You must be pretty lonely rattling round here on your own…'

Smooth bastard. I changed the subject, 'So is Sarah going to join us this evening then?'

'Do I detect a note of jealousy?' piped up Tom, laughing smarmily.

'No.' I cut him dead.

'Well as a matter of fact she's not,' he said. 'She's in London for a few days. Get your coat on, let's go,' he said.

I dived upstairs, opened my holdall and pocketed my trusty rape alarm with a malicious grin.

30

As Tom and I headed out into the rain that night, we saw a few other people huddling against the sides of the street, keeping out of the orange pools of the street lights. We were all making our way silently to the stables. No one acknowledged each other, but headed noiselessly towards the illicit rendezvous, heads down, bowed against the unbroken rain.

I was warm and fuzzy after my whisky and the edge had been taken off my anxiety about the protest. I had, I realised, almost fulfilled the role that I had planned to play that night. Tom had seen me prepared to protest, and was witnessing me turning up to help. It would only be a matter of half an hour before we set off with the other protestors and then I could set off the alarm and escape back to Alan's.

The rain had become heavier.

Tom and I said nothing as we slipped into the stable block. We stole into the back of his workshop, where there was already a substantial number of people, similarly dressed in black, huddled together in the dim light of a few torches and candles set on the tables.

The room was thick with whispers and anxious soft laughter. I could feel the tension in the air and it was intoxicating. I was actually excited and for a moment I forgot the purpose of the event and became caught up in the anticipation. When my eyes had become accustomed to the low light I could make out a few faces from the town that I recognised. Barbara from the butchers, and the two women from the post office… A couple of lads from the garage at the bottom of Castle Road and even some of the teachers from the primary school. Teachers, I thought, seemed out of place here. They seemed too respectable to be taking part in something like this.

Tom had thankfully left my side to go up to the front of the crowd and join one of Gloria's friends who was unrolling large white banners on the table. I wandered over and smiled broadly, hoping she would remember me and make sure to tell Gloria just how keen I had looked on the night. *What a good friend that Rosamund must be…*

I watched the assembly increase as one by one furtive black-clad townspeople slunk in through the back door. There were nods to acquaintances and arms outstretched to pull good friends over to the tight circles of whispering. No one raised their voices above a whisper.

'*…an' I just looks at him and says you can't buy two for the price of one and he just looks at me blank, like, and walks off…*'

'*…Tom says he's as good as gone, 'cause the Heritage are making him an offer…*'

'*…is that the jumper I gave you a while back…*'

I angled my watch to one of the torch lights and saw it was nearly ten. No one had come into the room for the last couple of minutes, which was just as well; it was packed.

'Thank you. Thank you all for coming.' It was Tom, now standing on his workbench and whispering as loudly as he could, torn between being heard and not wanting to alert outsiders. The murmur of voices had died down and everyone turned in the direction of their leader who stood proud above them, hands on his hips. Clearly Tom was in his element, loving the attention and the role he had to play.

'My friends, we've been through some appalling times these last few months…' There was a ripple of agreement from the room. 'We've been ignored by those acting for Richard Weston, and we've been misrepresented by the local council. We've had our efforts manipulated by the very people who were supposed to be listening to us, and our endeavours to date have been in vain.'

Here he paused while the murmur of consent and muffled clapping gave him a chance to get his breath.

'One by one you've joined together, to form the crowd of good people you see around you, because our legitimate actions have been fruitless. No one wanted it to come to this…' one or two people snorted and there was hushed laughter, 'but it has. If we're going to take matters into our own hands then by God we're going to have to give this everything we've got. We're going to show Lord Weston that we are *not* going to lie down and take it. We are *not* going to let him parcel up land piece by piece and ruin the fabric of our society here in Kings Newton. He cannot fob us off with any more smooth talking solicitors or with councillors who are so obviously in his pocket.

'It's true – right now he has only sold off one plot of land, but it's land in the heart of our town, on the very site of our old town; the place where our ancestors lived and in an area that we've always held close to our hearts. For no other reason than to make him wealthier. We've had to watch while his filthy diggers and trucks tear up the ground where our long-gone relatives once lived and we've had to watch while they pave the way for some faceless collection of commuter's houses.

'Look at Shelton. Look at Finden. They were once towns like ours and now they're part of the town of Ludlow. It's going to happen here. I tell you now that Richard Weston got tens of thousands of pounds from the sale of that land, and we know… we know that he's looking into the sale of lands further north of the town, up to the borders of Friarsby.' More mumbling from the dark crowd.

'That's right. Shaw's Wood, Stockett Fields and the area belonging to Townend Farm, that's all up for sale if he chooses, and I'm telling you, he's got the pounds and pence worked out. All he has to do is turn up for lunch with the building contractors, sign on the line and then where are we? We're just another part of a small conurbation!

'So I tell you what… The people of Kings Newton are not going to take it any more. We're here to say 'no' and we're here to say that we care about this town, and we care more than he or his family ever did. We're going to paste up these posters and string up the banners and when he wakes up tomorrow morning, the message is going to come through loud and clear. He can sod off out of our town, and he can sod off out of our lives, because we've had enough!'

Everyone started to clap and cheer and Tom had to hush them down. He'd certainly whet their appetite for a fight, and I could feel them itching to get started. I couldn't help feeling that the speech was a bit, well, contrived really. A bit Margaret Thatcher. I half expected some sort of 'the town is not for turning' coda, and was disappointed when it didn't come.

Tom continued, telling people what their role would be for the forthcoming evening. One by one he organised us into small groups and gave us specific tasks: pasting up posters, spraying trees with silly string, drawing chalk body-outlines on the patio slabs – 'to represent our ancestors in the old town' – and stringing up enormous banners from the roof of the actual building. That job, we were told, would be done by Tom and Tom alone. He would shin up the ancient drainpipes and crawl along the roof tiles to display the main banner for all the world to see.

'Right – Rosamund – I'll put you with Mike here, and Wendy, Lesley, Simon, Dave and Jenny. You are going to be responsible for tying up these small banners to the railings that circle the park to the front of the house beside the road. Got that?'

We all nodded.

By half past ten I'd met everyone in my group, collected the banners and string and we were filing out of the stables and into the hissing rain.

My heart was beating so loudly that I expected the team members to ask me to shut up. My breathing had speeded up alarmingly. Supposing Sarah, who surely must be the spy that Tom and Gloria had been talking about, had passed on details of this protest to Richard Weston, just like she had about the road block. Right this minute there might be eager policemen hidden in the rhododendrons, baying for blood and just itching to arrest me and throw me in a rat-infested cell. I almost smiled – imagine what my mother would say when I wrote to her from prison.

'Rosamund!' It was Tom. 'Good luck.'

I smiled a wan smile and peeled away from him, following my group and keeping to the hedge.

I was in charge of carrying the banners, which I reasoned wasn't actually protesting as such because I wouldn't be physically putting them up. As soon as I had given all but one of my banners away I would leave the group on the pretence of hanging up the remaining banner elsewhere, find a hiding place near the way out and set the alarm off. Then I'd make sure I looked as startled as everyone else before nipping back to Alan's and locking the door.

The ground had become waterlogged and soft underfoot. My shoes kept slipping and sinking into the soft earth and water oozed around the top of them and sucked around my feet. The little leather rose detail on the front of my pumps was now caked in wet mud and the petals were sagging pitifully in the rain. They would be ruined beyond repair this time – no miracle rescue from shoe polish for them. The banners weighed heavy in my arms, the strings slapping against my sleeves, which were already sodden, the rain having penetrated the mac. I hated rain, I never went out in bad weather and yet here I was outside in a downpour for the second time during my stay in Kings Newton. I took a deep breath and looked around. We had reached our rendezvous at the perimeter of the park by the railings. I could make out the Hall through the blur of the rain, a few windows lit up with a rosy glow of light. How I wished I was in there safe and warm and not outside in this miserable weather. My hand slipped into the pocket of Alan's jacket and closed around the seditious alarm. My fingers found the pin and I felt a new surge of confidence. This was bound to work…

I handed out banners, and string, to the protesters who then fanned out to find places to put them up. Everything was eerily still; there were no sounds except the steady hiss of the rain and my pounding heart.

I needed to set off the alarm now before any real damage was done so I backed away from the lawn and crept towards the boundary ditch. In an instant I lost my balance and slipped in the mud. I was left half kneeling in a puddle. I clung to a bush and tried to steady myself. A sharp pain shot up my leg and I fell back into the mud, letting go of my banner. I should do it. *I should do it now.* I looked around quickly and couldn't make out anyone near me, and crouched down by the bush which was as good a hiding place as I could have wished. I drew the alarm out of my pocket. My hands were shaking as I slid my finger through the pin and pulled.

The noise was terrific.

I thought my head would explode from the pain in my ears. After sitting there for a split second unable to move from the shock of it, I gathered myself together and threw the alarm as far from me as I could, scrambling up and trying my best to ignore the sharp pain in my ankle. Now I was half standing I could see people running out of the gardens, banners and boards abandoned. It had worked! Some of the protesters were shouting to one another, slipping and sliding in the mud and I laughed as I stood there, giddily happy that my plan had worked. I'd set an alarm off! I'd scared them away! So much for Alan's misgivings… Most of the protestors were running away in the opposite direction to where I was standing. They disappeared into the night and the driving rain. I hobbled towards where they were exiting but I'd misjudged the pain from my ankle and sank down into the mud groaning. I couldn't do it. From inside the house came the sound of barking and the shouts from the garden increased: '*Come on!*' I managed to crawl over the grass and towards the exit.

'Rosamund! Come with me,' it was one of my fellow protesters, drenched and alarmed, trying to pull me up onto my feet but my ankle wouldn't support my weight. I sank back down in agony.

'I can't. My ankle…'

'You've got to. Move!'

'I can't!'

'Oh for God's sake,' he panicked and fled from me, quickly lost in the sheets of rain. The alarm was waning now, the piercing shriek reduced to a slowly mournful whine and then nothing – the batteries had died. Thank God. It was driving me crazy.

The barking that had been muffled, inside, was now sharper, nearer. The barks were out in the grounds and I could hear paws pounding on the wet earth. I was crying big heavy sobs of frustration and pain, but it made no difference, the rain kept streaming down my face.

The weight of a dog landed on my injured leg and searing pain almost blinded me as I tried to scramble back up. I screamed and the dog drove me back to into the mud knocking the breath out of me. I curled up to protect myself against its attack. There was a pause. Nothing. And then as I opened my eyes, I saw Pilot sniffing me, his tail moving gingerly – wagging now that he recognised me.

Where there was Pilot there was Richard Weston, and sure enough I could see him now, emerging from the haze of rain, striding towards me.

I tried to pull myself up but only succeeded in twisting myself further into the mud. I turned round and he was standing above me, soaked, to the skin and gasping for breath in the cold night air. He looked worried, terrified even. And very angry.

'Get up!'

I scrambled around in the mud, sliding hopelessly against the earth in my dainty shoes, and finally managed to pull myself upright. Severe pain shot up my leg and I fell back onto the hedge. Richard Weston held out his hand and I took it – warm despite the wet, and he pulled me towards him, covering himself in the mud that had entirely coated me. He held me upright so I didn't put any weight on my left ankle.

I wanted to say something. I wanted to say: 'Isn't it funny, it's only recently your ankle had been twisted in the rain and now here am I…'

But there was nothing I could say. It was pitch black and now he had turned away from the house I could barely make out his expression, but I knew it was no time to make light of my predicament.

He held me tightly and walked me to the house. I hobbled as best I could, sinking every few steps with the pain.

Richard Weston didn't say a word. The dog bounded around us, well aware there had been people in the grounds, on guard, but keeping close. As I stumbled towards the Hall I saw and heard no one else, the others having had the sense to know where they were going and wear proper shoes. My heart sank and I realised I should have set the alarm off earlier. The protestors had already managed to hoist up a multitude of banners on many of the trees beside the house – flapping pathetically in the wind were 'Fuck off Weston' and 'King's Newton Land: help yourself'. There were many more, though, still lying in piles where the protesters had dropped them and fled. I had to explain, I had to tell him what I had done and why I was there. But I couldn't draw breath and I really, really wanted to get out of the rain. At least it had washed most of the mud out of my clothes and my hair. As we approached the house I was pretty much clean but soaked to the bone.

We walked through the French windows and into the library. He made me wait propped up by the mantelpiece while he covered an old chair with newspaper before helping me into it.

'I'll call you a doctor,' he said, and shut the door behind him as he left.

Alone with Pilot I closed my eyes and more hot tears ran down my cheeks, scalding against my frozen skin. Whether it was embarrassment or shame I don't know, but I couldn't stop them, and so I let them fall. As I sat in front of the fire, I thought over what had just happened. I wished I had explained my intentions to Richard. That I'd set the alarm off. What on earth would he be thinking of me right now?

My confidence had completely crumbled. My plan seemed so pathetic – I shouldn't have been at the protest at all. Stupid, stupid girl.

I wondered, as I sat there, dripping onto the newspaper and soaking the armchair whether I should just go, leave by the French windows and hobble back to Alan's. Then escape to Birmingham as the sun came up. But how I could drive with my ankle the way it was? I tried to put my weight on it, but it was no good, a shock of pain raced up my spine as I lifted my foot. I wasn't going to be hobbling anywhere anytime soon. *Oh God I am so stupid, and so very cold and wet.*

Richard appeared at the door to tell me the doctor was on his way, and left to change out of his wet clothes. Within twenty minutes a young, rather grey-looking doctor was in the room, examining my ankle. It was bruising, he told me, nothing more serious than that. I could see by the quick glances he kept giving me that he was curious as to why I was there, and why I was soaked to the skin. Coming from the main driveway he probably wouldn't have seen the banners, which was a mercy. But whether it was out of politeness or just the tiredness he didn't ask me any questions, stayed long enough to give me a few bits of advice which I didn't listen to, and within five minutes he was gone.

I heard Richard Weston show him out and apologise for having called so late, close the front door and slide large-sounding bolts across.

I knew he would be coming back to the room, and my heart beat faster, half in eagerness to see him, and half dreading the confrontation, which would surely put an end to anything that he might ever have felt for me. If, indeed, he had felt anything, ever. What a complete fool I was. What a bloody idiot. It was blisteringly clear now that I should never ever have gone on the stupid effing protest. What kind of friendship needed such a sacrifice to be made? I wanted to please Gloria and make amends for the scene at the wedding, but a real friend wouldn't need to have her friendship validated like that. I had been so stupid.

It was warm and dark in the library. There had been a fire in the grate earlier and the embers still smouldered, casting a glow on the old red walls. Pilot had muscled in on what remained of the fire and was drying out at my feet, eyes closed, breathing softly. His contentment made the events in the garden seem even more unreal. I watched him, concentrating on his softly rising and falling flank, trying to put out of my mind why I was there. I breathed deeply to relax, wiping back my tears on my damp sleeve.

Richard came back into the room and shooed the reluctant Pilot out towards the kitchens. Quietly he closed the door behind him.

'A towel,' he said, handing it to me.

'Thanks,' I mumbled, rubbing my hair and face into it. It was soft and warm.

He took up the chair opposite mine. The rattle of the rain against the old leaded windows and the pop and crack of the dying fire filled the silence. Self-consciously I dabbed my arms and legs with the towel. What was I supposed to do with it? I wound it in my hands and put them on my lap awkwardly.

He looked at me for a moment, his brown eyes shining by the firelight and his hair jet black with the rain, swept back off his forehead. I felt my eyes fill with tears so I looked down and tried to concentrate on the patterns in the rug.

'Do I need to call the police?' he asked, quietly.

'No.'

'Are there any bombs coming through my letter box, any man traps outside the front door sprung and waiting for me?'

I looked up at him, his tone was serious but I thought he was laughing

'No. Just banners. Look, I have to explain…'

'Why you?' he said it so softly that I almost wondered whether he said anything at all.

I paused, a lump in my throat.

'Why you?' he repeated. 'Of all the people who could have been out there tonight, I wouldn't have thought you'd have been one of them,' he bent his head down and nearer to mine, to try and see, no doubt, some truth in my eyes even though he didn't expect any to come from my lips.

'I took part so that I could ruin it,' I said, wringing my hands. 'It was me who set the rape alarm off.'

'That was you?'

'I thought I'd done it before anyone had had time to put up any of the banners and stuff but it looks like they were really quick.'

'But why were you there at all?'

'I know it seems stupid now…'

'Why didn't you just tell me about it and I could have got the police round or something?'

'Yes that would have been a good idea,' I said, 'it's just my friends expected me to go to the protest and I didn't want to let them down, not after what happened at the wedding and stuff. I feel really bad about it and I thought if I turned up at the protest then I could sort of make amends. And this way… well I thought this way I'd turn up and appease them and stop the protest and do you a good turn too…' my voice went wobbly.

He was leaning towards me, studying my face intently, which made me blush.

'Well it sort of worked, I suppose,' he offered.

'But I should have let the alarm off straight away. Then you wouldn't have any banners up…'

'Well your timing would have to have been spot on. I'm sorry but I don't think your plan was a very foolproof one.'

'I know. It seemed OK at the time. But it sucked.'

'Do you have any more plans that I should be aware of?' he said, a hint of amusement in his voice. He had leant back, his broad shoulders spanning the width of the chair.

'No. No more plans,' I managed with a smile, and tried to smooth my drying hair behind me. Already it was curling wildly round my shoulders.

'Well thank God for that. You and your imp-like ways – I never know where you're going to turn up next. In the woods, behind my sofas, up my trees and now in the bushes in the rain… Honestly, I live in constant fear—'

'I know I know!' I said. 'I wish I was more sophisticated than I am. I wish I wasn't the type of person who is clumsy and unrefined but I can't help it!'

'What on earth outcome did you imagine you would enjoy with tonight's festivities then?'

'Well,' I said cautiously, my heart racing each time I looked at him, 'I imagined I'd set off the alarm before any harm was done, you'd hear the noise and either call the police or just collect the unused banners up in the morning. Then tomorrow night at dinner I'd drop into the conversation that it was me who stopped the protestors from messing up your gardens.'

'And then what would I do?' he asked quietly

I paused: the image I had in mind wasn't something I could share with him just now. 'You'd thank me,' I said finally.

'I'd *thank you*? That's it?' he had the beginnings of a smile on his lips.

'Yes,' I said, more confident now. Was he playing with me?

'So are you waiting for me to *thank you* now?' He was laughing.

'Not *so* much,' I said. I could see he'd forgiven me. Relief came in a flood.

'I like the fact that you're so…' he searched for the word, 'unpolished! I think it's perfect.'

My heart skipped a beat.

'Do you want a drink?'

'Yes!' I said, overly eager.

'Brandy?'

'Yes. Anything. Brandy would be good. Thanks.'

He went over to the sideboard and poured us both a glass. He passed it to me and knelt beside my chair. I could smell the familiar scent of his aftershave and I breathed it in deeply.

'I'm so sorry,' I began, burbling, 'I really am. I just wanted to be the person that did you a good turn and helped you out. And this was the best plan I could come up with …'

'It's OK, it's OK,' he said gently, and laid a hand on my arm. 'Look at you – you're still soaking wet.'

'And so is your chair,' I said quietly, looking at the damage.

'I never liked that chair.'

I smiled at him. 'I really am sorry,' I said

'It's OK, really.' He was so close to me, his hand still resting on my arm, his fresh dry shirt spattered with drops of rain from his hair, which slid down his neck and out of sight. I reached out and gently brushed the water from his forehead. It was no use, I made his forehead wetter then before, but he leant towards me, and cupping my head in his warm hands, brushed my lips with his own. I responded and within a moment his arms encircled me, pulling me gently to the floor beside him where he held me close. I put my arms around his broad shoulders and reveled in his hungry kisses. I felt his hands move slowly down to my waist and gently lift my jumper, running his fingers across my skin and sending warm shivers up and down my chilly body.

I pulled back and began slipping undone the buttons on his shirt, one by one slowly working my way down his chest as he kissed my face and neck. I pulled aside the shirt, and he broke free from holding me, letting me slip the shirt cuffs over his wrists. As I ran my hands over his bare chest I could feel his heart, pounding just like mine.

31

I think I was woken by the honking of the geese on the lake, although I couldn't be sure because by the time I was awake the noise had stopped. I must have slept for a long time – bright light was flooding through the floor-to-ceiling French windows at the other end of the room, only half-dimmed by the thin linen drapes.

It seemed like hours but it must have taken a matter of seconds to work out where I was. Why I was hearing geese. And why I was lying in an enormous four-poster bed.

Richard Weston.

I turned over expecting to see his tousled black hair but I was alone. I hadn't heard him leave. I lay there for a few moments, feeling absolutely fabulous. For the first time in my life I felt wholly glamorous and just a hint debauched. I was a desired woman and somewhere downstairs was Lord Weston, knowing I was asleep in his bed. Upstairs in his enormous house. *How wonderful was that?*

He wanted me, and I wanted him. And, let's face it, this was a magnificent room to wake up in any day of the week. I looked around and took in the splendor of my surroundings. There was an enormous marble fireplace opposite the bed with an old silvered mirror above it, a large wooden chest at the foot of the bed, and a matching wardrobe against the wall.

And hanging from the door was a dressing gown.

What should I do now?

Was Richard making coffee? Would he be up in a moment?

Or had he been up for hours and was he wondering why I was still asleep like some lazy sloth. What time was it? Where was my watch?

It was in the library. It all came back to me now... the protest, the rain, the fire, Richard Weston... the horrors of the evening mixed with the pleasures at night. It was a strange feeling; confusing.

I would have tried to puzzle it out, but I began to feel increasingly guilty on account of staying in bed so long. It must be midday the light was so bright. Certainly lying around in bed all day wasn't going to impress anyone.

I hoisted myself out of the bed and winced with pain – bruised ankle be damned! My ankle hurt *a lot*. I managed to stumble over to the window, my feet padding on the bare boards. I peered out of the drapes of curtain: it was still raining. The sky was a dirty grey, despite looking so bright and cheery from behind the curtain.

'Weston OUT!' a banner announced, strung high from a tree near the window. My heart sank a little.

My clothes were not to be found, and it dawned on me that they were probably still in the library where I had abandoned most of them.

Damn.

This sort of thing never happens to sophisticated girls, I though bitterly. They never leave their clothes in another room; and not only another room but in another wing of the house, a host of complex corridors away. Sophisticated girls have evening dresses slung aesthetically over the back of a chair and tiny kitten heels kicked under the bed. I had a muddied Milktray-man ensemble waiting for me five minutes' jog away; soggy jeans and a faded black polo neck might be the perfect get-up for covert operations, but would surely put a damper on any ardour over breakfast.

What would a smart girl have done? I looked around me, frantically. Come on come on! I should put myself in her Manolo's and think how she would think.

The dressing gown! The sophisticated modern girl would swan downstairs in the thick luxurious dressing gown and perch daintily on the table as Lord Lovely ate his breakfast. The gown would fall open provocatively at the knee, exposing a glimpse of leg as she nibbled a *pain au chocolat*.

I pulled it on.

Horrors. It was too small. Much too small.

I started to panic. This can't have been his dressing gown? He was taller than I was, wasn't he? Broader?

And then it dawned on me. This was not Richard Weston's dressing gown. This was Sarah's. This was the dressing gown she would patter down the stairs in before perching at the breakfast table nibbling *pain au chocolat*…

It made me want to rip it off, made me itchy and made me feel cheap. But there was nothing else for it. I could hardly rifle through his wardrobes, and I was even less tempted by the idea of wandering around the house in the buff, so by the time I'd finished pacing up and down in front of the fireplace, I had decided on a plan. To sneak down the stairs in the Barbie-sized dressing gown, find my dirty black clothes and change into them. Yes they were disgusting, yes they had a whiff of the TA about them, but they were my own, and I could say my goodbyes and dash home and come out later cleansed and re-clothed as appropriate. *Ready for the meal tonight.* Perfect!

The house was quiet around me as I squeaked and clattered my way down the corridor as softly and subtly as a limping one-man-band, but thank goodness there was no-one near to hear me. I eventually navigated my way into the library and to my enormous relief saw that there was no one around. The grandfather clock was ticking away in the corner; it was half past ten. Thank God! I had thought it was gone midday. The fire had burnt down and was cold now. I hunted around, keeping an eye on the door in case anyone came in, and eventually I found my clothes behind the armchair, still muddied, still slightly damp. I managed to brush some of the mud off into the fireplace. Good job there was no guided tour this morning.

I checked that no one was nearby, inside or out, and put my clothes on, quickly, and checking my appearance in the old mirror above the fireplace. I looked like I'd just had a fabulous night! My hair was tousled and wild, my cheeks were rosy but most of all my eyes were shiny and bright. Ignoring the outfit itself I looked quite good I thought. I briskly combed through my curly hair as best I could with my fingers and fixed it up in a loose knot using a pencil I found on the writing table. I was ready to face the morning.

There was no one in the Green Room, the Drawing Room or the Breakfast Room. I headed for the kitchens, and as I walked closer, I heard voices.

Richard was standing at the window; Harold the estate manager – the man I had once mistaken for his lordship – was making tea at the Aga. He looked up at me as I went in, looking away again quickly, fussing with something on the table.

'Hi,' I said, rather sheepishly.

'Hello,' Richard came over to me, and kissed me softly on the lips. 'Are you OK?'

'Yes, yes,' I said. 'You?'

'Yes.'

'Well,' Harold hastily poured water into his mug and mashed the tea bag like a man possessed. 'I must be off now, plenty to do, plenty to do,' and he bumbled out of the room, eyes fixed on the floor all the time, as though I were Medusa and by my very sluttish-ness would turn him to stone.

I sat at the table and we waited until he was out of earshot.

'I was going to warn you about Harold, but you came down before I had the chance,' he said.

'Have you been up long?'

'No – you must have woken up just after me. I'm sorry I didn't wake you, but I knew Harold would be round for the books this morning so I thought I ought to get up,' he bent down to kiss me again. I responded and within a moment we were holding each other close and his hand was stroking my back.

There was a sharp knock on the kitchen door.

We parted and Richard went to open the door. Outside stood one of the farmers, sheltering beneath a knackered old Barbour jacket, a mangy collie at his heals. He stayed on the threshold and glanced into the house, but on seeing me he looked hastily away.

This must be a normal day for Richard Weston. His door would always be open to anyone and everyone and with no shred of privacy for himself. The reality of living in a beautiful house wasn't as appealing as it looked.

'I'm sorry to be disturbing you, sir, but there's a whole group of what I s'pose are newspaper people at the gates wantin' to talk to you and takin' photographs. I thought you oughta know.'

'Urgh! News of last night's activities no doubt,' Richard sank down on his chair. 'Thanks John. Did you say anything to them?'

'No. Wouldn't know what to say, to be honest with you. Energetic crowd though.'

'Right. Thanks. Well, I suppose I ought to go up and say something. Better to let them make me out the wronged man than hide away and piss them off.'

'Is that Sarah's philosophy talking?' I said, smiling.

'Something like that. Well, tea's in the pot. There's bread for toast just there and cereal somewhere about. Help yourself,' and with that he pulled a greatcoat on and headed out into the drizzle, talking to the farmer as he went. I watched them go then closed the door behind them.

Oh. That wasn't how it was supposed to go. There was no provocative leg showing or nibbling of pastries. All I was getting was an audience with estate managers and farmers, bread for toast and a solitary breakfast dressed in last night's damp clothes: it wasn't right.

I sighed. There was no point dwelling on it – these were strange circumstances and besides last night had been fantastically marvellous and it would take a whole lot to wipe the smile off my face this morning. I located the bread, the toaster and the butter and set about making breakfast. The house seemed oppressively enormous around me – so many empty rooms and so many empty corridors and just me rattling around in the kitchen. Spooky. I took my tea and toast to the Dining Room and looked out towards the gates at the top of the slope. I could make out Richard in an enormous grey coat talking to a crowd of people. It looked like there were TV crews there too: I thought I saw a boom mic. The garden was still covered with last night's spoils – rolls of banners on the grass, cans of silly string and even someone's shoe littering the ground. A few banners were flapping in the wind. I ought to do something. Swigging my tea and cramming the last of the toast into my mouth I set out for the entrance hall and grabbed a dry mac off one of the pegs behind the staircase; I'd seen Richard Weston get one from here before. Unbolting the front door I hopped down the steps and began to untie the banners that had been strung from the trees. It proved difficult so I limped back to the kitchens to get a pair of scissors and once armed with these I cut the offensive hangings down in no time. I bundled them in my arms along with the rolled up discarded banners and the shoe and went back inside. I piled last night's detritus in the kitchen and poured myself another cup of tea.

After I'd sat for a moment stirring my tea I began to wonder whether I should perhaps head back to Alan's. I wasn't going to be much help around the Hall and Richard probably wouldn't want me there anyway. Surely the right thing to do would be to leave him to it for the day and emerge butterfly-like tonight for dinner. If it was still on… This was not how it was meant to be *at all*.

32

It was all a bit of a blur...

I had made the decision to leave the Hall and head back to Alan's house and had been walking up the drive when I had bumped into Richard, who had been walking back down after having talked to the press. I explained – I'd left a note on the kitchen table, he was obviously busy, I was still in damp clothes, I ought to get back... And he had said yes, he was busy, there were solicitors to call – one of the protestors had gone to hospital with a broken arm and suspected concussion and the press were all over the story: would he sell the Hall, would he be sued by the protestor, how much damage had the protestors done...?

So I had said I'd better leave him to it and he had agreed. And then there had been a pause and I really wanted to say thank you – thank you for last night and how glad I was we had got together and how fantastic it was. And how I wished I could do something to help him but I didn't know how. But he just kissed me on the cheek in a friendly sort of way and asked if I was still on for tonight. So I'd said yes, that would be lovely, and we'd left it at that.

So it was that I emerged from Weston Hall into Kings Newton and the middle of the mob of newspaper reporters who were packing up after having spoken to Richard Weston. Looking back on that moment I suppose that there were various courses of action I could have taken; the sophisticated girl approach of holding a hand out to ward off questions: 'no comment' and tottering off. Or just claim to be a cleaner or estate worker and not know anything. But no, in a daze and thinking about the rather deflated ending to the last few hours I allowed myself to be stopped by them and stammered and hesitated, generally stuttering myself into a bit of a corner.

'Miss! Miss! Have you come from Weston Hall?' shouted one male reporter pushing to the front of the group and thrusting some sort of recorder in front of me.

'Err… yes?' I said, it being obvious where I'd come from so there was no point trying to lie.

'Are you close to Lord Weston? Were you there last night?' another began.

'Um…'

'Are you his girlfriend?'

'Well I…' what should I say? I couldn't and didn't want to get into the whole line of reasoning over what constitutes a boyfriend, although I certainly didn't think last night was sufficient but then what *was* he? No, I didn't want to ruin the thing we had by pigeonholing it into a category, if it was any sort of categorisable thing. It made it seem so *mundane*. And what we had was so—

'Lovers then?'

'Come on Miss…'

I stood there, mouth open, desperately hoping my brain would engage but not being able to think straight.

Click! Someone took my photograph and in a second there were more flashes from out of nowhere as photographers captured me open-mouthed.

'What about Thomas Mathews – do you know him?'

Who? The name was familiar and in my bewilderment I managed to recollect it was Gloria's Tom.

'Yes,' I said, 'I know him. Why?'

'Turns out he was one of the protestors involved in last night's activities. Broke his arm falling from a rotten drain pipe. What do you suppose he'll be thinking this morning?'

'How does my hair look?'

Goodness knows what the man would be thinking this morning. I fiddled with the pencil still holding my knotted hair in place. I desperately wanted to get away but was intrigued by this information. So it must have been Tom who had claimed he would sue Richard Weston, presumably for having faulty drain pipes and causing his injury. What an arse! I felt the anger well up and had Tom been in front of me I think I would have punched him. As it was I finally found my voice and, clenching my fists in my pockets, I pushed past the reporters, 'Look I'm no-one, you've got it all wrong!' I said. 'I don't know anything about the protest so don't bother writing about me…' and I hobbled down the hill towards the sanctuary that was Alan's house.

I was tired. I didn't know what to do. I knew that at some point I had to go back to the shop and open up. Gloria would have understood why I hadn't opened up today; she was a hard business woman but she would make an exception for this I was sure. And besides, even if she found out her shop had been closed for the day, it would pale into insignificance compared to the news that events at the Hall had stirred up trouble for Richard Weston, and that her erstwhile lover was nursing a badly broken arm. I wondered whether or not I should call her to tell her the news before she came back from her honeymoon.

I didn't call though. I sat in my still-damp clothes on the stairs in Alan's tiny empty house and cried and cried. I cried because I was homeless and because I was going to have to move again in a couple of weeks. I cried because just last night everything had seemed so rosy between Richard Weston and me, and now we were all awkward and distant with one another, he preoccupied with the house – and rightly so – and me not knowing what to do, hanging around uselessly. Besides which, the whole thing was futile given I was going to be moving to Birmingham. And lastly I cried because I'd lost a friend and however much Gloria and I had changed over the years it was still so sad that my oldest friend wasn't any more.

I wanted so much to be with Richard, but there was no way I could bother him right now. So I did the next best thing and called Alan.

33

'I can't believe it,' Alan was saying, 'I just can't believe what's happened.'

'I know,' I said, sipping the whisky coffee gingerly.

We were back in the shop, sitting on the high stools and staring out of the windows into the grey afternoon. It felt comforting to be back here again. Back where things were predictable and controllable and continued as if nothing bad had ever happened. Flowers arrived, bouquets were despatched, surfaces were dusted. I'd managed to find the number of Gloria's assistant, Deborah, who, thankfully, had agreed to come back to work sooner than planned, so things with the shop were looking fairly rosy.

Alan had raced down from Birmingham after I'd phoned him, in a bid to cheer me up. Fuschiarama was not yet open so he could afford to spend some time with me, and besides, he added, he wanted to nick as much information from Gloria's shop as he could. His departure had been swifter than he'd bargained for, so he hadn't had time to copy out exactly how Gloria had laid out her accounts, or the names and addresses of all her suppliers. So he sat with me, books open on the table and drinks poured, cheering me up, bless him, with his incessant chatter about his shop and his insatiable appetite for the gossip from the protest.

'Well, you do pick your moments,' he said, pushing my coffee towards me.

'I know,' I said, sighing. It's something I'd spent a lot of the morning thinking about, 'It's selfish, I know, but I can't help thinking that nothing can happen between Richard and me now, but I shouldn't even be thinking about it should I? I mean there are far more important things to be thinking about than whether or not there's anything more than a one night stand between us.'

'Do you want there to be something between you?'

'Yes! Yes I do. You know I do!'

'Despite all this?' he gestured to the newspaper spread out on the table in front of me. 'Could you share this kind of a life with someone surrounded by all these problems and all these people wishing they weren't here? Don't you think it would get to you?'

'I'm not even thinking about that. It's just background noise. I *really* like him Alan, and I know he likes me. A lot. But… God you're right, it's just awful timing.' I looked down at the paper Alan had brought earlier on.

Night-time Demonstration at Local Stately Home

Local man Thomas Mathews was in the Royal Infirmary last night receiving medical attention after an ill-fated night protest at Weston Hall, Shropshire. Mr Mathews, 36, had been climbing a drain pipe when the accident happened and he fell twenty feet into a bramble, breaking his arm in three places and sustaining considerable cuts to his face and hands.

'The drain pipe was rotten and crumbled in my grip,' Mr Mathews said this morning, 'I was lucky just to have my arm broken and my skin cut and scratched.'

He is considering taking legal action against owner Lord Weston to compensate for loss of earnings, as he makes a living woodworking at Weston Hall Craft Stables – something he can no longer do with a broken arm.

The protest took place at around 11pm on Monday night, with around fifty protestors putting up offensive banners and placards in the grounds of Weston Hall. The protest was thrown into confusion, however, when a burglar alarm was activated and people panicked.

The protest was carried out in response to the sale of land in the centre of the picturesque market town of Kings Newton, Shropshire. These events come at a time when government legislation on the sale and development of land around England and Wales' rural towns is being reviewed. Taking advantage of the current situation before legislative measures are put in place, Lord Weston of Weston Hall had recently sold land for development, a move that had proved unpopular with local residents whose concern over the future of their town prompted the demonstration.

The Heritage Trust, which is connected with Weston Hall and has been providing financial assistance for the restoration of the building, has refused to comment on speculation that Lord Weston has made the decision to quit Weston Hall and for it to pass solely into their responsibility.

For comment see p5.

'Where's Lord Lovely now?' said Alan, drawing me back to the present.

'In meetings all day I suppose. He said something about solicitors and I guess he'll be talking to the Heritage Trust as well.'

'Busy man,' Alan said dolefully.

'I know. And it's really heavy stuff that he has to do. Do you think he'll quit the house?'

'He must be really sick of it.'

'I think he is,' I said, closing the newspaper and throwing it onto a pile of folders stacked on the floor. 'But he has this really strong sense of responsibility about keeping it in the family. He's put himself under a lot of pressure over Weston Hall, but I wonder if this is going to push him over the edge. I mean – the place must be a money-pit. And with the prospect of a lawsuit against him…

I don't know. I have no idea how it must feel to let something go that has been in the family for generations.'

'Are you still going to go round for dinner tonight?'

'Yes. He said he wanted me to come round… and I really want to go. But urgh! I don't know what to say or do, do you know what I mean? It's all a bit weird…'

'Just be yourself,' Alan said

'Yes, you're right I suppose.'

'Well, not exactly "yourself",' he added, 'how about yourself but with a bit more confidence?'

'No. I don't think I can do that.'

34

Early that evening I had a long soak in the mini-bath and finally washed away the last of the mud from the protest. Goodness knows why I hadn't had a good wash earlier. I dried my hair so that it fell into long waves instead of tight curls, I put my favourite blue dress on and even found my make-up tin, buried deep in the bottom of my holdall, and touched up my eyes and cheeks.

I was dying to see Richard. I had been all day. The morning's awkwardness was probably a temporary thing – we'd been thrown off track by the events around us. Everything would be all right this evening. Wouldn't it? Good food, wine, candles...

I was as nervous as hell when I left the house.

Nevertheless the walk through the town in the early evening soon calmed me down. The rains had passed and left the earth smelling fresh and clean although there was a definite chill in the air signalling the onset of autumn. I passed one or two familiar faces and said hello, smiling sheepishly at a fellow protestor who was ambling innocently down the street.

I would miss this place, I reflected, as I wandered up the hill.

I would miss the sense of community, even if it was generated by rather militant characters. And I'd miss the winding streets and little redbrick cottages. And, of course, the beautiful countryside around and about. But I knew, realistically, I could never live in Kings Newton. It was too small and after a while I'd start to feel its limits. But for now, for the weeks I'd been there, it had been just right. If I hadn't managed to work out what I was going to do with myself then at least I'd drawn a line under my old life. Come to terms with all that had happened. That sort of thing. I wondered, fleetingly, if Greg was still with Rachel? Whether they had been anything more than a one-off? Who knows. Well Mum for one, but I wouldn't be troubling her with that question any time soon.

When I got to the Hall I skirted the front and headed straight for the kitchens where the smell of cooking wafted out from the open door. Richard was sitting at the table covered in paperwork, a deep frown on his face. His hair looked as though he had spent the day running his hands through it, and his eyes looked tired, black smudges beneath them.

'Hi!' I stood on the threshold.

'Hello,' he rose and came over to me. There was an awkward moment where I thought he might kiss me and I almost kissed him, but neither event happened and we both looked uncomfortable.

'I brought this…' I said, passing him a bottle of wine I'd bought on my way to the Hall. The trouble with mixing with someone of Richard's calibre is that one could no longer pop into the local off-licence for a £4 bottle of wine with a posh looking label. The man knew his stuff. So this wine, recommended to me by a *very* pretentious looking vintner, had a strikingly dull label (no gold lettering, no coat of arms) and a price tag of £15. I hoped it would be good.

'Lovely! I have some of this downstairs,' he said and I breathed a sigh of relief.

'Dinner smells lovely. What is it?'

'Oh nothing fancy. I was going to cook something up but I just got absorbed in all this stuff,' he gestured to the table covered in paper, 'so it's just toad in the hole I'm afraid.'

'That's great!' I said. 'Shall I open this?' and I hunted round the kitchen for the bottle opener and glasses. It turned out there were about ten different bottle openers on the sideboard, some of which would make it into his kitchenware collection and some of which were no doubt doomed to rejection. Hopefully the one I chose was going to be in the latter pile – it managed to chew through the cork and the metal bent as I pulled it out leaving me having to strain the wine through a sieve to remove the cork bits. Not a great start.

We chatted about his work and the merits (or not) of particular kitchen gadgets while he cleared away the paperwork and tended to the dinner. I saw letters among the mess of paper on the table. There were letterheads from the Heritage Trust, National Trust, an auction house and a firm of solicitors amongst others. These were mixed with one or two older looking documents with copperplate handwriting on thick yellowing paper and one document, the oldest I saw, looked like it was made of really old parchment, written in what must have been Latin with an enormous red wax seal suspended from an old ribbon at the bottom.

I desperately wanted to ask him about them but if he wanted to talk about them he would. And no doubt he'd say *something* about them. And the protest. And the reporters. So many big things to talk about and meanwhile we chatted about wine and mash and kitchen paraphernalia.

The meal was good – local organic sausages in a batter that, unlike any attempt I've ever made, stayed fluffy and light when it came out of the oven. Richard had made an onion gravy and buttery mash – all of which went very well with the, thankfully, good wine.

'So,' he said as we finished the main course and he went to get cakes from the pantry, 'how was your day? Here – have one of these. I asked Harold to stop by the baker's and pick some up on his way here this afternoon.'

I tried not to look too impressed at him having people to pick things up for him.

'It was OK. You know – the town is a bit strange after last night. Reporters everywhere, people being a bit cagey, that sort of thing. There was talk of the police getting involved but I didn't see any policemen about, did you?'

'They came up here about midday but I said I wasn't interested in pressing charges.'

'Really?' I said, putting my wine glass down. 'Not even against Tom, not even if he decides to sue you?'

'No. There aren't enough hours in the day to sort out my life, as it is, without having any more complications thrown in. Tom won't sue me anyway. He doesn't know I'm not going to take any legal action for trespass, so the threat of it is still there, which should stop him from doing anything. Anyway, one of my solicitors talked to his solicitor this afternoon so I think I can be pretty confident nothing is going to come of it.'

'Impressive…' I said, 'that was handled quickly.'

'Yes, well believe it or not there are some things I tackle straight away,' he laughed.

He was starting to look a whole lot better now that we'd had dinner and he was unwinding from the day. We sat back in the spindly old kitchen chairs and sipped a new bottle of wine which was, sadly, even better than my effort. He was smiling and his eyes were twinkly again, although the bags under them remained.

We reached a pause in the conversation and I fiddled absently with the stem of my wine glass. Was he ever going to say anything about the house? Maybe he'd had enough of it during the day and was happy to avoid talking about it that evening? But then, presumably he was talking about it to professionals in a business capacity, and maybe he wanted a softer shoulder to cry on? None of the solicitors, auctioneers or representatives from the conservation bodies would be interested in how he was *feeling* about the whole thing. So he'd probably welcome being able to talk it through with me. That was my reasoning, anyway, to convince myself it was OK to bring the topic up. I took a sip of wine and launched straight in.

'The, er, papers mentioned you might quit Weston Hall…'

It hung in the air for a minute.

'They're right,' he said quietly.

I looked straight at him, relieved that I hadn't overstepped the mark, and he was looking back at me.

'Really? You're really going to leave?' I was shocked. I thought he might be considering it, but to be so definite...

'Yes.'

'What, move down to London?'

'Yes,' he smiled rather sadly.

'Will you keep the Hall?'

'No.'

I leant forward slowly, 'You mean to say that you're letting go of Weston Hall?'

'Yup,' he said, tight-lipped.

'Oh…' I searched for something to say.

'It's not that bad,' he said eventually with a sigh. 'I thought it would be but it's not. It was only a matter of time before it happened and I think I've always known that it was going to happen on my watch. It's just been moved forward a few years, that's all.'

'Because of the protest?'

'Well I can't deny that's one of the reasons. The locals have been getting a bit revolutionary recently. I suppose you've heard about the road block?'

I nodded.

'Well first there was the road block, and now this. Where will it end? With my severed head on a park railing? I don't particularly want to live side by side with people who think they can act like that. And anyway, what is there for me here? There's no farm estate to manage, no people save a few part-time workers dotted about in decaying cottages. I can't really base my business up here so why am I here at all?'

'It must have been a very hard decision to make, though,' I said, a bit surprised at his laid back attitude. It must be a front. He must be devastated.

'Yes, it was. A very hard decision…' he admitted eventually.

219

And now that I really looked at him I could see that he'd been dealt a serious blow. He was slouched on his chair, his face worn and tired looking after a day of obviously wearing negotiations. The words might sound confident and off-hand but behind them was a man who had realised just what he was about to do, and felt the full weight of it on his shoulders.

I suppose it was down to the fact that I'd had almost a bottle of wine that I completely lost any inhibitions and dared to speak my mind at that point. I leant forward and said softly, 'I don't think it's solely your fault that the family house is being sold, really I don't.'

'How do you work that one out then?' he said, smiling forlornly.

'Well,' I began, tracing out the grain of wood on the table with a finger, 'I think it has a lot to do with your father, don't you?' I looked up from my tracings on the table and he looked interestedly at me.

'Go on,' he said.

'Well, if your father had kept the place in a better state of repair then he would have passed it on to you as a realistically workable estate. As it is, the minute you inherited it, it was only a matter of time before it got beyond your scope to keep it.'

He contemplated this for a minute.

'And,' I continued, on a roll now, 'you don't have to give up the place do you? You could be like you say your father was. A bit of a dreamer – not a very practical man. You *could* still live in the house, keep it ticking over and let the problems get worse. And then you could pass it on in an even worse state than it is now. But you *could* pass it on. It doesn't have to end here. But you're realistic. You're taking responsibility for it, which is something that probably hasn't happened much for a few years. Many years, even.'

I finished my little speech and sat back. Richard was quiet again.

'Yes, I suppose you're right,' he said at last. 'I don't think I'd ever thought of it like that before. You're right. Thank you.' He leant over and put his hand on my hand. Warm and soft. His thumb stroked my fingers up and down slowly. I thought my heart would explode in my chest it was hammering away so furiously.

'Oh, Rosamund! It's been a tough day!'

'Why? What happened?'

'Well… it started off well,' he lost his careworn look for a moment and shot me a cheeky smile making me blush furiously, 'but after the press interview I called up the Heritage Trust, my solicitors and so on and we set up a conference call and talked things through. And we all came to the same conclusion – that there is no workable alternative. I can't sell more land, I can't – and won't – open up more rooms to the public, I can't sell off the cottages unless I invest in their renovation, which I can't afford to do… So that's it. I have to sell.'

'Sell to whom?'

'The Heritage Trust: they've already quoted me an excellent price for it, pending a few surveys. Initially they assumed that they'd be able to buy it for a really knock-down price because of all the money they've invested in it, but my lawyers found a way out of that, meaning potentially I could offer it up for sale privately.'

'So you might do that?' I asked

'No. No private buyer would touch it given the state it's in. There's just too much wrong with it. But the National Trust and English Heritage are interested, so I could potentially hold a bidding war between all three charities.'

'So you could get a lot of money,' I said, choosing another cake from the box.

'Yes and no. The Heritage Trust really don't want it to go to anyone else or to get involved in a bidding war or anything so their latest offer reflects that – I'd be a fool to turn it down; given the timescales involved in going to auction I'm better off taking the money and letting the Heritage Trust have it.'

'When will the sale go through?'

'Oh God knows – there's so much paperwork and legal stuff to get through. But we're both wanting a quick outcome, so who knows, maybe a couple of months…'

'Wow – so quick.'

'I know. Probably for the best though – otherwise I'd start dwelling on it and fret about giving up the family home. And that wouldn't do anyone any good.'

'True. Do you want another cake? These ones are good,' I tilted the box towards him.

'Oh, absolutely,' he smiled and took out an egg custard.

'So will you be concentrating on your business then?'

'Yup. I can move down to London and put in the hours that I should have been doing a year ago or more.'

'Do you have a flat in London already?'

'Yes, my grandparents bought a house in Kensington years ago and I've still got that.'

'It's not a *large* house is it?' I asked. 'With a leaking roof and dry rot?'

'No,' he laughed, 'it's a very normal sized house, with a new roof and a tiny garden. Absolutely no room for a lake with geese in it. No locals. No conservation bodies. Nothing. It'll be marvellous.'

'So…' I began, frowning, 'if you don't mind me asking, how are you going to get all your possessions from the Hall into this tiny house in Kensington?'

'Yes, well that's the problem,' Richard took out his wallet and brought out a business card, pushing it across the table to me.

'Cecil Reese-Johns, Auctioneer,' I read out. 'You're going to get rid of everything?'

'No. Not everything. I want to hang on to as much as I can, but it's just not practical. So I'll have to take some things to auction. When I say the house in London is small, it's small by comparison I suppose. I mean, it's four stories and six bedrooms so I will have room to keep some of the furniture.'

'You're going to have a hard time deciding what goes and what stays,' I said, somewhat obviously. I could have kicked myself.

'Yes. But I have to be practical. They're only possessions after all. So this chap is coming on Friday. *That will be fun.*'

The rest of the evening was spent talking about auctions and paintings and what he thought he might keep and what would go.

I managed to make him laugh a few times and when it came time to leave, I felt really pleased with myself for having cheered him up and having been there to listen to his troubles. And that was it really – I had been a friend to him. Of course I wanted it to be more than that. More than anything I wanted to bound across the table and throw my arms around him and kiss him like I had just last night. But it felt wrong, and however much he enjoyed my company, I sensed he didn't want anything more than to talk. *Of course! The man had serious things to be thinking about, and anyway, didn't every magazine on every supermarket shelf tell you* not *to sleep with a man on a first date? That it doomed the entire relationship to failure?* Although, to be honest, last night wasn't a first date, not as such. In fact, tonight was the first real date I suppose. Or... you could count our various meetings as dates, we certainly had spent some time in each other's company and got to know each other pretty well before last night. God – why were these things so difficult?

Around midnight I got up to leave. We were both tired and, while he had more negotiations tomorrow, I had to open up the shop early. We said our goodbyes and he kissed me on the cheek, which was almost worse than nothing at all.

'I'll phone you!' he called as I walked off into the night. I turned and waved, continuing to walk away. It was a mistake as a second later I had toppled into an enormous stone trough filled with geraniums, and now me.

'Are you OK?' he shouted from the house, preparing to come outside and help me out of my predicament.

'Fine! Fine! Don't worry. See you soon,' I said, hastily withdrawing from the flowerpot and dashing off into the night before I could disgrace myself any more.

35

Dear Mum

~~Sorry but~~ I won't be able to make Sunday dinner next week. I can appreciate that you want to patch things up between Rachel and me, but to be honest I'm not particularly keen on seeing her ~~I saw so much of her recently (did you know that she has a tattoo on her...~~

Things are a bit strange in Kings Newton. Some people took part in some sort of protest (I don't really know much about it) but it's caused quite a sensation here. There are TV and newspaper people milling around all the time. ~~I've even been interviewed.~~

In answer to your question, I'm not sure what I'll be doing with myself in the near future. However, I'm happy drifting so ...

36

By rights I should feel sad. I should be mulling over all the things that were coming to a close and the fact that I *still* had as little direction in my life as I had done when I'd arrived in Kings Newton all those weeks ago. But no, I was *over* that maudlin period. Was it now the era of a new, stronger, more positive Rosamund? Maybe not. But it was feeling pretty good.

I should have felt sad, for example, that the fun I used to have working at Gloria's Flowers had dried up. Deborah was OK company but she wasn't a patch on the comedy duo that was Gloria and Alan. There was no Tom coming in to entertain Gloria and make us feel sick. And of course there would soon be no Richard Weston living up at the Hall. Did I feel sad about that? I don't know. It just didn't seem very real somehow.

Deborah, who was returning to work after six months' maternity leave, was happy for me to take charge, and I found I was happy to do so. I helped her pick up the threads of her old job as well as take calls from the new branch up in Shrewsbury, where all manner of things seemed to be going wrong. It was easy enough to sort out the problems though – and those that couldn't be sorted out were filed for when Gloria came back. Something to take her mind off things...

Deborah was a quiet little soul who could happily spend the day without uttering a word. I could see why she got on so well with Gloria. It made me realise just how much a sacrifice Alan must have made in staying on at the shop for so long. With such a quiet character as Deborah on one hand and the tempestuous Gloria on the other, the poor boy must have been horribly lonely during his working hours. No wonder he leapt at the opportunity to befriend me when I turned up. He'd called me yesterday, bless him, to tell me he'd found me an apartment for rent near to Fuschiarama. He was already networking in the city: 'a friend of a friend had just invested in a new waterside development' and had a one bed flat available. Where would I be without him?

Well, jobless and homeless for starters.

'Did you hear about the protest?' Deborah volunteered out of the blue while we were arranging the day's delivery.

'Er... yes,' I said

'Apparently there were nearly fifty people at it, according to the local paper.'

'No? Really?'

'Yes. They say it wasn't just yobs either. There were farmers and teachers and so on. Professionals. Makes you think doesn't it.'

'It certainly does,' I smiled and trimmed a few iris stems distractedly.

'I'm not surprised about that Tom being a part of it though. I knew he was bad through and through. Devious. Apparently he's got scores of women in the town. Married women, too!'

'You're kidding!'

'No I'm not. I don't know what they see in him myself. Too cocky for my liking.'

I had to agree with her there. She turned the conversation round to Richard Weston and the sale of the Hall, which by now was common knowledge. It was funny how things had changed in the past couple of weeks. All of a sudden Richard Weston was seen as the injured party. The one who had been wronged. People had crept into his grounds and violated his property, they were even talking about suing him too. And he was being forced out of his family seat because of them. Public sympathy was high and from those I spoke to while out shopping and our customers, too, people were actually sad about what was happening.

'It's the end of an era,' said Deborah, sighing into her hot chocolate. 'I reckon it's a shame he's going 'cause there's not many towns that have a traditional landowner as we have. Had. I reckon it's going to weaken the community,' she took a sip and let out another contemplative sigh.

'I suppose you're right,' I agreed, laying down my stems, 'I mean, it sort of held everyone together in mutual dislike for him didn't it? Everyone shared a common cause. And now the centrepiece of the town is going to be a museum rather than a home.'

'Gabby from the butcher's got me to sign a petition yesterday morning to get him to stay. They're saying opening up the Hall to the public is going to be a really bad thing. I don't know why exactly but anyway, I signed it.'

'Were there many signatures?' I asked, marvelling at the turn of events.

'Oh tons.'

I wondered whether Richard had any idea of what was going on now. How public opinion had changed. Such a British thing: backing a loser, sticking up for the downtrodden. And I wondered how he was feeling this morning. The auctioneer was due in the afternoon and it would be a hell of a day for him. To part with so many heirlooms, with your family's history… I was tidying up the wrapping table when an idea came to me. Not a rape-alarm type idea, a much more sensible one, one that a *sophisticated* person might come up with.

'Deborah, would you mind if I left you to it this afternoon? I have a friend who's in a bit of a pickle and could do with some help. I'll have my mobile on me so you can give me a call if you have any problems. And I'll still be in Kings Newton if you need me in a hurry.'

'OK,' she said, still nervous about being left on her own, it being the end of only her first week back. But she'd be fine. She was perfectly competent and she'd been working in the shop for three years before she left to have the baby. She couldn't have forgotten everything, even allowing for hormones.

At midday I gathered my things together, checked my hair in the mirror and applied some lipstick before heading off across town. Archie the baker, whose shop stood opposite Gloria's Flowers, had the most divine food so I bought a platter of various filled sandwiches and a selection of cakes, including Richard's favourite egg custards. Then I stopped off at the off-licence and bought a bottle of Bucks Fizz and a couple of tubes of Smarties. And, lastly, dropped into the newsagents, where Barbara managed to squeeze into my already laden arms a pack of brightly striped napkins.

It had been four days since I'd had dinner with Richard and I hadn't heard from him since. I remembered that he had promised to call – before I fell into the geraniums – but I hadn't really expected to hear too soon as he had a lot to be thinking about. Still, that hadn't stopped me looking up expectantly every time the bell went in the shop, hoping it would be him. And every time the phone went my heart leapt into my throat. Really, being smitten put a whole load of strain on the body; I was a nervous wreck.

Well, I wasn't going to sit at the wrapping table and wait for him to make the next move. Life was too short and my nerves wouldn't stand it, so if he wasn't going to call me then I would go and see him. Give him a picnic lunch in the Hall. After all, I knew he would be there today as he had the auctioneer to see, and what better time to be cheered up than before that particular trauma.

Heavily laden with bags I made slow progress up the hill towards the gates. The Heritage Trust wasn't kidding when it said it wanted a speedy resolution to the sale. I was waylaid for a minute at the entrance to the estate reading a laminated notice applying for permission to knock down the garages to the side of the building and gravel over the east lawns for car parking, to create disabled access etc, etc, etc. They must be working overtime to secure this house.

Now I felt sad, the spring had been taken right out of my step. The geese weren't funny any more, the lake wasn't beautiful and the house wasn't breathtaking. It was all so grim. The planning notice had suddenly made it all real. For some reason hearing Richard talk about it hadn't made it seem very tangible, more like something from Trollope, and the local gossip and newspapers just discussed the potential outcomes, but here was solid proof that the sale was going through, that plans were being drawn and permissions were being sought. Here was proof that very soon there would be no Lord Weston of Weston Hall. There would just be a kitchenware salesman living in a London townhouse who had once owned a very grand house indeed. It was a tragedy. He must be so upset. Car parking!

There were some tiny blue flowers growing near the lake that I couldn't resist. Putting my shopping down for a second I bent down and picked some and wound them into my hair, humming a melancholy tune to myself as I walked to the Hall.

I went round to the kitchen door and knocked as well as I could, what with all my bags and my platter balanced precariously. The door opened and Richard's face lit up when he saw me. I was over the moon that he was so obviously happy to see me. A girl can't help wondering what a man is thinking if she hasn't heard from him for a few days, whatever the circumstances.

'Rosamund!'

'I bring lunch,' I said, thrusting the platter into his hands, 'a selection of sandwiches, cakes, Bucks Fizz to perk you up and napkins to eat it all off. We can have a little picnic down by the lake, I thought. Get you out of the house. You must feel pretty cooped up in here.'

He laughed as he saw what I'd done: 'You are fantastic!' He bent over to kiss me on the forehead, cupping my head in his hands. A definite improvement on the peck on the cheek. 'I'm starving and there isn't a bite to eat in the place. Come on then, the auctioneer's due in an hour or so, let's crack on.' I took my bags out to the lake while Richard found a rug and champagne flutes.

In the end we moved the picnic to the back of the house as the geese got rather too excited at the prospect of bread. Pilot flopped down beside us, content with eating every other sandwich. I caught up with all Richard's news and then went on to tell him about the petition and the change of sentiment abroad. He'd caught a whiff of it from Harold, the estate manager, but he hadn't realised it had got to the petition stage. He laughed but dismissed it. It wasn't going to change his mind now.

37

It's larvely. A larvely house. How long did you say it has it been in your family?'

'About five hundred years,' said Richard, flatly. He hadn't made much of an effort to hide his dislike of the auctioneer, but whatever showed in his expressions was lost on the man who had been engrossed in the contents of the house the minute he walked through the door.

Cecil Reese-Johns had come recommended by the Heritage Trust and was one of the necessary evils of Richard's situation. He was already picking up objects and making notes in a large red notebook, muttering to himself like a well-bred lunatic.

I could see that he styled himself as a bit of a flamboyant country gentleman what with the tweedy jacket topped off with a yellow silk neckerchief, which emphasised his ruddy round face. His jacket pockets were pulled and distorted by their contents, which he would bring out every so often when needed: a magnifying glass, a small torch and a tape measure.

'Such a huge shame to be losing it. Such a pity. But then I see it a lot you know. Not so much of it lately, mind you. Calmed down a bit. Much better inheritance tax planning nowadays I suppose, people are better prepared. But it still happens. Heartbreaking. Gosh, is that a Latterworth?'

He waddled over to a painting of a Jacobean man and stood admiring it, 'Surely is! Latterworth's hand all over it. The richness of that gold detail work. Oh and look at the jewels on the fingers. So alive. So vibrant. Larvely.'

'Stay with me through this,' Richard whispered to me as Cecil launched himself on another painting. 'Please?'

I looked at him, standing close by my side, looking suddenly small and vulnerable in the big open hallway.

'Of course I will,' I said, thrilled. I was wanted, needed.

His hand enclosing mine in a firm hold felt warm. We were standing shoulder-to-shoulder, closer than we had been for days.

'Well, well, awful business, but must get on with it,' chattered the auctioneer to himself before turning round to face us, perching his large frame on the edge of the hall table.

'Now then, how do you want to play this? I usually suggest going through the main rooms on the ground floor first, they often contain the better stuff, before heading upstairs…'

'OK.'

'Not much in the kitchen I suppose.'

'No, not much.'

'Or outbuildings? Stables? Cottages?'

'No. It's all in here.'

'Anything on loan to museums? Galleries?'

'No. Nothing.'

'Good, good, that's how we like it. Should be over with in two or three hours I should imagine. I say,' he said, suddenly turning to me, 'you wouldn't be an absolute love and get me a cup of tea would you? I'm downright parched. Haven't drunk a thing since I got on the train at Kings Cross this morning. No milk. Two sugars. Ta.'

Richard squeezed my hand and I smiled at him. Gloria would

have burst a blood vessel if anyone talked to her like that.

'Absolutely. Richard?'

'Er… yes please. Thanks.'

I headed off and left the men to it.

When I returned with the tray of drinks they had moved on from the entrance hall and I heard Cecil's loud and chattery voice coming from the dining room. I was just heading there when I noticed a little yellow sticker on the corner of a portrait of one of Richard's ancestors. There were also stickers on the fruit paintings over the doorway and the Grecian scenes beside the hall table. Even the table had a yellow sticker, stuck midway on a leg.

'Oh thank you, thank you, you're an absolute saviour, really you are,' enthused Cecil, bounding over and sinking the tea in one gulp. 'Larvely. Right then, where were we? Ah yes, this family group here…'

He went over to join Richard in front of the fireplace and they both looked up at the enormous oil painting dominating the room.

'Difficult. Difficult to sell this one. Too large for most places and besides family groups aren't as popular as couples or indeed as men on their own. So it's really up to you. Do you want it or shall we flog it?'

'Put it up for auction,' Richard said, resignedly.

'Auction it is then,' and Cecil bumbled up to the painting and reaching up stuck a tiny yellow sticker on the bottom of the frame. He scribbled a note in his pad and moved across the room.

'OK. Now the last painting is the little rural scene over by the window there. Now if I'm correct…' Cecil went over to the painting and examined it and then looked down at his notebook, 'Yes, I think I'm right in saying that the Heritage Trust has shown an interest in this one.'

'Well I want to keep it,' said Richard.

'Right. Right. You're the boss. But could be valuable you know. Could be worth a lot of money.'

'I want it. I like it.'

'Surely so.' Cecil took a deep breath, 'let's move on to the porcelain then. Now then, this dinner service that you have on display, it's a beauty. Royal Crown Derby, late nineteenth century. Oh, a small chip to a dinner plate I see, but a really larvely collection. You've even got the cream jug and condiment set. Well that will add value.'

'Auction then.'

'Will do, will do,' and Cecil opened up the glass cabinet and stuck a sticker on the teapot. 'Now then, looks like I missed a couple of pictures here. These tiny oil paintings, they're not going to fetch much but we might get a—'

'I'm keeping them. They're my great grandparents.'

'Oh well, quite. Can't put a price on that now can you? But you'll be wanting to get rid of the fire screen I presume?'

'Yes. That can go.'

'Ye-es. Most people get rid of those. Not very popular nowadays. Don't sell very easily but we can try,' and on went the tiny yellow sticker.

And so it continued. Pictures, furniture and possessions were all discussed and stickers dealt out accordingly. Some decisions were easy and the pieces promptly bore stickers for auction. Other pieces, however, were more difficult. The family paintings were a hard choice. Some were enormous and would never fit in the sort of house Richard would be living in once he had left the Hall. These went for auction with regret. But the smaller paintings took a lot of consideration. The earliest paintings of the family dated from the late sixteenth century and Richard was adamant he would keep those. But some of the later ones were almost impossible to decide on.

'You can get them copied you know. Prints can really do them justice and you can get the varnish to mimic the paint effect, so really only you would know they weren't the originals,' said Cecil.

It was heartbreaking to have to watch Richard decide what would stay and what would go. A collection of objects that he had grown up with, that his family had bought and treasured down the years, meant more than its monetary value. And all split up and sold under his order. His short, low responses to Cecil spoke volumes.

One of the guest bedrooms had contained a lot of his parents' belongings, and much of it was not going to auction. Richard was determined to hold on to the objects even when Cecil tried to persuade him otherwise.

'Well the Heritage Trust really wanted that sampler,' the auctioneer said.

'It can't have it. My mother made it.'

'Quite, quite… But you have to think, what will you do with it? Where will it go?'

'I'll keep it on the wall,' retorted Richard, clearly hurt that he was having to defend his decision to keep something from the Heritage Trust.

'But will you have the space? That's what you've got to bear in mind.'

'But it's tiny!'

'Oh I know that. But you're keeping a lot of paintings. An awful lot. People don't tend to go for the number that you have and that's all well and good if you have somewhere to hang them, but will you have the wall space to accommodate all these?'

'Well no, but I can put some in storage.'

'Of course you can. But would they not be better left here where you could see them whenever you wanted to? For free. In fact you would be paid to keep them here. You see things like old paintings and this sampler here all take a lot of upkeep, with the humidity and temperature needing to be constant. And the light will need to be monitored to make sure that they don't deteriorate beyond the condition they're in now. I'm sure that they're of great sentimental value to you, as a lot of these things are, but you have to be realistic, sir. After all, it's not as though you'll never see the pieces again. The Heritage Trust has pledged to keep as many items here as it can, so you will always have access…'

'They just won't be mine.'

'Yes but what is ownership in the end? How much is it worth? The paintings come with a lot of responsibility and all that hassle would be gone if you agreed to keep them here under the watchful eye of the Heritage Trust.'

I stayed with them all the time. I went into rooms I'd never seen before. The rooms on the second floor were fairly empty, the damp and the condition of the floorboards not being conducive to storing antiques safely. I was amazed by the extent of the problems that were now obvious. The roof must be leaking all down one side of the corridor on the top floor: the wallpaper sagged and bowed and the rooms smelt of damp and decay. Floorboards were soft and some were even missing in the end rooms where it hadn't been feasible to replace them until the roof was repaired. Everywhere there were spiders' webs and layers of dust that indicated the rooms had not been in use or even visited in years. It was all so different to the rooms downstairs.

'Well that's about it then,' said Cecil finally, when we shut the door on the last rotten room. 'I can see why it's such a burden. Just like Haddenham Hall in the Lake District. Do you know it? Owner had a terrible time trying to make ends meet and in the end, well it's just like you have here…' he trailed off, seeing Richard was not in the mood to entertain him longer than he had to.

'Well I guess I'll be off then. Do you have some sort of photocopying device here in the Hall? I can leave you with an inventory of all the items you've requested to keep, auction and sell to the Heritage Trust and if you change your mind before the twenty-third then you can call me up on this number,' he twirled a business card in his fingers before giving it to Richard. 'I'll change it accordingly. Can I use your phone? I'll need to call a cab to the station. Do you have any cab numbers on you?'

Without answering any one of his questions, Richard led him downstairs to the study and the photocopier, and I headed out to the front steps to have a cigarette.

A taxi pulled up within a few minutes and Cecil lumbered into it, waving briefly in my direction and then barking instructions at the driver. Richard stood in the doorway, watching them go up the drive and out of the estate.

I got up and walked over to him, leaning against the doorframe, staring out to where the taxi had disappeared around the corner. Heavy tears were streaking down his face and fell onto the stone step at his feet. I pulled out a tissue and wiped them from his face but more came in their place. Feeling none of the inhibitions of the past few days I reached out and pulled him to me, holding him close and feeling his body heave with sobs. We neither of us said anything, standing in front of the open door. Pilot must have woken up from his sleep by the library fire and was bouncing around at out feet barking to be taken for a walk.

'Come on,' I said, pulling away from him and kissing the tip of his nose, 'let's take Pilot out.'

'OK,' he sighed. 'Thank you,' and he kissed me back as if he really meant it, a proper kiss, not a peck on the cheek by any means.

We wandered round the grounds, through the woodlands and up to the spot where we had first met all those weeks ago, he the preoccupied jogger and me the soggy dreamer. We joked about it now, but deep down I still felt a pang of shame for being so clumsy. Well, at least it had brought us together. It was dusk again now, but not raining and the sky was filled with orange streaks of cloud. We stood on the hill looking down at Kings Newton.

'You're amazing,' he said, leaning over towards me and gently lifting a strand of my hair off my face, 'you really are.'

'Thank you,' I said, loving the feel of his touch on my face and his hands running through my hair.

'I'm sorry that these past few days have been so awful. I wanted to tell you so many times that I think you're wonderful but I had so much going on in my head and so many things that I had to remember that I worried it would come out wrong. Or it would be the wrong moment and I'd mess it up. But the longer I left it the more difficult it was for me to tell you. Thank you for sticking by me, and helping me out the way you have. I love you. Please, please don't go to Birmingham. Come back to London with me.'

My heart was hammering against my ribs. He was inches away

from me and I leant over and kissed him, feeling the warmth of his body next to mine.

After a moment I pulled away slightly and traced his lips with my fingers. 'I don't really want to move to Birmingham, anyway,' I said. Alan would understand, he had Pierre and a whole bunch of new friends now…

'Good,' he pulled me close again. 'Stay with me, I want you to, always.'

38

The world was wonderful.

Everything was great.

And I couldn't stop smiling.

As promised, I stayed working in the shop until Gloria returned on the Monday. She'd wasted no time since getting back to Kings Newton and had already been round to see Tom and had gathered most of the gossip from him. She had breezed in at about ten on Monday morning, affecting to be all carefree and relaxed, but I could tell by the taut smile on her face that she was as tense as ever under that tan.

'You look very happy,' she said to me, trying not to sound too begrudging.

'I am,' I said, trying to busy myself and not be too obviously in love.

'So… get on OK at the shop?' she turned to Deborah while flicking idly through the order book.

Deborah shrugged and looked to me for an answer.

'Absolutely,' I said, matching her, cool-for-cool.

She shot a quick-fire round of questions at us, about orders, accounts, bunches and deliveries. Business, business, business.

After a few minutes of grilling we got to the point where Gloria knew everything there was to know. Business was OK, the receipts and orders were all recorded, Deborah knew what was going on and, really, there was no more need for me to be there. This was it. The leaving moment.

'Well,' I said, hopping down from the stool, 'I guess that's it really. You won't be needing me any more, will you?'

'No. No…' she busied herself arranging the paperwork on the wrapping table.

'So I'll get my stuff together…'

'OK…'

Neither of us looked at the other. There was nothing to say.

'Where are you off to now then?' she asked a minute later as I scrabbled around putting all my goods and chattels into my bag. How had I dispersed so much stuff around the place? 'Are you going to see Tom?'

'God no. How is he anyway?' I said, kneeling beside the Welsh dresser and retrieving a lipstick.

'Not so good. Apparently he won't work for weeks yet. He's teaming up with Sarah, you remember, my friend you met at the Hall, and they're working on some pieces together apparently.'

'Oh. Nice.' I hid my smile by shuffling everything around in my bag to make room for my diary.

'She's split up with Lord Weston,' she announced, more to Deborah than me.

'Why's that?' asked Deborah

'Apparently he's been seeing someone all along. Behind her back. Turns out he's moving to London with her and everything.'

'Who is she?' Deborah asked eagerly.

'Me!' I said and waltzed out into my fabulous new life.

39

All the apprehension and nervousness that had knotted my stomach since I had arrived in Birmingham left as I stood and stared at Alan's shop. It was everything that he had wanted it to be, and it looked stunning. Enormous, hot-magenta plastic letters above the door spelled out Fuschiarama, but the rest of the façade was the original Victorian shop front with freshly sandblasted brickwork and shiny, shiny black paintwork. The windows themselves were empty of the clutter and fuss that Gloria had liked; there were no buckets of flowers or cherub urns here, just barely-visible threads of cotton that held long stemmed lilies at intervals, cascading down the glass. It looked beautiful.

I stood admiring it for a long time, filled with a feeling of sheer pride at what Alan had managed to achieve. I could see him through the curtain of lilies, serving a customer who had just walked in. She was a cool, slick woman with dyed scarlet hair bound in two bunches. She was buying deep red roses and Alan was binding them together with thick brown wrapping paper and a long strand of thick magenta ribbon. Alan looked as cool as his surroundings, his hair lazily spiked in a Hoxton fin and his sunglasses, useless for indoors on a drab day, pushed back on his head. A natural poseur...

And as I watched him laugh and chat to this girl, I began to feel a pang of regret, even envy. I tried to work out why I should feel that way, because it was not something that I thought that I would have felt, coming here today. I suppose that it was because I was standing on the periphery of some great other life that I would never know, looking in. Now I would never be part of it, part of the trendy shop with the cool customers in the heart of a vibrant city; I wouldn't pop out to the new bar across the road after work, and I wouldn't rub shoulders with Birmingham's emerging funky scene.

Deep down though, and more powerful than the regret at not taking part, was the realisation that I would miss Alan's company and the closeness of our friendship, which had been so important over the past few weeks. It had been Alan who had dragged me back to my feet after Greg's dodgy performance by the fridge, and it had been Alan who had taken me out and cheered me up when I felt bleak and directionless. Yes, Gloria had provided the practicalities, but it was Alan who had taken an interest in me, and had cared about me. He had made me appreciate that it was OK to not have a direction, and it was OK to drift so long as I was happy to do it. He had given me my confidence back, and I would miss him enormously. I felt a pang of sadness as I watched him zip around his shop with an energy unlike anything I'd ever seen.

I would miss him so much! I would miss the giggling in Gloria's shop, sticking our fingers up behind her back and playing filthy-word hangman on the receipt book when there was a lull in the day. I would miss going out for cider and staggering home through the streets of Kings Newton.

The red-haired girl emerged from the shop with her bunch of flowers and walked off with a group of friends, deftly avoiding the little canals cut into the pavement. Alan was on the phone, perched on his enormous wrapping table, twiddling the phone cord in his fingers and chatting away. He looked up suddenly and saw me standing there. His face lit up in a big smile and he beckoned me in. With a lump in my throat I walked towards the shop, ready to hand in my notice before I'd even started.

40

I'd spent a long lunch with Alan in Birmingham, and as I was in the area, sort of, I somehow found myself at Weston Hall without a sensible excuse not to visit.

The first thing that I noticed was that the driveway was much smoother than it had been, all the ruts and bumps had been filled in and shiny cream gravel laid out and hemmed in everywhere by neat terracotta borders.

But it was the Hall itself that looked completely different, a thousand subtle changes taken together had completely changed it. The brickwork was sharper and newer looking, the repointed mortar exactly framing each brick with a neatness that suited the look of the house. The huge stone columns had been cleaned and repaired so the detailed carvings could once again be seen. The woodwork around the windows and doors was newly painted and gleamed in the afternoon light and everywhere there were huge tubs of smart looking bay trees and miniature fir trees.

In the short walk from the bright, white, gravelled car park I was bombarded with dark green signposts telling me where to go and where not to go; I should keep to the paths and not go on the lawns. I should pay at the main entrance but the gardens would cost me £2.50 extra. The stables were around the side and they had refreshments and toilets with disabled access.

This was no longer a softly crumbling family home. It was a family day out.

Of course the Heritage Trust had offered the Weston family the opportunity of keeping an apartment here, but the offer had never been taken up, London being the focus of Lord Weston's new life and business. His lordship had been allowed to keep the rights to the name *Weston Hall Tableware*, although he couldn't sell his products from the estate shop, which was where the Green Room used to be, as that was owned by the Heritage Trust and stocked with their own mass-produced tat. It didn't matter though. His business had taken off in leaps and bounds since he'd moved down to London and he would have considered an outlet at Weston Hall too small to make commercial sense. Anyway, he never visited the place. Never needed to.

'Would you like to come on the tour? It's just about to start,' a lady with an aggressive fringe came out of the front door, having seen me standing there, apparently lost and helpless. 'Oh now she's a pretty little thing isn't she? What's her name?'

'Jessica,' I said, letting the woman take my daughter's tiny hand in hers.

'Oh she's beautiful. How old is she?'

'Nearly three.'

Jessica smiled politely and had her head patted by the harsh-fringed woman, before we went indoors and I paid my fee.

'Would you like a guide to Weston Hall? It explains the history behind the place?' the old man at the desk said when he gave me my entry ticket.

I smiled and declined.

With Jessica trailing behind me, a group of us were guided around the rooms. Even though they had been stripped and sanitized since I had last seen them, a glut of memories came back to me with each different room; the dining room with the polished table where Gloria and I had arranged flowers was now set out with the full dining service and candelabras polished like glass.

The library! The place where I'd found my grimy clothes and dressed for my first Weston Hall breakfast. The room was much more orderly than it had ever been when I had known it. The horrid old chair that I'd slumped on, covered in mud, was now repaired and cleaned and had a tiny little 'do not sit here' sign on the cushion. The novels and magazines had all gone, as had a lot of the newer books from the shelves; their place was taken by older-looking books that must have been sourced from the archive room and the estate office. They were books that had no place in the Hall library; a Gardener's Almanac and an early automobile mechanic book now sat beside more weighty tomes such as Forsters's Encyclopaedia of Mammals. The only deciding factor on what had stayed in the library and what had gone had obviously been age, the look of the books' spines, rather than the content, being most important.

Wire so thin it was almost invisible held them on the shelves; books never to be opened again, except to check that they weren't rotting away. How sad, I thought, that they were now just part of the furnishings and no more useful than wallpaper.

There was no toast lying abandoned on the dining room floor, and further on in the tour I saw that the study's neon strip-lights had gone, along with the computers, the disfiguring power points mounted half way up the walls and all the grey filing cabinets and piles of papers and discarded envelopes.

The paintings had been rearranged and a couple of them were copies, Richard had steadfastly refused to part with the originals however inappropriate it had been to keep them. Odds and ends from other nearby houses padded out the collection that was on display, arranged in a weirdly formal way that would have been totally impractical to live with but looked good to the visitors behind their rope barriers.

Rather nicely, I thought, Richard had been asked to leave a photograph of himself, which I found just above the mantelpiece in the kitchen. It was too small an object to merit the guide talking about, and as a consequence none of the people on the tour bothered to look at it. I picked Jessica up and pointed it out to her.

It was black and white, and I had taken it in the gardens beside the copper fountain, the day we moved to London. Richard was holding three month old Jessica up to the camera, kissing her wispy hair. In the background you can just make out the corner of one of the removal vans parked near the front steps, but you would have to look very closely to see it.

Summer Shadows
by award winning novelist, **Siân James**

A touching novel of heartbreak and hope

Bel lives quietly working as a gardener in the Cotswolds village
she grew up in, looking after her brother David, but this summer
is about to change everything..

Bel is struggling in the aftermath of the end of her relationship
with a married man; her ex-model sister returns from London in
need of her support and even her best friend, the happy-go-lucky
Gloria has a sudden, urgent problem of her own. What ensues is
a summer of growth and change for all three.

ISBN 1-870206-64-69   £6.99

*"Siân James has a fine ear and an acute eye. She writes with warmth
and compassion, "* **Glenda Beagan, Welsh short story writer and poet**

Siân James is one of Wales's most respected novelists. Born in
Rhydcymerau, she was brought up in Aberystwyth, where she went
to University. *Summer Shadows* is her twelfth novel and is set in Wales
and in the Cotswolds. In 1997, her short story collection, *Not Singing
Exactly* (Honno,1996) won the Book of the Year Award in Wales, her
fifth literary award. In 2002, she was awarded an honorary doctorate by
the University of Glamorgan, for her services to literature.

" She writes with grace, as to the manor born " **Susan Hill**

Also by Sian James :
The Sky Over Wales – An autobiographical account of her Cardiganshire
childhood in the 1930s, beautifully illustrated by Pat Gregory.

ISBN 1-870206-28-2   £ 5.95

Published by Honno, the Welsh Women's Press